Mad Dad, Fun Dad

Mad Dad, Fun Dad

Finding Hope that Things will Get Better

Doug Draper

Elm Hill

A Division of
HarperCollins Christian Publishing

www.elmhillbooks.com

Mad Dad, Fun Dad

Finding Hope that Things will Get Better

Published in Nashville, Tennessee, by Elm Hill, an imprint of Thomas Nelson. Elm Hill and Thomas Nelson are registered trademarks of HarperCollins Christian Publishing, Inc.

Elm Hill titles may be purchased in bulk for educational, business, fund-raising, or sales promotional use. For information, please e-mail SpecialMarkets@ThomasNelson.com.

Library of Congress Cataloging-in-Publication Data

Library of Congress Control Number: 2018930965

ISBN 978-1-595541987
ISBN 978-1-595556257 (eBook)

To my wife, Linda, for her daily love, support, and advice and to my friends with OneTeam Leadership for their encouragement to share this story.

Chapter 1

On a scorching summer day in 1965, Ben Baker stood next to his mother, Rachel, taking wet dishes from her and drying them before making a handoff to his big brother Joe who put them away. The team worked silently and quickly, cleaning up from the family's big Sunday lunch—the same thing they did every week after attending church.

Joe, age ten, and Ben, a year younger, knew their roles and performed them efficiently. Their parents had taught the boys how to work. When Rachel's sons grumbled about working too much, she always gave the same answer—"Idle hands are the devil's workshop." And she did her part to make sure her boys never had time to make anything for the devil. Keeping her boys busy also helped maintain the family's five-acre farm, located about two miles northeast from the small town of Alma, Utah.

After taking a lengthy bathroom break, the head of the family, Al Baker, strolled into the kitchen. "I thought you'd be done by now," he said. "But, I'm glad to see my boys working without their usual whining and complaining."

Al turned to the far corner of the kitchen and noticed his daughters—Debbie, age five, and Becky, less than a year old—playing. "And soon, you girls will be doing your fair share of the work," he said.

To soothe hurt feelings from an earlier argument with his wife, Al approached Rachel from behind, wrapped his hairy arms around her chest, and whispered, "When are you going to stop being so grumpy and give me a happy face to look at?"

Rachel kept her hands in the dishwater but swung her elbows away from her body to loosen Al's grip. "Don't touch me. I'm still mad at you."

"Is that the proper way to treat your sweet, loving husband?" Al asked and then roughly pushed her toward the sink.

"Please leave me alone for now," Rachel cried. "That's all I'm asking."

Al cursed and hit her with one of the firm slaps to the back of the head that he often delivered to his children. She retaliated by spinning around and slapping him across the face with a wet dish rag.

Joe managed to slip away, but Ben became trapped in the combat zone. In case the anger shifted to him, Ben dropped to a sitting position and held the dish towel against his chest with one hand and tightened the other into a fist at the side of his face to block any blows.

As soap suds and water streamed down Al's furious face, he grabbed his wife's chin with one hand and cocked the other above his head in a fist. With a roar that thundered across the kitchen, he yelled, "I try to be nice to you, but you do everything possible to make my life miserable!"

Tears covered Rachel's flushed cheeks. "Why can't you leave me alone?"

While shaking his clenched fist at her, Al shouted, "Why can't you just shut up!"

Silently, Rachel turned back to the sink and resumed washing the dishes. Al responded by delivering a quick jab to her right shoulder blade. She fell forward and let out a mournful sob.

A second later, Rachel spun around to face her attacker, but this time she held a paring knife. She pointed it at Al, dripping soapy dishwater on his boots. "Leave me alone."

He slapped the knife out of her hand, bouncing it off the refrigerator and onto the floor next to Ben. Rachel ducked her head and darted past Al, leaving the kitchen. "Stand up and get back to work!" Al shouted at Ben. "You look like a baby sitting on the floor like that. What's wrong with you?"

Ben quickly stood up, waiting for the next order. Joe had retreated to the far corner of the room when the battle began and remained on the floor next to his sisters. All of them looked terrified.

Al, red-faced and breathing heavily, picked up the dropped knife and tossed it into the sink. Snatching the towel from Ben, he dried his face and then kicked the cabinet under the sink, leaving a black scuff mark on the white paint. He glared at the few dishes, glasses, and utensils still in the sink. "I suppose your worthless mother isn't coming back to finish this job, so we'll have to do it."

Ben nodded in agreement, having learned that cooperating fully and enthusiastically with his father kept him safe in such moments. Al tossed the towel to Ben, saying, "I'll wash. You dry."

Ben prepared to get back to work, but his mother returned to the kitchen with the family's shotgun braced against her shoulder and pointed at Al.

"You're never going to hit me again," she stated with a steely blue-eyed stare. "And I'm not bluffing."

Seeing the shotgun aimed at him, Al seized the barrel and yanked the gun out of Rachel's hands. In a single motion, he spun the gun around and clubbed his wife in the forehead with the butt.

The blow dropped Rachel to the floor where she rolled to her right side, holding one hand to her quivering mouth and the other to her head. Ben stood inches away, frozen in fear, and watched as blood began to flow across his mother's forehead. She stayed on the floor, sobbing and groaning.

"That's a lesson for all of you!" Al shouted. "I'm in charge here and you had better learn that right now. Things will be a lot less painful if you do."

To reinforce his message, he kicked the refrigerator, making it rattle. Then, he spouted reasons why his wife deserved to be punished.

Rachel endured his vile deluge of insults until she recovered her senses and could stagger to her feet. She took the dish towel from Ben and held it over the bloody gash in her forehead, but blood continued to roll down her face and drip on her blouse and the floor. Without a word, she walked to the far corner of the kitchen, picked up Becky, and waved at Debbie to follow. They left the kitchen while Al did nothing but watch. A few minutes later, she left the house and drove away.

Joe continued to sit in the far corner of the kitchen and Ben held his position near the sink. The boys didn't move or make a sound.

Al muttered a series of profanities, which often served as his way to recover from one of his "mad Dad" outbursts. At this point, Joe usually took charge of helping his father calm down, but on this day, Joe had no solution and remained silent like Ben, waiting for orders.

"Boys, it looks like you'll need to finish doing the dishes," Al said unemotionally, waving his hand around the kitchen. "Make sure everything is clean and put away."

Pointing at a trail of blood from the sink to the kitchen door, he added, "And wipe up this mess your worthless, stupid mother made."

Joe and Ben obeyed and worked quickly to finish the dishes and remove the evidence of their mother leaving the house injured, which included blood drops from the kitchen to her bedroom and to the front door. Al avoided his sons for the next few hours, fiddling in the kitchen with an old radio that he had been trying to fix.

In a whisper, Ben asked Joe if their mother might be dying, but Joe scolded him for talking. "Keep your mouth shut unless you want your head bashed in with that gun."

For the rest of the day, Ben hovered near the front door and looked for a car to pull into the gravel driveway, but none arrived. And no phone calls came in from his mother or grandparents to let him know that everything would be all right.

Three days passed with no news. When Rachel and her daughters returned home, they came unannounced, acting like nothing had happened. The homecoming received less fanfare than a trip to the grocery store. Ben wanted an explanation of the violence and a promise that it would never happen again. Instead, he received silence and stone faces.

Chapter 2

Four days after the fight in the kitchen, George Oaks ambled across the narrow country road that separated his family's house from the Bakers' farm. Bored with listening to his teenage sisters argue about which boy in Alma was the dreamiest, George searched for Ben to see if he had time to play or go for a hike. As always, he found Ben at work—this time, picking weeds from a twelve-foot-long flower garden behind the house.

"What are you doing?" George asked, slowly taking a seat on the top step of the back porch next to the flowers. The cracked and chipped concrete porch had absorbed so much heat from the summer sun that George could barely sit on it.

"What else? I'm working," Ben said, glancing up to acknowledge his neighbor who occasionally left his house to see if Ben could take a break from his chores.

George had plenty of reasons to stay home—toys that every boy his age coveted, subscriptions to popular comic books, and a color TV with a clear picture. As a result, he spent little time outdoors and looked as white as one of his favorite cartoon characters—Casper the Ghost. George also limited his excursions because other kids teased him about his spindly arms and legs, thick glasses, and cleft palate. They mocked him for how his birth defect twisted his upper lip and made the way he talked a little different from everyone else. George hung out with Ben because he never made fun of him.

Except for his library books, Ben had no distractions to keep him indoors and plenty of chores to keep him outside, especially in the summer when the animals needed more water and weeds overwhelmed the farm. On this day, Ben worked to save his mother's wilted flowers. During the school year Ben had a fair complexion, but he was tanned in the summer from spending most of his daylight hours outdoors. His tan matched his light brown hair and made his dark blue eyes stand out. Ben liked being tanned. He thought it made him look like a tough Apache brave.

Instead of tackling the weeding project with a lightweight garden hoe, Ben used a much heavier pickaxe, to dig up the hardy weeds that threatened to conquer his mother's flower garden. The pickaxe sliced deep into the sandy soil and allowed Ben to remove the weeds by their roots and keep them from coming back soon.

While the weeds embraced the intense sunlight and dry air, his mother's bed of yellow marigolds and pink petunias failed to thrive with no rain and temperatures near one hundred degrees. The flowers turned their faces to the ground and many drooped so low that they rested on the baked soil.

"Do you want to build a fort in the gully or go hiking?" George asked as he continued to watch Ben swing the pickaxe and use his bare hands to grab weeds and throw them into a pile. Sweat poured down Ben's face and soaked his T-shirt, and splotches of dirt covered the bottom of his shirt where he had wiped his hands.

"I'd like to, but I have to finish this project for my mom," Ben said while swinging the pickaxe. "The flowers will be dead by tomorrow if I don't get the weeds out today. Do you want to help?"

"Oh, I don't know. It's kind of hot and my mom would get mad if I got as dirty as you."

Ben paused to examine his filthy shirt, shorts, and socks. Dirt covered every inch of them and his bare arms and legs, except where tiny rivers of sweat had cut lines.

"Yep, she probably would. I could throw you in the cow trough to clean you up."

George laughed, remembering the last time that happened. After building a castle behind the Baker's barn, the boys had used the trough as a bathtub.

When Ben returned to digging up weeds, George's patience faded. "Why isn't your mom doing this?" he asked. "I thought these were her flowers."

"They are, but she has a headache today and asked me to do it."

"My mom gets headaches too—usually from listening to my sisters playing their Beatles' records too loud."

While pounding the flowerbed with the pickaxe, Ben said, "My mom got her headache from getting hit in the head with the butt of a shotgun."

"What? A shotgun?"

"Yep, it happened just like this," Ben said, turning to face George and using the pickaxe to demonstrate the blow. "Dad grabbed the gun out of mom's hands and slammed the butt into her forehead. Pow! She fell down and blood gushed out all over the floor."

"You're making that up," George said. "Why would your dad do that?"

"Because Mom aimed the gun at his head and promised to pull the trigger."

"That doesn't sound like something your mom would do."

"Before getting the gun, she tried to stab him with a knife."

The screen door on the back of the house suddenly swung open and Rachel stepped out next to George. He jumped off the porch and turned to look at her. Ben dropped the pickaxe, put his hands in his pockets, and bowed his head.

With a large bandage on Rachel's forehead, George could see that Ben's story might be true, not a tall tale to entertain him. He stared at the bandage.

"George, I think you'd better go home now," Rachel said flatly.

Without waiting for an explanation, George dashed for home. Rachel took a few steps off the porch to gain a better view of his retreat, and she watched as George ran down the gravel driveway that led him away from the Bakers' home.

While taking a deep breath, Rachel faced Ben and said, "Benjamin, look at me."

He obeyed, and Rachel said, "There are some things that must stay secret. Do you understand?"

Ben nodded but Rachel continued to frown, making it clear that her son had committed an enormous mistake. "I'm surprised you thought it was acceptable to tell George about something that happened in the privacy of our home. Do you want his mother spreading rumors about our family up and down this road?"

Rachel pointed at George's house across the street and added a sweeping gesture to include the nearby homes, trailers, and farms scattered across that dirt-poor slice of Utah. Ben looked down at the pickaxe. "No," he whispered sheepishly.

His mother continued without a reassuring smile. "You need to do your part to keep family matters private. Will you?"

Ben nodded and muttered, "Yes."

"What do you think your father would do if he found out that you started a rumor about us?" Rachel asked, before going back into the house.

Ben returned to weeding the flowers but with much less vigor. He couldn't stop worrying about what his father might do if he found out that he had blabbed about the fight in the kitchen.

The next day George showed up and, when away from potential eavesdroppers, he asked Ben to finish the story about the fight.

"I'm not supposed to tell you anything about it. So shut up before you get me into trouble again."

Chapter 3

Ben's earliest memory took place at the same place where his mother made it clear that the Baker family keeps secrets. Shortly before his fourth birthday, he stood next to Joe as they watched their father fall from a ladder while trying to fix a rain gutter. The boys stared in horror as Al plunged face-first to the concrete porch below. When he stood up, blood trickled out of his mouth and dripped on his white shirt.

"Ben, run to the barn!" Joe shouted, grabbing Ben's arm and pulling him away from their father.

As the boys sprinted away, Joe delivered a statement that became a motto for the Baker children. "*When Dad is mad, someone is going to get hurt.*"

From experience, Joe knew "mad Dad" would blame and punish the boys for what had happened. And Ben had already learned to trust Joe.

Al called them sissies for running off and added, "Haven't you seen a little blood before?"

Despite the stench of cow manure, Joe and Ben hid in the barn until their father drove off in his truck. Later, they found out that he went to the dentist because of chipped and loosened teeth.

Rachel Baker had the lead role in Ben's next memory. While sitting on the back porch and watching his mother mow the lawn, Ben played with a small plastic horse and did something a typical four-year-old might do to test a parent. He tossed the horse to a section of the lawn yet to be mowed. As Rachel passed Ben during her next lap around the lawn, she pointed at the horse and shouted over the lawnmower engine, "Move your toy or it'll get run over!"

Ben shrugged his shoulders to let her know that he didn't care. Rachel came by again, cutting another swath through the grass and coming very close to hitting the horse. She repeated her warning. Ben shook his head defiantly to let her know that he wouldn't be moving the horse—that was her job.

With Rachel's next trip around the lawn, she didn't offer another warning or even glance at Ben. She mowed over the horse, spraying chopped-up horse parts—hooves, head, tail, and body—across the grass. Devastated, Ben cried and ran to gather the pieces.

He wondered how his mother could so cruelly shred his horse. She had the chance to pick it up or easily kick it out of the way. Instead, she delivered on her threat and destroyed his favorite toy. Ben stored that moment as a long-term memory with a simple message—*this woman means what she says.*

Ben's other early memories came from activities related to "the church," which was how everyone in his hometown described the only church in town—the Church of Jesus Christ of Latter-day Saints. Also known as the LDS Church or the Mormon Church, the Baker family attended it every Sunday as members of the local congregation, which was called the Alma Ward.

The weekly schedule included "primary" for children, the young adult program for teens, and Sunday school and sacrament meetings for everyone. The content for these meetings and programs came from the King James Version of the Bible and from other sources considered to be "scripture," including the Book of Mormon, Doctrine and Covenants, and Pearl of Great Price. For Ben, the Book of Mormon stood out because his favorite song learned in primary was about "the golden plates." Joseph Smith said he found these plates and translated and published them as another testament of Jesus Christ. Cities in Utah were named for the prophets of the Book of Mormon, including Ben's hometown of Alma and the nearby towns of Nephi and Lehi.

While Ben's early memories included Bible and Book of Mormon stories, his favorite church-related moments took place in the "cultural hall," which was an indoor basketball gym and a large stage in the center of the church. That's where he played games and appeared on the stage in dramas that taught church doctrine. Easily, his best times in the cultural hall were watching Disney films such as *Old Yeller* and *20,000 Leagues Under the Sea*.

Other standout memories included his mother telling stories about her pioneer ancestors who pulled handcarts across vast plains and over tall mountains to start new lives in Utah. To reinforce her stories, she arranged visits with her grandparents and other relatives who had grown up in pioneer communities. These people recalled stories they heard from their grandparents about what it was like to make the journey to Utah and build farms and towns in a desolate, harsh land.

Ben came to view "the church" as much more than a place to go on Sundays. It represented his family's pioneer heritage—dominated by sacrifice, perseverance, and achievement. The church gave him a connection to five generations of family members who followed Mormon prophets to a place nobody wanted and turned it into a place he was proud to call "home."

Joe also had weighty influence on Ben in his early years. Within a few weeks of Ben's fourth birthday, Joe started school. To his surprise, Ben wasn't allowed to go with him. Rachel held three separate chats with Ben before he finally understood that he wasn't going and that they wouldn't be discussing his request again.

On Joe's first day of school, Ben spent a quiet lonely morning in the gully at the southern edge of his family's farm where he usually went with Joe to dig small caves and build roads and forts. Using his imagination and sticks, rocks and sand, he created an Aztec village and a World War II battlefield. He ended the day covered in sand and the gully's dark red soil.

The Wasatch Range provided a beautiful backdrop for his solitary morning. The Bakers lived in a small, drab farmhouse next to a makeshift barn, chicken coop, and hog pen, but they had superb scenery behind them. Their property filled a narrow gap between Foothill Road and the base of Loafer Mountain. The narrow winding road that ran in front of their house led to small towns in both directions.

Loafer Mountain looked tall from where Ben played in the gully, but it didn't reach nearly as high as some of the nearby landmarks, including Mt. Nebo—the tallest mountain in the Wasatch Range. The Bakers' farm included a barn that Al built using old boards, rusty sheets of corrugated steel, and other scrap material. It contained a section for hay bales and a large stall for the family's milk cow, Daisy. The stall led to a corral for Daisy to roam in during the day. At night and for her twice-a-day milking, Daisy stayed in the stall.

Next to the barn sat a small chicken coop with a fenced-in, outdoor run behind it. It was usually home to about fifty chickens, providing the Bakers with a steady supply of eggs and a weekly chicken dinner.

Farther away from the house, the pig pen held a momma pig and six piglets that survived on feed purchased from the grain store and discarded produce the Bakers scavenged from dumpsters behind grocery stores and restaurants. The family also planted a large garden each year and fed the pigs some of the crops.

When money for groceries ran out, the family relied on the meat, eggs, and vegetables produced through their endless work on the farm. The days when Ben could play for many hours didn't go beyond the first grade. By then, he had a list of daily chores to complete and any spare time would usually be filled with additional tasks or schoolwork.

Ben learned to never utter the words "I'm bored" or to give the impression of being less than fully productive. Shoveling manure, picking weeds, or dusting the house could always be added to his chore list if he had spare time. And both of his parents believed that if anyone does not work, neither should he eat. So, Ben worked.

Chapter 4

Besides working on the farm, Ben spent many hours helping his father at the family's full-service gas station. Al opened the business in 1962, taking over an old station on Alma's Main Street that had been closed for a few years.

Joe and Ben witnessed the new sign—Al Baker's Service Station—being added to the exterior of a faded, worn-out building. "Wow, that's cool," Ben said. "We're going to be rich."

"We'll see," Joe said with a smirk.

The service station became an exciting place for adventures. Joe and Ben fell in love with two old rusty cars parked in the weed-filled vacant lot behind the station.

"Let's get in and drive!" Ben shouted, waving Joe toward the cars.

"OK, but I get the cool blue one," Joe said. "That green thing is yours."

Despite being assigned a hideous lime-green beast, Ben gladly opened its rusty door and climbed in. He grabbed the steering wheel and started bouncing up and down on the seat while making sounds to simulate a powerful racing engine. Joe did the same thing in the blue car.

"Joe, do you see those bank robbers heading out of town?" Ben asked. "We need to catch them before they reach the Salt Lake County line. Let's go!"

Their imaginations led them on many high-speed chases to capture notorious criminals and to make trips through enemy lines in Germany to blow up bridges and shoot Nazis. Joe and Ben never complained about spending long days at the garage because their father gave them short breaks to take the cars for a spin.

During the summer and on weekends, Joe and Ben often spent all day at the station where they helped their father by cleaning his tools and sweeping the two service bays. Al usually had a car in each bay and used dozens of tools to complete repairs. He also sold gas, which required him to put his repair work on hold when a customer arrived.

"I wish you boys could pump gas for me," Al said in the summer of 1965, when hurrying out of the station to assist a customer. Help came about a week later with the arrival of Derek Dean.

From the first moment, Derek mesmerized Ben with his sly smile, wavy black hair, and cocky attitude. Being tall, handsome, and broad-shouldered, he looked like someone who belonged in Hollywood, not a small town in Utah.

Derek showed up riding a loud motorcycle and wearing Levi's, a dark T-shirt, and sunglasses—no helmet. Ben kept his eyes on Derek as soon as the roar of his motorcycle shattered the tranquility of the station's neighborhood. He parked his bike near the gas pumps and strode into the service bay where Al worked on a car.

"Good morning, Mr. Baker, I'm here to turn this garage into a gold mine," Derek said, overflowing with confidence. "The name's Derek Dean. Sir, it is my sincerest pleasure to meet you."

Derek initiated a handshake, which Al cautiously accepted after wiping his greasy hands on a rag. "Al Baker," he said. "Nice to meet you."

"I know you're Al Baker," Derek said with a deep voice and sly wink. "Folks in town have told me about you and said you've been working hard to get this new business up and running. But they said it hasn't taken off yet because you're trying to do it all by yourself. I'm here to change that in ways that go beyond anything you've imagined."

"Well, I haven't considered adding any help because cash has been a bit tight," Al said, shifting his focus from Derek to Ben and then back to the car being repaired.

Derek recognized that he had caught Al by surprise and pounced like a roaring lion. He confidently presented details of his plan for doubling the amount of business. Most of what he said made no sense to Ben, but Al kept nodding and agreeing while smiling nervously. Ben had seen this look before—when his father committed to purchase more unneeded tools from a salesman.

"All right, you've got a new job," Al said. "Can you start tomorrow morning?"

"Yes, boss. I'll be here and help you turn this place into a money-making machine."

As promised, Derek came to work the next day. After a few minutes of training, he began helping by pumping gas and handling office tasks that included writing service orders and accepting payments. He also entertained customers with hard-to-believe stories.

Ben assisted Derek by answering questions about the location of things like the keys to the soda machine and restrooms. Even though Joe didn't trust the new employee and kept his distance, Ben tagged along with Derek wherever he went.

While Derek was pumping gas on his first day at the station, Ben noticed three sixes tattooed on each hand. "Why do you have six hundred and sixty-six on your hands?"

Whispering so the customer nearby couldn't overhear the conversation, he replied, "That's six-six-six—the mark of the beast. That's my nickname—the beast. Do you like it?"

"Sure. It's supercool."

"Do you know about the beast?"

"Not really."

"Do you read the Bible?" he asked, after filling the customer's car and hanging up the gas pump nozzle.

"Yep, in Sunday school."

"Then, go to the last book in the Bible. That's where you can read about the beast. You'll see that he's the smartest, toughest, and most powerful dude on the planet."

After the customer had driven away, Derek showed Ben his tattoos again. "I got these when hanging out with some thugs and needed to make it clear that they shouldn't mess with me."

"Why did you hang out with those guys?" Ben asked. "Couldn't you just stay away from them?"

"No, that wasn't possible," Derek said nonchalantly as he walked back into the station. "We were in the Utah State Prison together."

Ben watched Derek open the cash register and ring up the customer's purchase and sort the bills into the slots designated for each denomination. Seeing an ex-convict touch his family's money made him very nervous. And he knew that it would certainly upset his mother.

Three days passed before a neighbor called Rachel and asked if she knew that her husband had hired an ex-convict to work at the service station. Ben only heard his mother's side of the conversation, but he could tell by her short answers that it wasn't a social call. She kept repeating, "I'm sorry. I'm so sorry."

As the call went on, Rachel said, "I don't know anything about this Derek Dean. You're the first person to mention his name to me."

Rachel listened for another minute, shaking her head and twisting the phone cord. "I'm as shocked as you are. And please believe me that I'm even more upset than you."

She hung up the phone and told Joe and Ben to finish the dishes. "I have to speak to your father and I want you boys to stay here—and keep your sisters in the room," she said with tears in her eyes and her voice quivering. "Do you understand?"

Joe merely nodded, but Ben couldn't resist sharing his opinion about the phone call. "Mom, don't worry about Derek. He's really cool and plans to make us richer than anyone in Alma."

Rachel halted in the kitchen doorway and glared at Ben. "How do you know him?"

"We're pals," he said, brimming with enthusiasm. "Derek and I take care of the customers together. You'll really like him—all the ladies do."

"Oh, I'm sure that I won't like him at all," Rachel said. "I've already heard from one customer who thinks he's a huge problem. She found out that your friend Derek has spent time in prison. I bet you didn't know that."

"Yeah, he told me and showed me his prison tattoos—six, six, six, for the mark of the beast," Ben said, touching his hands to show where the matching tattoos were displayed.

Rachel looked at Ben with sad eyes, pausing to take a deep breath and then letting it out slowly. "Ben, I'm so glad we had this little chat before I talk to your father. Now I know that he has hired an ex-con, and the stranger spending all day with my husband and sons is a fan of the devil."

Rachel hurried from the kitchen, closing the door behind her. Al was in the bathroom, doing what he called "worshiping on the great white throne"—code for making sure he wouldn't be disturbed while sitting on the toilet.

Even though Ben stayed in the kitchen, he still heard his mother knock on the bathroom door and shout, "Al, hurry up and finish your business in there. We need to talk."

He yelled back angrily, "I'll be finished when I'm finished!"

His wife's anger had unleashed "mad Dad" and somebody was going to get hurt. Joe took charge of the kitchen, demanding that the girls stay there and barking orders for Ben to finish the dishes—"right now!"

"Everything needs to look spic and span by the time Mom and Dad are done talking," Joe said, hurrying to the baby's small crib in the corner. "I'll keep Becky from crying when she hears the shouting."

Joe knew what was coming and how to prepare for it. Uncompleted chores and a crying baby would make matters worse and needed to be prevented. Ben followed Joe's lead and worked as fast as he could to finish the dishes and ensure the kitchen looked spotless.

"Debbie, you need to sit at the kitchen table and read one of your books," Joe said, pointing at her usual chair.

"No. I want to go to my room," Debbie whined, heading for the kitchen door.

Joe raced to the door and blocked Debbie's exit. "If you go out there, he's going to hurt you and then come in here and take it out on me. Do you want that to happen?"

Debbie frowned and stomped back to the table where she took her seat and pouted.

"Debbie, you need to put on a happy face before Dad comes through that door," Joe said. "If you don't, he will slap that frown off your face."

She displayed even more unhappiness and turned away from Joe. Ben fought the urge to walk over to Debbie and slap her pouty face. He wanted to do it, but he knew it would create a chorus of crying and shouting—the last thing that should happen with his parents ready to argue. And they went at it immediately and loudly in the living room.

Ben only heard the fight and didn't see whether his mother took any punches or kicks, but the battle held his complete attention. Ben listened intently, worrying about his mother's safety and cringing when he heard his name inserted into the argument about "Derek Dean, the ex-con."

Before the fighting ended, Joe told Ben, "Read to Debbie and get her to cheer up." Having finished the dishes, Ben understood the purpose of his new assignment and did it.

When Al ended the argument by bursting through the kitchen door, he saw a sleeping baby being tended by Joe and a happy Debbie listening to Ben read. Joe's leadership worked. Seeing four well-behaved, quiet children had the same effect as dumping a five-gallon bucket of water on a campfire. Al reacted with one of the sheepish smiles he used after having made a mistake. Next, he checked the stove, sink, and countertops. Everything looked perfect.

Satisfied with his inspection, Al made a little grunting sound and walked through the kitchen toward the back door. As he passed the kitchen table, he slapped Ben in the back of the head.

"Six, six, six. You didn't need to tell that ridiculous story to your mother. Why don't you grow up and stop being so stupid?"

Before leaving the house, Al looked at Joe and said, "Tell your crazy mother that I went back to the station. I'll need to work all night to keep this ungrateful family out of the poor house."

Joe said "OK" and Ben watched his father close the door and soon drive away. Ben wondered if he was going to the station to work or only needed a place to hide. Ben didn't care. He liked to see his father leave and always had the same thought in these frightful moments. *Why does he keep coming back?*

Chapter 5

After his father's departure, Ben followed Derek's suggestion and read the last book in the Bible—Revelation—to learn more about "the beast." While not understanding much of the book, he could see that the beast starts off with great power and gains the world's praise, but he eventually loses a war and gets tossed into prison for eternity. Ben wondered why Derek chose the beast as his hero.

At the station the next day, he watched Derek pumping gas and mentioned having read Revelation. "You're right about the beast being strong, but did you know that he ends up in prison?"

"Yeah, you can't win every battle," Derek said. "But while the beast is the boss, he lives the high life and takes crap from nobody."

After hanging up the gas pump hose, Derek quickly washed the windshield of the customer's car and then accepted five one-dollar bills for the payment.

"Sir, I hope you have a glorious day," Derek said with a broad smile and snappy salute. He stepped back to allow the customer to drive away and then strolled toward the office with Ben walking alongside him.

On the cash register, Derek rang up a sale for four dollars and placed that amount in the cash drawer before closing it. He stuffed the remaining dollar into his pocket.

Derek winked at Ben, and said with a chuckle, "That dollar is a small tip to keep me a happy and satisfied employee."

Derek then pulled a quarter from his pants pocket and flipped it toward Ben who caught it. He whispered, "And here's your tip, with more to come if you keep our deal a secret. OK?"

Ben grinned and nodded, wiping grease off the quarter before hiding it in his pocket. "Thanks! I've never had money handed to me for doing nothing."

"Keep quiet about it or the money train will no longer be stopping for you. Got it?"

"Yep."

"That means nobody, including your brother, can see you with extra cash. And if someone catches you with it, make up a story about how you found the money on the side of the road."

Ben said "OK" and shuffled around the station for about fifteen minutes before he couldn't wait any longer and ran across the street to Benanti's Groceries. The quarter matched his weekly allowance, which was only paid if he completed all his daily chores. With a week's wages in his pocket, he knew what he wanted—a large apple turnover.

After making his purchase, Ben took the exit that faced away from the station and found a shady place on the store's loading deck where he sat on an empty milk crate. He gobbled up the turnover before Joe found him and asked where he got the money to buy such an expensive treat. Ben enjoyed the fruit of his deal with Derek for three days despite feeling guilty about taking the money. But a visit to the station by his mother brought it to a sudden end.

While carrying Becky in her arms and holding Debbie's hand, Rachel walked through the station, checking out the displays for tires and car accessories. Through side glances, she watched Ben trailing Derek and laughing at his crude jokes while they assisted customers at the pumps.

After about twenty minutes, Rachel called Ben to her side. She bent down to look him in the eyes and then solemnly delivered one of her favorite sayings. "Benjamin, remember that bad company corrupts good morals."

She didn't elaborate, but her words reminded Ben of the two quarters he currently had in his pocket from "tips" that Derek had given him that morning. He reached into his pocket and caressed the warm metal in his hand, dreaming of all the snacks he could buy with so much money. This pleasant thought vanished as his mother's searching stare churned up a wave of shame. He knew his secret deal with Derek was stealing.

Later in the day, overwhelming remorse kicked in when Ben munched on the fifty-cents worth of snacks he bought with the stolen money. His mother's comment made the pastries and candy turn from sweet to bitter in his mouth and he shuffled back to the station buried in guilt.

When Derek skimmed another dollar from a customer's purchase near closing time, Ben looked away, pretending not to notice.

"Hey, partner," Derek said quietly. "Catch."

Derek tossed a quarter from across the office, bouncing it off Ben's chest. The quarter rolled to the middle of the office floor.

"Pick it up! It's yours."

Ben complied, but then he handed Derek the quarter and said, "I don't want to take any more money."

"Why?" he asked, stuffing the quarter into his pants pocket.

Ben shrugged his shoulders and said, "Don't know."

Derek scowled and grabbed Ben's left arm, mashing it with his firm grasp. "If you blab about this to your dad, you'll regret the day you double-crossed me. I'll crush your nose and tell your dad that you've been taking his money."

He clenched his right fist and held it under Ben's nose, so he could clearly see the 666-tattoo. Ben nodded and fought back tears, being disappointed by his friend's harsh behavior and feeling foolish for having been duped into stealing.

Derek's threat worked. Ben said nothing and avoided being near Derek when he handled money. Ben decided to stay out of the way and expected his father to eventually discover the missing money or catch Derek in the act. But the station's sudden prosperity hid the thefts.

As Derek promised, the volume of business picked up after his arrival. Customers liked not having to wait for help when they pulled in.

And with Derek always available at the pumps, Al finished repairs more quickly. His gamble on the handsome, charming stranger paid off.

After a few weeks, Rachel became more accepting of Derek and smiled at him when she visited the station. As with all the ladies, Derek poured buckets of praise on her.

"Mrs. Baker, you look lovely today as always," Derek would say. "And your beautiful children are eternal jewels in your crown. I've never met such well-behaved children."

Rachel enjoyed the flattery and the increased volume of cars and trucks pulling up to the pumps. But she didn't see Derek taking "tips" and finding other ways to steal from the station.

"Hey, if it isn't the one and only Denny Siegen—welcome to Al's!" Derek said, greeting the driver of an old, rusty car. "It's about time you stopped by to see me at my new job."

Ben stood nearby, watching the conversation but keeping his distance. He had witnessed a similar greeting with another friend of Derek's who left the station without paying for gas. "Are you here for a fill-up?" Derek asked.

"No, I only have two dollars," Denny said, holding up the money. "And I'm running on fumes right now."

Derek snatched the dollars and tucked them into his pocket. "That's good enough. I bet this old thing has a small tank."

Ben glanced at the pump for the sale price when Derek returned the hose—more than four dollars. And yet, Denny didn't hand Derek additional money and drove away with a sneaky grin.

As Derek strolled to the office, he glared at Ben and said, "Hey, Benny: just so you know, I don't appreciate you keeping tabs on me. And don't forget that I learned how to deal with squealers in prison. If you're smart, you'll keep your mouth shut."

He returned to the office and took a chair in the shade but didn't approach the cash register to complete the sale. While Ben continued to worry about these thefts, a more severe problem had its roots in a conversation he overheard a few days later.

"Al, do you know what marketing is?" Derek asked.

"Uh, I guess so," Al said. "It's telling customers about your products."

"Much more than that," Derek said. "Marketing is what you do to get people excited about coming to your business because you have something they desperately want. It's exactly what you need to make this station the top business in Alma."

Derek continued after unfolding a piece of paper and showing it to Al. "You should use your mechanical skills to build a stock car and showcase it at the Utah County Speedway on Saturday nights."

Al seemed interested, so Derek blazed ahead. "I know that you could build the fastest stock car in the county and dominate the competition at these local races. And then we could move up the ranks to the races at the state fairgrounds and show everyone that Al Baker is the best mechanic and driver in Utah. You'll be famous."

Derek held a big smile while Al studied the paper that described the races. Ben peered over his father's shoulder to see what it said, not trusting Derek but liking the idea of his family being involved in auto racing.

"Well, I don't know," Al said. "How could I keep up with all the work I have now, plus build a stock car?"

"Come on, Al, you need to think big like me. With the money you make from racing, you could hire three or four more mechanics to do the dirty work here at the station while you're taking care of the easy stuff. And before you know it, we'll be opening Al Baker Service Stations across the state—with me as your business partner, of course."

Ben missed the conversation between his father and Derek that sealed the deal, but he witnessed the arrival of a car four days later that needed extensive body work.

"You can use the engine in this monster to create the fastest stock car west of the Mississippi," Derek said while Al handed Denny Siegen a cash payment for the car.

Al noticed his son watching the transaction. "Ben, don't tell your mother about this car. It's our little secret. Do you hear me?"

Ben nodded and honored the pledge, but his mother visited the station about two weeks later and asked why the car in the far service bay only had a chassis, engine, and four wheels—no doors, hood, or fenders. "Where's the rest of it?"

"That's the foundation of a stock car that's going to put this station on the map," Al said. "Dear, we're going into the racing business."

As soon as they started to argue, Ben retreated to one of the old cars behind the station. He drowned out the quarrel by making sounds of racing engines, squealing tires, and honking horns. He stayed in the car until his mother drove off. His father must have won the fight because he kept working on the car and it slowly began to look like something seen on a racetrack.

The finishing touch came on a hot evening after the station closed. Al and Derek painted the car dark blue and added a giant eight on each door—the number assigned to the car by the racetrack director.

"Al, we've created a mobile billboard," Derek said, admiring the paint job. "Let's park the car out front so people can see it."

"Oh, I don't know," Al said. "Somebody might damage it."

"Not with me and Ben keeping our eyes on it during the day and then parking it inside the garage at night," Derek said.

Al agreed, and Ben enjoyed keeping kids from playing on the car even though he realized that they only listened to him when Derek gave them a fierce stare. "Look but don't touch," Derek said to the kids who violated the hands-off policy.

When the crowd included a couple of Derek's friends, he climbed inside and started the engine, pumping the gas to get it to roar and delight the onlookers. Ben loved the sound and smell, swelling with pride that his father had made this powerful machine. Many kids from Ben's school joined the spectators checking out No. 8. He chatted with them at the station and looked forward to the summer break ending so he could go back to school with something to talk about.

No. 8 already gave his parents plenty to discuss. They argued about the car frequently with his mother expressing fears that it would bankrupt the family. "And what will happen if you're injured driving that thing?" Rachel asked.

"Oh, don't get so worked up over nothing. I'll wear a helmet and I have a roll cage in the car to protect me if there's an accident. Plus, I plan to be in front of the pack, leading the way and taking the checkered flag. Nobody is going to touch me."

Ben wanted his father's boast to be true. In his mind, he saw the racetrack stands filled with cheering fans and No. 8 crossing the finish line first. And he could hear the racetrack announcer saying, "And that's Al Baker in Number Eight, the fastest car in Utah County, leaving the competition behind for another easy victory."

Chapter 6

"I have absolutely no interest in watching you race," Rachel said in response to Al's request that she attend his first race. "What makes you think it would be fun for me to sit on bleachers for two hours with a baby on my lap and three other kids to keep under control? And the entire time, I would be worrying that you are going to get hurt or something worse will happen."

"Come on, don't be such a dark cloud," Al said. "I thought you'd want to be there to cheer me on."

"Why would I cheer for something that puts your health and our finances at risk?"

While delivering a stern look, Al said, "Fine. Stay home, but I'll be taking my boys with me. They believe in me."

Joe and Ben rode in the back of their father's pickup truck while Derek sat in the cab. No. 8 trailed behind them, secured to the truck with a sturdy hitch. When approaching the track, Al parked on the side of the road and pulled a tarp from behind the truck's bench seat.

"Boys, you need to hide under this," Al said. "Kids aren't allowed in the pit area, so you'll have to stay out of sight until we get inside."

After parking in the track infield, Al told his sons to jump out and sneak into the grandstand. "Don't get caught. I'm not buying tickets for you."

With Joe taking the lead, the boys hurried past the other race teams, attracting a few stares but no commands to "get out of here." When they reached the track, Joe took off at a full sprint and arrived ahead of Ben at their targeted exit point—the tall, chain-link fence that separated the racetrack from the grandstand.

When Joe started to climb it, a security guard on the other side shouted at him. "Hey, junior, what do you think you're doing? Get off the fence."

After spotting a possible escape, Ben ran away from Joe, aiming for a small section of the fence that had pulled loose from the bottom of the grandstand. Ben slid to a stop and pulled on the fence to create a gap so he could slide through. When on the other side, he pushed the fence with his feet to make a bigger hole.

"Joe, over here!" Ben shouted to his brother who had dropped off the fence and stood on the racetrack while the security guard reprimanded him.

Joe followed Ben's lead and dashed toward him. He dropped to his hands and knees, sliding through the gap and landing on his back next to Ben. Joe spun around and pulled the fence back into place to hide the entrance.

"Now, what?" Joe asked.

Ben pointed at a faint distant light slightly to their left. The boys moved toward the light as fast as they could go. At first, the grandstand stood three feet above the boys, which required them to crawl. The grandstand's solid wood planks held closely together by steel brackets only allowed tiny beams of light to enter the space below.

"I hope we aren't crawling over rattlesnakes and black widow spiders," Ben said as they hurried toward their goal.

Soon the boys could stand up and walk, because the grandstand had risen much higher over their heads. They reached the light, which was coming through a small hole in a series of large plywood sheets that formed the grandstand's back wall.

Joe and Ben searched for a loose board when a much better exit appeared—a door. Ben twisted the handle and, to his surprise, found it unlocked. He led his brother through the door and into a crowd of spectators near the grandstand stairs.

"Clean yourself up," Joe said as he wiped dirt off his pants and shirt. "You look like a bum."

"No, I don't," Ben said, giving his clothes a quick brush down. "If it was up to you, we'd be getting thrown out of this place."

"That still could happen," Joe said. "What are we going to do if someone asks us for our tickets?"

The boys entered the grandstand and found empty seats on the opposite end from where the security guard had caught Joe on the fence. After a long wait, the roar of powerful engines shook the grandstand and a loud cheer went up. The stock cars entered the track one at a time and began running laps. The last car out of the infield—No. 8—caused Ben to jump to his feet and cheer. Joe held back on his applause.

The track announcer's introduction of the drivers included, "Al Baker, a rookie racer, who will be starting at the back of the pack."

When the dozen competitors lined up for the race, Al pulled into the outside position in the last of six rows. To win, he would need to pass all the other cars on the short, narrow track. While the drivers waited, the crowd rose for the singing of the national anthem and remarks from the announcer. Then, a pretty blonde woman wearing shorts and a tight blouse waved a flag from behind the infield guardrail and the race began with a thunderous charge.

Ben cringed on the first turn when the driver next to his father's car slid sideways and bumped him. No. 8 received its first blemish. The car's beautiful paint job didn't survive ten seconds on the racetrack.

Ben swore and shouted to Joe, "Hey, that's not fair. Did you see that jerk? He hit Dad on purpose."

Joe scolded his little brother for swearing and looked around to see if anyone had heard him, but his concern didn't fit the setting. The air soon filled with vulgar expressions as the other patrons had opinions to share about the race. And the air became thick with cigarette smoke. Most of the spectators shared another habit—drinking beer—and they had been at it well before the race began. As a result, most of them tossed off any restraint, yelling at each other and the drivers. Having grown up as Mormons and in a town dominated by Mormons, Joe and Ben had rarely seen people use tobacco or drink alcohol because those things and others were prohibited by the LDS Church's health law, known as the word of wisdom.

Ben ignored the "sins" of the race fans and matched their zeal with his cheering. "Go Number Eight! Put the pedal to the metal!"

A couple of men with bushy beards and hunting caps stood next to the boys. When Ben shouted, they looked at him and grinned. The man nearest to Ben tipped his beer can at him and said, "Son, you must be crazy cheering for that driver. He's never raced before."

"I'm not crazy. That's my dad and there's nobody on that track with a faster car. I know because I helped him build it."

"Is that really your dad?"

"Yes, sir," Ben said with pride.

"Then, we're cheering for him too. I'm Curtis and this here's my buddy, Tom."

Curtis and Tom switched their attention to the track and cheered for the rookie driver. When No. 8 went high on a turn to pass another car, Curtis splashed beer on Ben as he waved his can in the air to salute the move. As beer dripped from Ben's hair and soaked the front of his shirt, he stood on his toes to watch his father avoid spinning out when a car bounced off his rear bumper.

When the pack sailed past the grandstand, the inside car in the front row surged ahead. With that move, the pack broke apart and the race's first wreck occurred. No. 8 ran into the passenger's side door of a car that had spun out in the turn. Ben watched in horror as his father's car started to slide after the collision and ended up stopped and facing the wrong way on the track. Somehow the two cars behind No. 8 raced by without hitting it head-on. After they passed, Al turned his car around and continued the chase—in last place except for the car he had hit and pinned against the guardrail. When Al tried to catch up with the pack, his car's engine showed off, surging ahead with a mighty roar.

"This kid built that car!" Curtis shouted while pointing at Ben. A few spectators turned to look at Ben and sneer with barefaced skepticism.

While the rest of the cars shot through the back straightaway and into the far turn, the damaged car remained next to the guardrail. The driver signaled with his hands that he couldn't continue. A race official waved a red flag to stop the race when the cars approached the grandstand. With the cars halted, a truck entered the track and towed away the damaged car.

The race resumed, with No. 8 at the back again. The cars stayed together for the next six laps with only a little bumping in the turns. When one of the front-row cars pulled ahead, it kicked off a series of moves that resulted in the cars circling the track single-file.

"This will help Dad," Ben said to Joe. "He has the fastest car out there and can start passing the others now."

"We'll see," Joe said.

Ben grinned when his prediction came true. Al passed cars in the straightaways through aggressive maneuvers that put him in fourth place. His progress stalled there because the driver of the third-place car blocked him every time he tried to pass. Nothing changed until only a few laps remained, and that's when the second-place driver spun out and fell behind No. 8.

"Lucky move for your dad," Curtis shouted. "If he can hold onto third, he gets three hundred bucks."

Thinking big, Ben asked, "How much will he get for first place?"

"Five hundred bucks, but I can't see that happening," Curtis said.

The race continued, and Al made another attempt to move up, but the other driver swerved to keep Al behind him. The checkered flag came down with No. 8 in third place.

"Third place for a rookie isn't bad," Curtis said. "Congratulations! If you were a little older, I'd give you a beer to celebrate."

Within a few minutes, the top three finishers received prize money.

Al earned $300 for driving thirty laps around the short track. To Ben, it seemed like a fortune that would help pay the bills and fill the refrigerator with groceries.

When the ceremony ended, Joe and Ben said goodbye to Curtis and Tom, letting them know that they couldn't stay for the next race. While walking out of the grandstand, Ben started chatting about the race, focusing on the $300.

"Mom will be thrilled!" he shouted.

Joe shot down Ben's enthusiasm with a stern command. "Keep your mouth shut about the money. Do you really think Mom is going to see any of it?"

Joe's downbeat view reminded Ben of past times when their father and his money were soon parted. And he didn't argue when his brother added, "Dad has a better chance of making the long drive home with ice cubes in his pocket than three hundred dollars."

CHAPTER 7

Five trucks towing race cars passed Joe and Ben before their father and Derek showed up at the exit. No. 8 had gone from beautiful to battered in less than an hour, with dents, scrapes, and dirt all over it. Ben walked around the car, groaning as he noticed more and more problems until his father's patience ran out.

"Get into the truck—pronto!" Al shouted.

Joe had already climbed into the back and gave his little brother an urgent wave to join him. Ben jumped in and Al sped away from the track—still in race mode.

"Do you think Dad will get to start up front at the next race?" Ben asked, shouting over the road noise.

Joe shrugged his shoulders and stared into the darkness along the highway. As he often did, Joe showed no excitement because he didn't like to get too high when things went well. It helped him deal with the disappointment when everything plunged downhill.

Before going home, Al dropped Derek off at his apartment in Alma, which made room for Joe and Ben to climb into the truck cab. Ben finally had a chance to talk to his father about the race.

"Fantastic job, Dad!"

"Thanks! Were you surprised to see me nearly win?"

"No, I knew you could do it. You had the fastest car out there and would've won if you had started in the front row."

"Yep, but starting in the back is the way it goes for first-timers."

"Will you get moved up to the first or second row the next time?"

"I don't know. They didn't make any promises."

"And what are you going to do with the three hundred dollars?"

"Well, boys, I hope we can keep that money a little secret between the three of us," Al said, glancing at Joe to make sure he paid attention. "I had to pay track fees and give money to Derek for helping me. So I barely have enough left to get the car ready for the next race."

When turning into their driveway, Al asked a pair of questions that Joe and Ben took as firm orders. "Do we have a deal about the money? Is it our secret?"

They both mumbled "Yes" and then Joe elbowed Ben in the ribs. He didn't need to say a word. As always, Joe had predicted the future. No money for their mother.

Al left No. 8 hitched to his truck, telling his sons that he planned to take it to the service station in the morning. With the station closed on Sundays like most businesses in Alma, he could make the repairs without customers interrupting him.

"Can I help you?" Ben asked, still excited about his father's racing career.

"Sure, I could use assistance from both of you."

Joe faked a smile to indicate his status as a cheerful volunteer.

"Of course, your mom will drag us off to church first. But we'll go right after lunch and get the car running smooth."

When the race team approached the back door, Rachel came out of the house carrying Becky with Debbie following her. From a distance, she looked toward No. 8, but Al had parked near the barn where the lights from the house didn't reach. The darkness concealed the damage.

"How did it go?" she asked.

"We're all still in one piece," Al said. "And I took third place. Not bad for a rookie."

"Dad had the fastest car on the track," Ben said. "You should have seen him fly."

"Oh, that's nice," Rachel said.

"I heard a lot of good things about the car," Al said. "People who know this business think I have a future in racing."

"It's true!" Ben shouted with enthusiasm. "Curtis and Tom said that Dad had the fastest car on the track."

"Who are Curtis and Tom?" Rachel asked as the family entered the house. Before Ben could answer, Rachel sniffed and then moved closer to Ben and sniffed again.

"Oh, Ben, you smell like beer and cigarettes. What have you been up to?"

"Nothing. Curtis got a little excited is all and spilled some beer on me when cheering for Dad. And everybody smokes at the track—except for me and Joe, of course."

"Oh, Al, what kind of people did you let our boys hang out with?" Rachel asked with a pained expression before pulling Joe closer to smell his clothes.

She didn't wait for Al to respond, attacking the odor issue instead. "Boys, take off your clothes and leave them on the back porch to air out. And then you will need to get into the bathtub and scrub with lots of soap. I don't want our house smelling like a bar."

Joe and Ben obeyed and then quietly slipped into the front room to watch TV even though their normal bedtime had already passed. Rachel let them watch for a few minutes while she sat with her hands clenched in front of her. Al had dozed off on the couch.

Being exhausted, Joe and Ben didn't protest when she led them to their room. She usually told the boys to go there by themselves, but this night she went in to make sure they settled down.

"Mom, you would have been proud of Dad," Ben said.

"I'm glad," Rachel said, gently touching Ben's head. "It's good to be proud of your father."

"Do you think he's proud of me and Joe?"

"Sure, your dad might not show it when he loses his temper, but he's proud of both of you and loves you very much. I hope you remember that when things don't go as well as they did today."

She quickly left, wiping her eyes and whispering "Good night."

Sleep came slowly for Ben as he thought about crawling under the grandstand, listening to the cars roar and seeing his father take third place. The night had more excitement crammed into it than any he could remember.

Chapter 8

Fourth grade began two days later, with Ben receiving the same day-one greeting that he had heard from his teachers since kindergarten. "Oh, you're Joe's little brother," Mrs. Adamson said with a beaming smile. "I'm so excited to have you in my class. Joe was my best student last year."

Ben grinned nervously. By this time he had learned that Joe, a truly gifted student, had created lofty expectations that Ben would fail to match. Joe impressed his teachers by being smart, hardworking, and polite, but Ben struggled to pay attention, especially during math class, and fell below the class average.

As in previous school years, Julie Winters sat next to Ben and smiled as soon as she saw him. Since first grade when Julie's family moved to Alma, Julie and Ben sat next to each other on the classroom's front row. Their teachers placed them there because they were the shortest kids in the class and needed to be in the front to see the chalkboard.

While the other boys preferred the back row, Ben never complained about his seat because it placed him next to Julie, who he regarded as an angel and the prettiest girl in the school. She always added a spark of hope to his day with encouraging words and her kind, gentle spirt.

Alma didn't have any wealthy families, but some did better than others and Julie belonged to one of them. She came to school in clean clothes that never looked old and tattered like the hand-me-down stuff that most of the other kids wore. Her beautiful brunette hair always appeared clean and carefully brushed, and she adorned it daily with a pretty bow. Despite Julie being tiny, the other kids considered her size an asset. It made her cute and adorable. Every boy in the class loved Julie.

When Julie mentioned having seen his father's stock car at the station, Ben beamed with pride and explained how hard he worked all summer to help build it. He also shared an exaggerated story of the trip to the racetrack.

"Wasn't it frightening to see your dad in a crash?"

"Oh no, he wears a helmet and the car has a steel cage to keep him safe," Ben said. "His next race is on Saturday. Do you ever go to the races?"

"No, that's not something my family would do."

Ben wanted to share more details, but Mrs. Adamson shouted "Class!" and fourth grade began. When announcing her plans for the school year, Mrs. Adamson mentioned publishing a monthly magazine that her students would help create by writing articles. Ben immediately made plans to write an article about his father's racing career.

When school let out, Ben looked for his brother because they planned to walk to the station to help their father until closing time. He looked for Joe in the fifth-grade classroom, but he had already left. So he searched the playground and found Joe being shoved and taunted by two boys from his class. They insulted him about being a "grease monkey" and living in "a shack with pigs and chickens." It surprised Ben to see his big brother being picked on because he thought everybody liked Joe.

When Joe noticed Ben watching, he asked, "Where have you been?"

Joe then turned away from the boys and started walking briskly toward the station. Ben ran to catch up and asked, "Why are those guys giving you a hard time?"

"Shut up and walk faster."

Joe increased his pace so that Ben needed to run to keep up with his brother's longer stride. Joe remained silent and focused on the sidewalk in front of him while Ben peeked over his left shoulder and spotted the two boys following them.

"Those guys are right behind us," he said, anticipating an attack based on his years of experience with bullies. "Should we run?"

"No, and don't look at them again."

Ben resisted the urge to look back, but his ears warned him of an attack. The boys charged forward, pushing Joe and Ben in the back. The push caused Ben to fall and drop his books and lunch box. Joe stumbled, but he kept his footing and took off at a fast run toward the station.

Knowing that Joe usually had the right idea about what to do in all situations, Ben scrambled to pick up his stuff and then sprinted for the station. Joe always outran Ben and most other kids his age, so Ben knew he would be left to deal with the bullies. This realization motivated Ben to move his short legs as fast as they could go.

The bullies quit trying to catch Joe, but they continued to follow Ben while laughing and making squawking sounds like chickens. Ben tried to run faster, but the boys stayed with him until they passed a large hedge that had blocked their view of the station. As soon as they saw the station, the bullies stopped.

"Nice run for a little girl," one of them said. "We went easy on you today, but we'll catch you tomorrow and you'll be sorry. Tell your chicken brother that we'll be looking for him too."

The boys turned and walked away laughing and calling Joe and Ben cowards. Ben had been through many similar incidents, but this time it was different. Seeing Joe picked on bothered Ben more than when it happened to him.

Ben walked into the station where Joe sat behind the office desk and Derek stood nearby. The station had no customers at that moment. Ben dropped his books and lunch box on the desk. He asked Derek, "Where's my dad?"

"He's gone to the auto parts store for a carburetor to put on that old Buick," Derek said, pointing at a large car parked in the far service bay. "Why? Need something?"

"No, I was just wondering where he is," Ben said, wanting to tell his father about the bullies. His body shook with anger, and he shouted an obscenity in frustration.

"Hey, cowboy, what's up?" Derek asked. "Is there something you aren't telling us?"

Taking the lead, Joe answered, "Nothing's wrong. Ben needs to learn to keep his big mouth shut. That's all."

Message received. Ben stopped talking and picked up a broom to sweep the service bays. They weren't dirty, but he needed a distraction.

Joe continued to sit behind the desk and act like a whipped dog. Ben hated his brother looking that way and the rage kept building inside him. He swung the broom with all his force hitting the empty oil barrel being used as a garbage can. Derek stormed into the service bay and snatched the broom out of Ben's hands.

"Man, get yourself under control or you're going to break something," Derek said, tossing the broom into a corner.

"Let's go for a walk," he said. "Joe, watch the place. We'll be back soon."

Then Derek used Ben's shoulder to guide him out of the service bay and toward the road. He remained silent until about thirty yards away. Releasing Ben's shoulder, he asked, "Are you having some trouble with your big brother? Is he roughing you up?"

"No."

"Come on, you can be honest with me. What's happening?"

Ben wanted to remain compliant with Joe's no-talk rule, but he blurted out the story about the bullies. Derek listened and then calmly said, "Your problem is something that every guy runs into at times. There's always someone bigger, stronger, and tougher than you. That's when you need to be *meaner* to take care of yourself."

He told Ben to follow him back into the station where he sorted through Al's massive tool collection. After a few minutes, Derek pulled out a steel pipe about three feet long and an inch in diameter. Al used it to slip over the handle of a wrench to give him more leverage when trying to loosen a rusty bolt.

"This here is what I call an equalizer," Derek said. "Use this piece of steel to drop someone bigger than you to his knees. When you bring him down to your level, then you'll be equals and can win the fight."

Ben looked at the pipe and thought that he wouldn't be able to hit somebody with it. He mumbled about it being a terrible idea and started to walk away from Derek.

"Hey, kid, come back here and do exactly what I tell you," Derek said with a touch of anger.

Ben turned around and faced Derek, being worried about what might happen if he refused.

"Take the pipe in your hands. Remember how you felt when those jerks chased you—and then think of them as you hit that barrel. Give it all you got."

Ben did it, and the pipe stung his hands and the noise caused Joe to yell. "Knock it off, dummy. You're going to get us into trouble."

"See, it's that easy," Derek said, ignoring Joe's concern. "If you swing the pipe that hard and land even one shot to the guy's chest, he won't remain standing—guaranteed."

"That would be nice," Ben said quietly while studying the pipe and imaging what it would be like to swing it when face-to-face with the boys.

Derek watched Ben for a few seconds and then pushed him away from the station. "Now, go hide the pipe in the bushes up the road and it'll be waiting for you tomorrow."

Ben regretted the last time he went along with one of Derek's plans, but this one needed to be done. He didn't have any other ideas for protecting Joe.

Ben followed Derek's instructions, completing his return to the station about the same time his father arrived. Al stepped out of his truck with a couple of boxes that he carried to the office. While standing behind a customer's car at the gas pumps, Ben watched his father and brother to see if they talked about him. He worried that Joe might have seen him go up the street with the pipe and told his father about it, but his secret appeared to be safe. Joe focused on homework and his father filed receipts from his purchase.

After filling the customer's car with gas, Derek smiled and said, "Man, I'd pay good money to watch the show you put on if those clowns chase you again."

Derek simulated a batting motion. "I can see you hitting a homerun and sending those boys crying all the way to their mommies with broken ribs and wet pants."

Chapter 9

Despite being furious the day before, Ben hoped the bullies would leave him alone. Overnight, he had grown uncomfortable with Derek's plan, worrying that he could seriously injure the boys with the pipe. Before leaving the classroom at the end of the day, he whispered to Julie that he might not see her for a week or longer.

"I'll probably be getting into a fight after school with two fifth-graders and expect that'll get me suspended," Ben said.

"Ah, Ben, you should tell Mrs. Adamson about your problem and let her take care of it," Julie said. "Fighting is a bad idea. You could get hurt."

"Don't worry about me. I've been getting help from my friend at the station and he taught me a trick he learned in prison."

"No. You need to talk to Mrs. Adamson or the principal and do what they say. Don't listen to someone teaching you terrible things. I've always thought you were a good boy and wanted to stay out of trouble."

Julie gave Ben a concerned look and headed for the classroom door, briefly pausing there. She gestured toward the teacher and nodded at Ben. He understood the message, but he didn't want to get Mrs. Adamson involved. Word would spread that he tattled.

After Julie left the classroom, Ben made his exit, avoiding eye contact with Mrs. Adamson. He looked for Joe in the hallway and on the playground, but he couldn't find him and walked toward the station alone.

When starting down the street that led to the station, he noticed Joe running four blocks ahead of him with the two bullies about a half block behind. Seeing Joe easily outpace the bullies gave Ben some relief, but he still hated watching his brother run away from a fight. As soon as Joe reached the station, the bullies made obscene gestures at him and then turned and walked in Ben's direction.

By walking on the other side of the street, Ben tried to pass the bullies without being noticed, but one of them spotted him. "Hey, Joe's little brother, you'd better start running. We already chased your sissy brother down the street."

Ben took off with a mix of fear and anger driving his legs. The boys crossed the street and charged down the sidewalk about forty feet behind him. Ben noticed a car coming his way and dashed across the street a few seconds before it reached him.

Cutting in front of the car caused the driver to shout and honk at Ben. It also forced the boys to stop chasing him while waiting for the car to pass. The risky move placed more distance between Ben and the bullies, but they gradually closed the gap.

By listening to their footsteps and taunts, Ben knew they would catch him before he reached the hedge where the steel pipe waited. To run faster, he tossed his books and lunch box into the yard of a house as he sprinted by.

"You're such a momma's boy," one of the bullies said. "I bet you're going to have her come back and pick up your stuff for you."

The other bully shouted a couple of names—"wuss" and "pansy"—to reinforce his friend's insult. The humiliation of being chased and disrespected triggered deep anger in Ben and convinced him to use Derek's plan. As he approached the hedge, he looked over his shoulder to see how long he had to dig out the hidden pipe.

"We're right here and going to beat the crap out of you," one of the boys said.

If all went well, Ben would have barely enough time to grab and swing his weapon. To gain an extra second, he added a sprint to the end of his run and then thrust his hands into the hedge, grabbing the cool steel pipe and yanking it out with one motion.

The two boys, running side-by-side, were nearly on top of Ben when he spun around to face them. As Derek had taught him, Ben held the pipe in two hands like a baseball bat, pulled it back over his right shoulder, and then swung it as hard as he could. The chest of the boy nearest to Ben served as his first target.

The boy saw the pipe coming and uttered a little whimper as he held his books in front of him to block the blow. The pipe whistled through the air, knocking the books out of the boy's hands. The pipe continued undeterred and made a loud thumping sound when it connected with the boy's upper chest. He had run into the blow, so his feet continued moving forward while his head and shoulders went backwards. The boy landed flat on his back and let out a loud gasp.

Homerun!

Energy surged through Ben's body. With a growl, he jumped over the fallen boy and tried to hit his friend, but the boy jumped sideways and ran into the street. Ben chased him, taking a swing at his back and delivering a glancing blow. The boy yelped and changed directions to evade the menacing pipe. Still furious, Ben continued the chase for about half a block before the boy sprinted away.

Ben turned to look for the fallen boy and saw him picking up his books. He charged toward him with the pipe above his head like a sword. The boy noticed Ben coming and took off, leaving one of his books behind. Ben chased him, scooping up the book and holding it up in one hand with the pipe in the other.

"Hey, you left your book here. Why don't you come back and get it?"

After taking another dozen steps Ben gave up the chase, having grown tired from running with a heavy pipe in his hands. He also started to regret what he had done. Julie's advice came to mind that he should be a "good boy" and not listen to Derek. He returned to the yard where he had thrown his books and lunch box. After gathering them, Ben walked to the station.

Derek was pumping gas for a customer and spotted Ben's arrival. "Hey, how did it go?" he asked.

Ben paused at the pumps, shrugged his shoulders, and said, "Fine."

"I don't see a black eye or any blood. What does the other team look like?"

"They ran home. I think it's over."

"Good for you. Now give me the pipe and I'll put it back in the tool bin. We need to keep quiet about what you did. It's nothing your dad needs to hear about."

Without replying, Ben handed Derek the pipe and then walked into the office where Joe sat behind the desk doing his homework. Ben placed his things on the office desk and showed Joe the book left behind by his classmate. "This belongs to one of those guys who chased you down the street. Please give it to him tomorrow and say I'm sorry."

Joe glanced at the book but didn't take it and asked, "Sorry about what?"

"Tell him I'm sorry. That's all."

"Do it yourself. I'm not getting messed up in whatever you've been doing."

Ben decided that Joe was right. Having committed the foul, he should deliver the apology. That night, sleep evaded Ben for hours as troubling thoughts kept circling in his head. Once again, he let Derek convince him to do the wrong thing. Even though the victims deserved it, he wished that he hadn't set up an ambush. Being "meaner" than the bullies brought him no satisfaction.

Chapter 10

Ben's apology took courage but only fifteen seconds to deliver. He found the two bullies in their classroom and walked to the desk of the one he had hit in the chest with the pipe. Being in the fifth-grade classroom scared Ben because he had been picked on by many of these students. He also knew that students visiting a classroom must have the teacher's permission to enter it. And Joe sat nearby, watching him break this fundamental rule.

He plunged ahead and handed the boy his book. "You dropped this yesterday. I'm sorry about what happened with the pipe. I won't do it again."

Before the boy could respond, Ben left the room without either of the bullies saying anything or following him. They didn't want to explain why a puny fourth-grader had walked into their classroom, dropped off a book, and apologized. Any discussion of the incident would seriously damage their reputations.

When the day ended, Ben hurried to meet Joe for their walk to the station. Without exchanging words, the brothers headed off at a faster pace than normal. Joe still hadn't asked any questions about what happened the previous day. After a couple of blocks, Ben looked back to see if they were being followed.

"Stop it," Joe said, poking Ben in the shoulder to reinforce his command. "Keep your eyes straight ahead and ignore anything they say or do."

"Quit punching me," Ben said. "I'm tired of it."

Joe ignored his little brother and kept walking.

"You can slow down," Ben said. "Those guys aren't following us. And I don't think you'll have to worry about them again."

No response from Joe. That didn't surprise Ben. His big brother often ignored problems. Joe would pretend his classmates had never taunted him and that Ben hadn't gotten involved. Joe's skills included making undesirable things vanish from his life.

The boys walked in silence the rest of the way to the station. When they arrived, Derek was helping a customer at the pumps. He whistled and waved at them.

"Hey, boys, why aren't you running today?" he asked with a laugh. "It looks like my plan delivered as promised. Listen to me and nobody will mess with you ever again."

A week later, Ben stood alone during recess watching a group of boys from his class throwing a football and taking turns trying to catch it. It looked fun and Mrs. Adamson had often encouraged him to try fitting in better with his classmates, so he jumped in front of one of the passes. The other boys had been doing the same thing, so he thought it was part of the game. When Ben went for the ball, he surprised himself and caught it, feeling a wonderful sense of accomplishment. His proud moment didn't last long.

Mike Omanski, the boy who had been waiting for the ball, pushed Ben in the back and then reached around and slapped the ball out of his hands. Before Derek strolled into his life, Ben had always lowered his head and walked away from such incidents, but this day he turned around and pushed back as hard as he could.

After recovering from the surprise of Ben retaliating, Mike lunged forward, wrapping his arms around Ben's head and tackling him. Landing on the concrete playground stunned Ben and left him unable to keep Mike from sitting on his chest and pinning his arms to the ground.

Mike held Ben in this degrading position while taunting him with threats to break his nose and knock out his teeth. Other boys quickly formed a circle around Mike, encouraging him to punish Ben for touching their football.

Ben started squirming and trying to break loose of Mike's strong grip. In response to the resistance, Mike tightened his hold on Ben's arms and mocked him with an exaggerated laugh. The sneering faces that surrounded Ben triggered a hatred for his classmates and an intense desire to punish them for this humiliating moment.

"Get off me, you stinking, fat pig!" Ben yelled.

With an arrogant expression, Mike asked, "And what are you going to do if I don't?"

A spark of creativity gave Ben a way to bring down his opponent. Even though Mike sat on his chest, Ben's legs had complete freedom. With all his might, he kicked his right foot up as far and as fast as he could. Ben's foot caught Mike at the base of his skull.

Ben and his tormentor still had eye contact when the blow caught Mike from behind. Mike's first reaction came as a look of shock. A second later, his eyes rolled back, and he tumbled off Ben without making any effort to soften the blow of his face hitting the concrete playground. Mike uttered a moaning sound but not a word.

Furious, Ben jumped to his feet and kicked Mike in the face and then several times in the torso with all his strength. The rage that gripped Ben's brain rocketed to a higher level than anything he had ever experienced—beyond the anger triggered when bashing the fifth-graders with the pipe. Deep hatred for this boy exploded and Ben wanted to make him pay for every hit and insult that he had suffered in his life—at school and home. Ben's muscles tightened, his face turned red, and his mouth spewed a steady stream of filthy words—everything from the vast catalogue his father had taught him.

While teachers had overlooked the daily blows suffered by Ben since kindergarten, they didn't miss this attack. It helped them that Ben didn't take the sneaky approach of the bullies. He attracted the attention of the entire school by shouting profanities that many of the kids and some of the teachers had not heard. Mrs. Adamson and another teacher rushed to the scene and grabbed Ben from behind.

Not knowing who held him, Ben shouted, "Get your hands off me or I'll kill you!" Except he included an adjective to describe "hands" that Principal Smith and Mrs. Adamson later told him was highly offensive and should never be repeated.

The teachers who rescued Mike had to restrain Ben for several minutes until his head cooled and chest stopped pounding. During the brief fight, Ben experienced a strange excitement that made him feel powerful—ready to take on every bully in the school and to hold nothing back when teaching them an unforgettable lesson. This new feeling electrified but scared him. He didn't understand where it came from or what he should do with it.

The fight ended with a one-week suspension for Ben and the requirement to apologize to Mike and his parents. Ben spent the week working at the service station. Al lectured his son about the need to "fight fair" and "never kick a man when he's down," but he didn't ask why Ben kicked the boy.

After listening to Al's reprimand, Derek pulled Ben aside and said, "There's no such thing as a fair fight—forget that nonsense. The point of a fight is that you either give the pain or you feel the pain. And it sounds like you're starting to understand which side is best—the pain giver."

At home, Rachel delivered a much different message, saying, "Ben, you shouldn't behave like a criminal. I can't begin to describe how much your actions disappoint me. What were you thinking?"

Ben mumbled, "Sorry."

"Please promise me that you'll never fight again."

"OK," Ben said, despite knowing that what happened came from a place hidden inside him, not something he knew how to control. He expected to break his promise the next time that impulse escaped.

Chapter 10

A few days after the playground fight, Ben heard his mother whispering to his grandmother about it. "I'm so worried about what will happen if Ben doesn't learn how to control his temper. I'm afraid he's going to become exactly like his father."

His mother's words echoed a fear already growing in Ben's heart.

Chapter 11

"Life isn't fair, so quit bawling about it," Derek said to Ben as they sat in front of the service station on cheap lawn chairs, enjoying a cool breeze coming off the mountains. The rest of the kids in Alma were in school but not Ben. While suspended for the kicking incident, Ben received his education from Derek.

"Nobody is going to hand you stuff because you deserve it," Derek continued. "What you get is what you take and then you have to be ready to fight hard to keep it."

That's the advice Derek gave Ben after listening to him gripe about his suspension. Ben found it unfair to be punished for beating up Mike even though nothing ever happened to the two dozen boys who had kicked, punched, slapped, pushed, tripped, and spat on him since kindergarten.

"Missing school doesn't bother me," Ben said. "I'd rather hang out here than have to put up with all the crap that goes on there. But I'm mad because my mom isn't letting me go to the race on Saturday."

"She's just trying to be a good mom and doesn't want you to turn out like me," Derek said with his hearty laugh. "You need to look at this situation differently. On the negative side, you're only missing one race, and there will be many more to come. On the positive side, you got to kick a jerk in the head—twice, front and back! Now, that's what I call a good deal. And if you want jerks to leave you alone, you'll keep showing them that you're nobody they should ever mess with."

"That's easy for you to say because you're huge, but I'm smaller than any of the other boys in my grade and even smaller than most of the girls. Everybody thinks picking on me is a lot of fun and, if I fight back, I'll always be fighting and getting into trouble."

"Not if you do it right. You need to make it very painful for them and they'll stop. And I don't want to hear any excuses about how tiny you are compared to the giants picking on you. Haven't I already taught you that there are ways for you to be as big as you need to be?"

Ben briefly thought about Derek's question before replying. "Yeah, you taught me how to use a pipe to beat up a bigger guy, but taking a pipe to school every day wouldn't be allowed."

Derek turned to face Ben, flashed his huge smile that charmed the women who visited the station, and asked quietly, "Do you have a switchblade?"

"No, I have a pocket knife, but we can't take knives to school either."

With a laugh, Derek said, "Man, if you keep worrying about the rules, you're never going to have any fun."

Derek reached into his pocket, pulled out a switchblade, and pushed the lever that caused the blade to shoot out from the handle with a loud click. He handed the knife to Ben.

"Now, there's something you can hide in your pocket until you need it, but it's important that you only pull it out at the right time—that's when you want to scare the crap out of someone and there aren't any witnesses."

While Ben studied the knife, a new model Chevy Impala station wagon pulled up to the gas pumps, driving over the pressure-sensitive rubber cord that rang the station's bell. After hearing the bell's "ding, ding," Derek slowly rose from his chair and headed to the pumps.

"When I come back, I want you to give me examples of how you've been picked on at school. Then I'll tell you how to use a switchblade to put an end to it. And I guarantee you that my way will work."

Derek sauntered to the car, waving and smiling at the middle-aged female driver and then moving ahead with filling the tank, washing the windshield, and checking the oil. He did it all while chatting with the driver about what a beautiful car she had and asking questions about her children. Ben overheard the woman ask, "Why isn't that boy in school?"

"Oh, he's been bad, but I'm getting the young man back on the straight and narrow path," Derek said with a beaming smile and wink at Ben. "He'll return to school next week fully prepared to deal with his many challenges thanks to the new tools and techniques I'm teaching him."

The customer seemed interested in what else Derek had to say, remaining parked at the pumps while Derek leaned against the car and chatted with her. The long delay gave Ben time to think about Derek's question.

Many of the boys in Ben's grade and above had teased and attacked him whenever they could get away with it. They especially liked throwing punches or kicking him when in the restroom, at lunch, and on the playground. For self-defense, Ben avoided crowds and kept his back to a wall or fence. If he saw an attack coming, he had a better chance of dodging it.

In the first grade, Ben's attempts to sidestep the bullies created a problem. To avoid being harassed, Ben stayed out of the restroom until his need became urgent. When he held out too long, he ended up damp. His wet pants became obvious to everyone and gave his classmates another reason to insult and punch him. One boy even held Ben on the ground and slapped his face until he did what the boy demanded and wet his pants.

Ben's first-grade teacher, Mrs. Ford, would quietly pull him aside after these accidents and send him to the school office to get cleaned up. The office staff put his wet pants in a bag to take home and gave him dry ones. The replacements came out of a giant box of old clothes donated to the school for students in need. After a few trips to the office, Mrs. Ford kept Ben after school and asked, "Is there something keeping you from going to the bathroom on time?"

He shook his head no.

"We need to find out what the problem is. Perhaps I should talk with your parents about it, so we can work on a solution together."

"I'll try harder," Ben said. He presented his appeal frantically, knowing that his father would be furious about Ben being a "pee-pee pants boy" and would "knock some sense" into him.

"Let's see how it goes over the next two weeks and then we'll chat again if necessary."

Ben agreed and tried to stay dry all day by avoiding the drinking fountain and cutting his lunch short, so he could go to the restroom while the other kids ate. His strategy worked well for nearly two weeks, but then his body betrayed him by finding another way to release the tension. He threw up during class.

When Derek finished his chat with the customer, he placed the payment in the cash register and then dropped back into the chair outside the office. "Do you have the example I asked for?"

"Yeah, if I go to the bathroom at the same time as the boys in my class, they'll sneak up behind me and push me into the urinal, getting me wet. It's gross and everybody laughs at me. I hate it."

"That's an old trick. I've done it, but nobody would ever try that with me because they know that I'd make them pay. But your problem is that you let them get away with it—every time!"

After taking the switchblade out of Ben's hand, Derek closed the blade and then said, "I'll show you what you need to do."

Derek told Ben to stand up and then he walked behind him. "When somebody has pushed you around, look for the right time to send the jerk a message. Follow that guy into the bathroom when only the two of you will be in there. After his zipper is down and his thing is hanging out, step up behind him and open your knife next to his ear, so he hears the click—loud and clear."

Ben flinched as he heard the metallic sound of the switchblade opening next to his face. Derek continued. "And then you hold the blade against the side of his neck like this."

The cold blade pressed the side of Ben's neck, causing him to stand very still. He worried that any movement would result in a cut.

"You now have his complete attention," Derek said. "So you let him know that if he ever touches you again, you'll slit his throat from ear to ear and then castrate him like you do the little pigs on your farm. Got it?"

Ben nodded slightly, not wanting to move too much while Derek continued to hold the knife against his neck. Derek pulled the knife away, closed it, and then handed it to Ben before sitting down.

"You can borrow my knife for now. I'll want to get it back after you've had a chance to scare off the jerks bothering you."

"Thanks," Ben said, stashing the knife in his pants pocket and then taking a seat. "But won't that get me into deep trouble?"

"Only if you're not smart about it," Derek said with an amused tone. "After you use the knife, hide it outside where only you can find it. When the kid squeals on you—and he will—tell the principal that the boy must be lying and show him your empty pockets and let him search your desk. If there's no knife to be found, then it's your word against his."

Ben patted his pocket with the knife in it and said, "Thanks. I'll keep it safe."

"And what are you going to say if someone finds your switchblade and asks you where you got it?" Derek said, making eye contact with Ben.

"Uh, that I found it in the parking lot of Benanti's Groceries," Ben said, pointing at the store across the street from the station.

"Cool, I like your quick thinking and that you didn't mention my name. There's hope for you yet."

Chapter 12

After his suspension, Ben returned to school without much commotion. Principal Smith started the day with a brief discussion before sending him to class. There, he took his seat next to Julie, exchanged smiles with her, and jumped back into the lessons as if he had merely missed school due to a bad cold. Mrs. Adamson patted him on the shoulder and whispered, "It's good to have you back."

Mike Omanski ignored Ben in the classroom and hallway, but his face spoke for him. A large bruise on Mike's right cheek marked the spot where Ben had kicked him. Seeing this reminder of their fight prompted Ben to try apologizing again, but Mike made it clear that he preferred not to hear a word from him. All the other boys in his class also avoided him.

When the long school day ended, Ben walked with Joe to the station to help their father. After dropping their books and lunch boxes on the office desk, the boys strolled into the first service bay where Al worked on the engine of a large flatbed truck.

"Dad, do you need any help?" Joe asked. As usual, he took the lead in volunteering.

"Without a doubt," Al said, sounding irritated. "Joe, I need you to fetch tools for me. And Ben, hold the work light so I can see what I'm doing."

Al was using a portable light to see inside the truck's engine compartment. The light included a lightbulb on the end of a long black extension cord with a small metal cage surrounding the bulb to protect it from being smashed. The top of the cage had a hook to hang the light. Al already had the light hanging from the truck's hood, but he complained that he still couldn't see well enough to make the repair.

"Ben, set up the small step ladder next to me," Al said, pointing at the spot where he wanted it. "I need you to stand on the ladder and shine the light into the area where I'm working."

Ben hurried away to get the ladder, but he couldn't find it in the usual storage place. Knowing that his father's temper would be rising to the boiling point due to the delay, he rushed through a search of both service bays. Still, he had no success.

After returning to his father's side, Ben said, "I can't find the ladder. It's missing."

Al shouted a profanity and then said in a tone that oozed with contempt, "How hard can it be to find a ladder? You truly are the stupidest and laziest boy in the world."

Ben fought back tears, knowing that any display of emotions would make things worse. His mind froze while he wondered what to do. Al spotted the confusion and shook a wrench in front of Ben's face.

"Well, don't just stand there looking stupid. Go find it. Ladders don't disappear."

Ben ran off to search again and noticed Derek sitting on a lawn chair outside of the office. "Where's the small ladder?" Ben asked breathlessly. "Dad needs it right now."

"Oh, I used it to clean the office windows this morning," Derek said with his usual relaxed style, ignoring Ben's sense of urgency. "Your old man complained this morning about me loafing, so I cleaned the windows even though that's not my job."

From having witnessed similar episodes, Derek recognized how nervous Ben would get because of his father's anger and grinned when Ben squirmed in front of him. Then he lazily pointed to the far corner of the office. "It's over there."

Ben ran, grabbed the ladder, and hustled to his father's side. Al continued to lean over the truck's engine, straining to reach the failed part. Ben set up the ladder exactly as instructed.

When Al saw him, he said, "Time's money! You're killing me with your dawdling. Get on the ladder and hold the light for me."

Ben complied without blaming his delay on Derek. He knew that his father would view any excuse as arguing and smack Ben for having a "smart mouth." So, he silently soaked in the criticism.

Al handed Ben the light. "Come closer and don't worry about getting your hands dirty. Shine the light on whatever I touch. Got it?"

Ben mumbled "OK" and tried to follow his father's instructions. He came as close to his father as he could bear, hating to feel his father's body heat and to smell his Old Spice aftershave mixed with the odors of a mechanic—motor oil and grease. When this close, it became more difficult to avoid a blow to the head or ribs. Despite Ben's effort, his father's body still ended up in between the light and the side of the engine.

"Move the light lower. I can't see anything the way you're holding it. Come on! Get with it! You're not helping at all."

Ben stretched even lower, nearly falling off the wobbly ladder, but it still wasn't enough. He let the light cord slide through his hands, so the bulb dangled below the point where he guessed his father's hands were.

"That's better. Now, move it a few inches closer to me."

To make that happen, Ben had to get into a position where he could hold the light's extension cord under his father's body instead of next to it. When Ben tried to squeeze deeper into the engine area, the light swayed like a pendulum.

"What are you doing? Stop swinging the light. That's driving me crazy."

Ben tried to reach lower to stop the motion, but the cord slipped out of his hands and the light fell to the floor. Before he had time to pull it up, Al threw his right elbow into Ben's shoulder. The blow caught Ben by surprise, preventing him from dodging it. He lost his shaky footing on the ladder and kicked it over as he struggled to regain his balance.

Without the ladder to hold him up, he slid off the truck's fender and fell backwards, landing across the fallen ladder's legs.

The ladder made painful contact with Ben's back from his shoulders to his hips. Ben had already been on the verge of tears when trying to cope with his father's frustration. Now, as he rolled off the ladder and onto the floor, he could no longer control his emotions. Ben cried and sobbed as his mind reacted to a combination of pain, fear, and humiliation.

Al validated his fear by dropping his tools and kicking the ladder away from the truck. It sailed across the service bay and banged off the wall. Anticipating more pain to come, Ben started to scramble away.

Before he could retreat, Al took a step forward and tried to kick his son in the rear. Ben lunged to the side, but Al still connected, delivering a punishing blow to Ben's left thigh. The kick caused Ben to stumble and land on his hands and knees. He crawled away from Al to the back of the truck, continuing to sob and shed tears.

"Stop acting like a baby! What's wrong with you? Why does everything you do have to turn into a pathetic crying fit?"

Ben jumped to his feet and turned to face his father, getting ready to run if he came after him. He didn't and suddenly calmed down. As often happened, his father turned off the anger as quickly as it began.

"Go sweep the floor or do something useful," Al said in quiet disdain.

The remark further wounded Ben, but he preferred to be dismissed and limped to the other service bay. Joe became the light-holder and, being much taller, did exactly what his father wanted. Peace returned to the garage.

While looking for a broom, Ben spotted the pipe he had used to attack the bullies. Derek had left it leaning against the wall instead of putting it into the tool bin. Ben picked up the pipe and took a practice swing, imagining a new target—his father's back. He followed up with a blow to his father's knees and pictured the next one smashing his nose.

Ben's tears and sobbing stopped when anger and hatred knocked his shame aside and gave him a surge of energy. While embracing these powerful emotions, a dark thought popped into Ben's head that made him tighten his grip on the pipe.

Teach your dad a lesson and bring him to his knees.

Ben spent a few minutes practicing his swing with the steel pipe. Then he quietly stashed it in the tool bin and found the broom. He didn't sweep with enthusiasm that day because his mind became preoccupied with planning his revenge. He made a vow.

Someday I will make my father pay for every beating and insult and he won't like the price.

Chapter 13

Within an hour of Ben being elbowed and kicked, Al acted like it never happened. Ignoring the incident followed his pattern. He soon gave the impression that his violent outbursts were insignificant events and certainly nothing to cry or talk about. After closing the station and heading home, he merely chatted about the weather and neither apologized for hurting Ben nor criticized him for having dropped the light.

Al's silence about the temper tornado clearly stated that he wanted the matter closed. No further discussion would be necessary or tolerated. Ben understood that his mother should not hear about it. As Ben had often done, he went along with the lie that nothing happened.

While driving home, it became challenging for Ben to bury his emotions because each bump in the road sent sharp twinges of pain up his injured back. To conceal the abuse, he avoided any facial expressions that might be interpreted as discomfort or unhappiness.

The next day came with an amazing surprise. Rachel decided that the entire family should go to Al's next race. "That's great," Al said with authentic excitement. "The boys will show you the best place to sit in the grandstand."

"But we can't go with Mom because we'll be in the truck with you," Ben said.

"Not tonight," Al said. "You and Joe need to help your mother find a seat by nice people who won't be doing a lot of cursing."

"Or, smoking and drinking beer," Rachel said.

Ben didn't know how that would be possible, but Joe nodded and said, "Got it."

Despite not being allowed to ride to the race in the truck, Ben remained excited about going and kept thinking about it while spending the morning and afternoon of race day doing chores. With Al's schedule at the station growing longer each week due to his racing career, he spent less time on farm work. To address that problem, Al gave Joe and Ben a lengthy list of things to do.

While Al still milked the cow every morning and evening, he hadn't raked Daisy's stall and corral recently. Joe and Ben completed that task before moving on to the less challenging work of cleaning the chicken coop. After lunch, the boys repaired damage to the hog pen caused by the pigs trying to dig under a fence and then spent the rest of the day weeding.

By dinner, exhaustion overtook Ben and any movement created so much back pain that he couldn't take deep breaths. Still, he remained silent about his injuries. After having endured a full work day, he wanted the reward of going to the race and said nothing that might take it away.

Ben took a shower to get rid of the cow manure smell that had followed him since morning. While in the bathroom, he noticed a giant bruise on his thigh where he had been kicked. Then he used the bathroom mirror to inspect the many dark purple bruises on his back. He looked battered and quickly put on his clothes before his mother noticed his injuries and asked any questions.

By the time Rachel and her children arrived at the racetrack, they encountered a full parking lot and crowds of partying fans. After Rachel paid for the tickets, Joe took charge and found a group of seats in the grandstand without any obviously intoxicated race fans nearby. Ben scanned the crowd for his friends Curtis and Tom but couldn't find them. Because Becky stood out in a sea of adults, it didn't take long for the Bakers to meet new friends.

An older woman sitting behind the family tapped Ben on the shoulder and asked, "How old is that baby?"

"She'll be two in December."

"Wow! I guess your family believes in getting an early start on becoming race fans."

"Not really. I only started coming a few weeks ago because we have a car in the race."

"Is your pa a driver?"

"Yep, he drives Number Eight—the fastest car on the track."

"Oh, yeah, I remember him from last week. He took home prize money. Didn't he?"

Despite having heard from Joe that his father had finished in third place again, Ben paused, debating what to say. With his mother listening to the conversation, he didn't want to break his promise to keep the prize money a secret.

"Well, I don't know. I had to miss the race because of a problem at school," Ben finally replied.

"I hope your pa gets the first-place prize this week," the woman said. "With four kids to feed, I'm sure that money would come in handy."

The woman stood up to let two men take seats in the middle of her row. The gap in the conversation allowed Rachel to lean over and ask Ben, "How much money did your dad win last week? Tell me the truth."

Ben looked at Joe who frowned in return but said nothing. He understood. Joe didn't want to be the one to break the news that No. 8 had already collected prize money twice.

"How much did he win?" Rachel repeated, expressing her agitation with Ben's delay.

"I think it was three hundred dollars."

"I appreciate you telling me the truth."

After a few moments of silence, Rachel again leaned toward Ben and asked, "What does he get for finishing in first or second place?"

"Five hundred for first and four hundred for second."

"Well, that's good. We surely could use that money."

The woman behind the Bakers had listened to the conversation and reached over and patted Rachel on the back. "Ma'am, I'll be cheering for your husband to win the top prize. And by the way, I'm Gloria and this is my husband, Conrad."

"Thank you. It's nice to meet you both. I'm Rachel and these are my sons Joe and Ben and daughters Debbie and Becky."

"What a wonderful family. You'll hear me cheering for your husband to roll all the way to victory. I want you to go home tonight with five hundred bucks in your purse."

When the announcer introduced the cars, Ben jumped to his feet and cheered, especially when his father came onto the track in the third position. His past races had impressed the track officials and led them to give him a more favorable pole position.

After the prerace ceremonies, the race began with the deafening sound of supercharged cars when they headed for the first turn. During the early laps, the cars stayed in a tight pack and in the original order. The excitement began when Al took a low path through the near turn and shot ahead of the top two cars. The move caught the frontrunners by surprise, and Al zoomed ahead of them before they could block him.

Ben swelled with pride that his father had taken the lead even though he had only been racing a few weeks. And he made it happen in a car he built himself—with some help from his sons. Everything Derek had promised about racing suddenly appeared possible. Ben's excitement grew as his father circled the track, holding the top position and looking invincible.

Al's dash to the lead position paid off until the sixteenth lap. That's when two cars in the middle of the pack bumped and spun out. The last-place car hit both, creating a tangled mess of cars. They ended up in a pile against the guardrail. None of them could drive away from the collision, so the red flag came out and the race stopped until tow trucks could clear the track. After about ten minutes, the race resumed.

Because Al had been in first when the red flag came out, he began in the lead position and held it without a serious challenge. With six laps to go, things changed. The driver running next to Al lost control of his car and smashed into him. The collision caused No. 8 to start skidding toward the outside of the track, but Al regained control of his heavily dented car and avoided hitting the guardrail.

Despite the hit, Al still held first place and accelerated to get away from the pack. When he came through the front straightaway, the entire grandstand crowd cheered for him. With five laps to go, Ben couldn't imagine any possible outcome for his father besides victory and the $500 prize.

Al completed the next lap with a full car-length between him and the next two drivers. When the cars headed into the first turn, Ben noticed his father's car slide more than normal. When going down the back straightaway, the other cars suddenly closed the gap and tried to pass, but Al blocked them.

As No. 8 entered the front straightaway, Ben shouted to his mother, "Four laps to go. He's going to win it. We'll be rich!"

With all the crowd and car noise, Ben didn't hear her reply, but he suddenly lost his confidence when he turned back to the race and watched No. 8 pass. His father's car continued to move at a high speed, but it shuddered. The chassis appeared to have a major problem. To keep his lead, Al accelerated when heading into the next turn—a risky maneuver even without a shaky car. The other cars accepted his challenge and picked up their speed.

When Al hit the turn, the front end of his car suddenly dipped, as if the front axle had snapped and the tires buckled. The nose of the car started plowing the track. Dirt flew over its roof, landing on the windshields of the cars behind. The plowing served as a brake, bringing No. 8 to a sudden halt and causing it to roll. The two trailing cars had no time to avoid a collision and slammed into the bottom of Al's tumbling car.

The impact created a loud bang and crunching sound. Within a split second, another loud bang shot across the racetrack as No. 8 went airborne and its roof struck the outer guardrail. The fence behind the rail stopped the car's flight and tossed it back onto the track. The cars that had rammed No. 8 spun around and hit the outside guardrail.

While furious with his father the previous day, Ben suddenly felt a sense of panic because he could be dead. He glanced at his mother who accepted a hug from Gloria while both cried. Joe took charge of attempting to calm Becky, who screamed because of the anxiety around her. Debbie stared at Ben as if he could provide answers about what had happened to their father. He decided to find out.

Ben ran to the back of the grandstand, down the stairs and to the door that led underneath the structure. After stepping inside, he hurried toward the front. By reversing his path from his first trip to the track, he reached the place where he had slid through the fence and did it again. He started running toward his father's wrecked car. An older, heavyset security guard spotted Ben and charged from the infield to catch him.

Easily outrunning the guard, Ben headed for his father's car, but he stopped abruptly when passing a white object on the track—his father's helmet. He picked it up and then dropped to his knees, holding the helmet and crying loudly. The dirty helmet had several deep scratches, tire marks, and a splash of bright red blood. He also noticed the broken strap that failed to keep it on his father's head.

The security guard kneeled next to Ben and, after struggling to catch his breath, asked, "Do you know this driver?"

"Yep, he's my dad and we've got to save him."

"We're doing our best. You need to help by staying out of the way."

The guard gestured toward the infield and asked Ben to follow him. Ben stood up, clutching his father's helmet, and walked to the infield. He kept looking toward the wreck to see if he could spot his father in the swirl of activity around the mangled car. About a dozen men worked on No. 8, trying to pry open the door and using fire extinguishers on the engine.

The security guard allowed Ben to watch the rescue attempt from the infield. All the drivers had climbed out of their cars and stood in a pack next to the ambulance. While Ben and the guard watched the flurry of activity, Derek came up from behind them.

"Hey, Ben, what are you doing here?" he asked. "Aren't you supposed to be in the stands with your mom?"

"I came to find out what's happening," Ben said.

Derek shrugged his shoulders, pointed at No. 8, and said, "I'm sure he's fine, but the car is in terrible shape."

Offering to shake hands with the security guard, Derek said, "Sir, I'm Derek Dean, business partner of Al Baker, and that's our car—Number Eight."

"Good, then you can take charge of my little friend and keep him off the track," the guard said, patting Ben on the head before leaving them.

Ben's eyes remained fixed on the car and he ignored Derek when he began describing what he thought had caused the accident. Ben didn't care about the cause. He only had one concern—seeing if his father had survived.

After what seemed like a long wait, the rescue team lifted Al out of his car. Medics with a wheeled stretcher hustled toward him. From what Ben could see, his father could be dead or alive. Al's head was slumped on his chest, blood covered half of his face, and his arms hung limp at his sides. He showed no signs of life, but the urgency of the rescue team gave Ben hope.

When the medics placed Al on the stretcher, the grandstand crowd politely clapped and a few fans shouted out encouragement to No. 8. Within a minute, the men slid the stretcher into the ambulance and the vehicle sped toward the racetrack exit.

When the ambulance disappeared, Derek said, "I guess we might as well pack up the truck and get out of here. There's not much more we can do."

Ben scowled at Derek, feeling that his father could be dead or dying because of Derek's racing idea. "This is your fault!" he shouted.

"Whoa, Benny, simmer down," Derek said with a laugh. "Your dad is a big boy and makes his own decisions."

Ben wanted to punch Derek, but he had no doubt that Derek would strike back and didn't want to see the big man's 666-tattooed fists coming at him.

A race official joined them, introducing himself as Rex and saying, "The medics will take Al to a hospital in Provo where he'll receive excellent care. We're going to tow his car to an area outside the infield gate and will let it sit there until you have time to haul it away."

"Thanks for letting me know," Derek said. "I'll come get the car soon."

"It's a shame that car has run its last race," Rex said. "But I have good news for the Baker family. We're calling the race complete and awarding your team five hundred dollars for first place."

Derek grinned and shook hands vigorously with Rex. "Thanks for your generosity!"

Rex looked at Derek with unveiled annoyance. "It's the least we could do, and all the other drivers agreed with our decision."

"That's sporting of them and much appreciated," Derek said, continuing to grin.

Rex asked Derek to follow him to his office where they would settle accounts. Before walking away, he looked at Ben. "Are you Al Baker's son?"

"Yes, sir."

"Well, he's a tough guy. Don't worry. I'm sure he's going to be OK."

"So, he's still alive?"

"Yes, no thanks to that cheap helmet you're holding. He's knocked out right now, but I expect he'll be back on the track with a new car soon."

Ben took a deep breath and exhaled slowly, feeling an enormous amount of tension leave his body. He appreciated the man's optimism. At the same time, he stood with his mother when it came to stock cars—*racing is a bad idea.*

Chapter 14

Derek took off with the race official and left Ben standing in the track's infield even though he had promised the security guard to watch him. Ben suddenly thought about what his mother must be going through and headed back to the grandstand. As soon as he climbed over the inner guardrail, a security guard started shouting and running toward him. Ben decided to aim for the gap in the fence and tried to slip through before being caught, but he heard his mother's sharp, piercing command over the crowd noise.

"Benjamin, stop right now!"

Ben hit the brakes and looked for his mother. She stood in the grandstand's first row with his brother, sisters, and a pair of security guards. They all frantically waved to get his attention. The guard chasing Ben caught up and grabbed his left arm.

"Bring him to the ticket office," one of the guards near Ben's mother shouted. "We'll meet you there."

The guard delivered Ben to the ticket office where Rachel received directions to the hospital and the Bakers left for it immediately. When they arrived at the emergency department, Joe and Ben took charge of the girls while Rachel sought information about her husband's condition. Equipped with a few details from a nurse, Rachel gathered her children in the waiting room and said, "Your father is alive but in a coma. It's serious."

"But the man at the track said he was only knocked out," Ben said.

"A coma is a bigger problem than what that man said," Rachel said. "That's why I'm going to stay here tonight, but your grandparents will be coming soon and take you to their house. Please make me proud of you by being on your best behavior."

The Baker kids liked staying with their grandparents, so they didn't complain about the plan. They also looked forward to getting away from the uncomfortable hospital, but leaving their mother alone bothered them. She had red eyes from crying and her hands trembled.

After delivering her brief update, Rachel gestured for Ben to follow her as they walked a few steps away. "What else did that man at the race-track say?" she asked.

"That Dad won the race and gets five hundred dollars."

"Oh, that's a miracle because we're going to need every penny to pay for the hospital bill."

The kids' grandparents soon met them at the hospital. When saying goodbye to her children, Rachel took Al's helmet from Ben and tossed it into a nearby trash can.

"Wait! Dad can put on a new strap and it'll be like new."

"No, that helmet is a piece of garbage and will never be worn again."

Anticipating Ben's interest in keeping the helmet as a souvenir, she added, "And I don't want to ever see it again."

Getting rid of the helmet saddened Ben because he viewed it as an important part of his family's history, but he silently let it go and remained quiet all the way to Alma.

In the morning, Grandma Thorne gently woke the children by filling the house with the smell of buttery cinnamon rolls baking in the oven. Ben slid out of the bed he shared with his big brother and shuffled into the kitchen.

"Good morning, Ben, would you like to taste one of my cinnamon rolls to make sure they're all right?"

"Sure, but your rolls are always delicious," Ben said, watching his grandmother use a spatula to lift a roll out of the baking pan and place it on a small plate for him. She handed him the plate and a fork, which was the only way to eat her cinnamon rolls without getting the sugar coating, cinnamon, and butter all over hands, clothes, and furniture. Ben dove in, taking a big bite and showing his pleasure with a satisfied grin.

Soon, Joe joined the sugary breakfast buffet and then Grandma Thorne received a phone call. After a brief conversation, she hung up and announced, "That was your mom calling to say that your father is still in a coma, but the doctors are seeing signs that he might wake up soon. So, that's good news and something we can share with the bishop at church this morning."

"Oh, do we have to go?" Ben asked.

"Yes, there's never a more critical time to go to church," Grandma Thorne said. "We'll ask the church members to pray for your father. Now, I need you to get your sisters out of bed and try to clean up your shirt."

Ben looked at his shirt, remembering how he had hugged his father's bloody, dirty helmet after the crash. Following his grandmother's instructions, he hurried to his sisters' bedroom, woke them up, and then went into the bathroom to try cleaning his shirt. He failed to make an improvement and went to church with dirt and bloodstains on it.

While attending his Sunday school class, Ben had to explain his dirty clothes, which led to a long story about the race and his father's first-place finish. All the kids liked the story, but his teacher, Sister Peterson, said that she didn't understand why Ben's father would do "something so dangerous and risky."

After church and lunch, Ben asked his grandmother if he could walk to the service station to make sure the doors and gas pumps were locked. "That's fine," she said, "but don't stay too long. We need to drive to your house this afternoon and pick up clean clothes for you kids and your mother."

Upon arriving at the station, Ben noticed Derek's motorcycle and his dad's truck behind the building. He knew that Derek drove the truck back to Alma after the race, but he found it odd that Derek would be at the station on a Sunday. When Ben approached his father's truck, he could hear voices inside the station. They included Derek's unmistakable drawl. He peeked inside the open back door to see what was happening.

"Hey kid, get away from there!" a man behind Ben shouted.

Ben flinched and spun around to see Denny Siegen, one of Derek's friends—a small man about thirty-years-old with long hair, a beard and squinty eyes. He recognized him as one of Derek's friends who received free gas at the station.

Denny quickly approached Ben. He looked agitated instead of flashing his usual sly grin—the same one that Derek used when trying to give the impression that *hey, we're all friends here, and friends take care of friends.*

When Denny recognized Ben, he quickly switched to his "friends" routine and said, "Oh, it's you—Al's kid. I thought you were some punk trying to break into the place."

"It's just me, Ben Baker."

"Hey, I'm so sorry to hear about your old man busting up his car last night. That was a tough way to end a race."

"What are you guys doing here? The station is closed."

"I'm helping out a friend of mine in his time of need," Denny said, reaching for Ben's left arm.

As Ben backed up to avoid being grabbed, Derek stepped out of the station and placed his large hands on Ben's shoulders.

"What's going on?" Derek asked. "I thought your family would be at the hospital."

Ben looked down and noticed the 666 tattoo inches away from his face and involuntarily shuddered.

"My, oh my, this little boy is shaking like a leaf," Derek said with a chuckle. "Benny, I hope I'm not making you so scared that you mess your pants."

Ben tried to pull away from Derek, but he tightened his grip and Denny wrapped his right hand firmly around Ben's left arm. He used it to guide Ben, with Derek's help, toward the station's back entrance, but not before Ben glanced at the truck bed. He noticed that it held his father's air compressor, welding equipment, and tool boxes. He had interrupted Derek and Denny robbing the station.

After pushing Ben inside, Derek backed him up against the office desk. Susan Meadows, a high school student, sat behind the desk. Ben knew Susan because she was beautiful and worked at the Burger Barn. With her long blonde hair and skimpy shorts, Susan always caught Ben's eye when he ate there with his family. She smiled smugly at Ben while she leaned back in the office chair with her bare feet on the desk, showing off her brightly painted toenails.

"Before you get the wrong idea, I need to explain what we're doing," Derek said. "We're packing up a bunch of tools and then driving to the racetrack to fix your poor daddy's car. I want to surprise him with a ready-to-go car when he gets out of the hospital."

Ben knew that his father would be pleased if that happened, but he also recognized that Derek's story stood as far from the truth as the sun is from the moon. Derek wasn't a mechanic and even an excellent mechanic wouldn't be able to fix No. 8.

When Ben didn't respond to Derek's explanation, Derek glared at him. "If you don't want us to do this helpful thing for your dad, just say 'No thanks' and we'll put all the tools back. But it'll be your fault that your dad missed out on our neighborly kindness."

Derek paused before asking, "So, what do you say? Should we go fix that car?"

"No thanks," Ben whispered.

"Wrong answer!" Derek slapped Ben in the face with enough force that he bit his tongue and could taste blood in his mouth.

Before Ben could recover, Derek slapped him again and then punched him in the middle of his chest. Ben had been hit by his father and boys at school many times, but he had never experienced the pain delivered by this heavy blow. It dropped him to his hands and knees.

Derek pulled Ben back to his feet and smiled while watching him struggle to not fall again. "I'll ask you nicely one more time. Will you please help us load the truck, so we can go fix your dad's car?"

Ben took a deep breath and uttered "OK." Then, he helped Derek and Denny finish carrying nearly all the tools and other valuables out of the station to his father's truck. Due to this work, he added grease stains to his already well-marked shirt.

Derek then surprised Ben by telling him to ride in the truck with Denny. Until that moment, he thought Derek would tie him up or club him over the head with a tire iron and leave him in the station.

Before departing, Derek locked the station's rear entrance. He noticed Ben watching and said with a laugh, "Don't worry, Benny. I'm locking it up. We wouldn't want anything to get stolen."

Derek laughed, spinning the keys around his right index finger while walking to his motorcycle. Ben recognized the keys as his father's set. Of course, Derek had ended up with them after the race. It suddenly struck Ben that Derek also had the $500 in prize money, which his mother counted on to pay the hospital bills.

Riding his loud motorcycle, Derek led the truck south on Main Street, brazenly leaving Alma with a teenage girl and a truckload of stolen tools behind him. When Derek turned south on Highway 91 and Denny followed him, Ben knew for certain there was no plan to fix the car. To reach the racetrack, they should have gone north. Ben considered pointing out the error, but he kept his mouth shut and focused on the scenery as they continued driving south, passing Payson and Santaquin and soon entering Juab County. He wondered where Derek planned to take him.

The answer came a few minutes later. Derek made a left turn from the highway and took a dirt road marked by a sign for the Bald Mountain Trailhead. After about two miles, the dirt road ended in an empty parking area that bordered the base of the mountain. Sagebrush, scrub oak, and juniper trees were scattered across the mountainside and valley.

Denny parked the truck next to the motorcycle, took the keys, and jumped out to chat with Derek. While Susan stretched next to the motorcycle, Derek and Denny slowly walked up the trail, never looking back at the parking area. After they had gone about one hundred yards and entered a wide canyon, Ben decided to escape.

He quietly slipped out of the truck and then dashed straight south, away from the two men and toward the mouth of a nearby canyon. Ben hoped it would include a trail too steep for Derek's motorcycle to climb. If not, he would go off-trail and straight up the mountainside. Derek and Denny could follow him on foot, but the difficulty of the climb might discourage them from chasing him.

After running as fast as he could for two minutes over the sandy, rolling terrain, Ben heard Derek's mocking laugh in the distance. He dropped to his hands and knees behind a lone juniper tree halfway between the parking area and the canyon he wanted to reach. Looking back, he could see Derek pointing in his direction and laughing.

"Hey Benny, I hope you enjoy your hike," Derek shouted. "We're taking off now to go fix your dad's car. We'll look for you on our way back."

For a moment Ben almost believed Derek's story, but he knew that they wouldn't leave him in this deserted area if they truly planned to go the racetrack. So he ignored what Derek said and focused on what he did. He watched Derek and Susan get on the motorcycle and Denny return to the truck. They drove away from the parking area at a fast pace, leaving a cloud of white dust behind.

Ben realized that Derek wanted him to escape and felt stupid for making it happen so easily. He climbed to a higher point, which gave him a clear view of the entire dirt road. While sitting on a limestone ledge, he watched the motorcycle and truck finish the dusty trek back to the highway where they turned south, going away from the racetrack. Within a few minutes, Ben lost track of both vehicles.

"Now, what?" Ben asked himself while picking June grass seeds out of his socks. The seeds came from running off-trail during his dash to freedom. Being stranded more than twenty-five miles from home, he struggled to come up with an easy answer to his question. Sitting on a rock in the middle of nowhere clearly wouldn't solve his problem.

"Time to get moving," Ben muttered, standing up and wiping dust off his pants. Unless he hitched a ride, it would take hours to get back to Alma. The thought of making the long walk overwhelmed Ben, but he knew he could do it. He had already taken a ferocious punch from "the Beast" and survived.

Chapter 15

Walking back to the highway and catching a northbound ride took Ben nearly an hour. He fretted about every minute of the trek because it delayed his plan to get the sheriff to chase Derek and Denny and retrieve the stolen truck, tools, and money. While still in Juab County, the driver of a bright red station wagon pulled over next to him.

"Climb aboard," the driver said, waving Ben toward the car. The oldest of the driver's three kids opened the door to the backseat, stepped out, and told Ben to sit in the middle. Ben slid in next to a girl about his age with a younger boy sitting behind him in the cargo area. A woman was in the front seat with the driver.

"What's a youngster like you doing out here all by yourself?" the driver asked.

"I caught three people robbing my dad's service station and then they brought me out here to get rid of me while they ran off with all the stolen stuff."

"What? That's the most unbelievable story I've ever heard," the man said, pulling back onto the highway. "Where do you live?"

"Alma."

"Never heard of it. We're heading back to Orem. Will we pass it on the way?"

"Yep, it's in between Payson and Spanish Fork—up against the mountains."

The woman asked, "How old are you?"

"Nine, but I'm small for my age, so most people think I'm younger."

"Hmm, I've never met a nine-year-old who tried to stop a robbery, been kidnapped, and went hitchhiking all in one day," the woman said, giving Ben the impression that she didn't believe a word of his story.

"That's what happened," Ben said defensively. "You can drop me off at the sheriff's office in Santaquin or Payson, so you don't have to go out of your way. I'll ask him to start looking for the people who robbed our station."

"Nonsense," the woman said. "You're too young to be doing such things on your own. We need to take you home and let your parents call the police."

The man agreed, and the woman turned in her seat to look at Ben. "Your parents must be wondering where you are by now and probably looking for you."

"No, my dad is in the hospital in Provo and my mom is with him. I'm staying with my grandparents in Alma."

"This story keeps getting better," the man said, glancing over his shoulder at Ben. "I hope you don't mind me asking why your father is in the hospital."

Ben told the story about his father's race and how another driver caused the wreck that put him into a coma. "My dad had the lead when the race was called off, so he ended up in first place," he said with pride.

While traveling to Alma, Ben learned that his new friends, the Nelsons, had attended a family reunion in Nephi over the weekend and were returning to their home in Orem. The man introduced himself as Chuck and his wife as Helen. He talked the entire way to Alma, telling Ben about the games they played at the reunion and the mountain of food they ate.

When entering Alma, Ben pointed out Al Baker's Service Station and then guided Chuck up the road to his grandparents' house. His grandmother must have been expecting visitors because the Nelsons had barely set foot out of the station wagon when she hurried from the house to greet them.

"I've been praying for someone to find Ben. Thank you, thank you! We had no idea where he had gone."

"Glad to help," Chuck said. "We were traveling from Nephi to Orem and barely had to go out of our way to bring Ben here."

"Where did you find him?"

"Hitchhiking south of Santaquin. He looked way too young to be out by himself, so we picked him up."

Ben's grandmother turned to face him and asked, "Ben, what in the world were you doing way down there?"

He quickly told the story about Derek and Denny robbing the service station and let her know that she needed to call the sheriff.

"Please hurry up so the sheriff can find Derek or else we'll be broke," Ben said. "He cleaned us out—and even took the prize money from the race last night. It's all gone."

The Nelsons stayed with Ben while his grandmother went into the house to phone the sheriff. When she returned, she invited the Nelsons inside for punch and cookies. She said the sheriff wanted Chuck and Helen to wait for him, so they could talk.

The sheriff arrived about fifteen minutes later. He disappointed Ben by showing up at a normal speed, without his siren wailing and lights flashing. He quietly pulled up in front of the house and slowly got out of his car. While his grandmother chatted with the Nelsons, Ben let the sheriff in.

"Are you Ben Baker?" he asked, bending down to look at Ben's face as soon as he entered the house.

"Yes, sir," he said, feeling intimidated by the stern sheriff who examined him closely and touched his face where Derek had slapped him.

"Did someone hit you?"

"Yes, Derek Dean, the man who works for my dad."

"Derek is someone I know well," the sheriff said. "Did he cause you to bleed?"

The sheriff pointed at the dried blood stains on Ben's shirt.

"I had a little bit of blood in my mouth after he slapped me, but the blood on my shirt is from holding my dad's helmet after the crash at the racetrack."

"Tell me why Derek hit you."

"Derek was mad about something and slapped me—twice. And then he hit me in the chest."

The sheriff carried a form attached to a clipboard and made a few notes on it before shifting his attention to the Nelsons.

"Good afternoon, I'm Sheriff Tom Kort and appreciate you folks waiting for me," he said. "I only need to ask you a few questions and promise to keep it brief."

"No problem, Sheriff," Chuck said. "We're glad to help."

Sheriff Kort nodded and uttered a quiet "Thank you" before turning toward Grandma Thorne and saying, "Mrs. Thorne, after I finish talking to the Nelsons, I'll have some questions for you and then need to spend more time with Ben."

The sheriff proceeded with his plan and did it quickly, but Ben continued to worry about how far Derek had already traveled. He wanted Sheriff Kort to jump in his car and track down the thieves immediately.

Before the Nelsons left, Chuck patted Ben on the head and Helen gave him a hug and lecture. "Be careful in the future, young man. You were lucky that we found you instead of someone who likes to hurt children."

The sheriff conducted a short interview with Grandma Thorne and then asked her to stay in the room while he interviewed Ben. Before getting started, Grandpa Thorne and Joe returned to the house.

"Mr. Thorne, I'm collecting information about a theft from your son-in-law's gas station," the sheriff said. "I'll fill you in on the details as soon as we're done here."

Grandpa Thorne patted Ben on the shoulder and said, "Glad you're all right." Then he sat nearby, listening to Ben's interview with the sheriff.

Sheriff Kort continued to ask Ben questions about what happened at the station. When Ben repeated his mention of being hit in the chest by

Derek, the sheriff said, "Pull up your T-shirt so I can see if the blow left a mark."

Ben complied, and the sheriff kneeled in front of him to get a closer look. "Wow! You're going to have a giant bruise there in the morning. I'll need you to come to the station tomorrow, so we can take a photo of that for evidence."

The sheriff turned to Ben's grandfather and added, "When we catch Derek, he's going to prison for a long time. I plan to request charges of burglary, theft, assault, kidnapping, and whatever else I can throw at him."

Grandpa Thorne stood up and approached Ben. "I want to see the mark that coward left on you."

Ben twisted toward his grandfather. As he did, the sheriff lifted Ben's shirt higher and leaned behind him. Ben could tell that he was looking at his back and realized what he had discovered—the bruises from his fall on the ladder. Knowing where the sheriff's interest in those bruises could lead, he pulled on his shirt to hide them.

"Hold on there, Ben," the sheriff said. "I need to check out your back. It's covered with bruises. Did Derek do this to you too?"

Ben made the quick decision to lie. "Yes, sir. He did that too."

"How?"

"With a board. I didn't want to help Derek load the truck, so he started beating me with a board."

"Did he hit you anywhere else?"

"Uh, yeah, kind of."

"Can you show me?"

"Sure, but I need to pull down my pants."

Grandma Thorne asked, "Would you feel more comfortable if I left the room?"

"Sure," Ben said.

After she left, Ben slowly pulled his pants down to show the sheriff the large dark bruise on his thigh where his father had kicked him.

"How did that happen?" the sheriff asked.

"Derek kicked me."

"Why?"

"When leaving the station, I told Derek that I didn't want to go with him."

Ben felt guilty about lying to the sheriff, but he didn't know what else to say. The truth could get his father into trouble. The sheriff made additional notes, asked more questions, and then scheduled a time in the morning for Ben to be at his office for photos.

"I can't go in the morning. I have school."

"I'll write you an excuse for school. This is important. I want photos taken while those injuries are fresh. I'll see you in the morning."

As the sheriff prepared to leave, Ben let his frustration out. "When are you going to start looking for Derek? It seems like you're not even trying to find him."

With a kind smile, Sheriff Kort pulled a sheet of paper from behind the form on his clipboard and handed it to Ben. "As soon as your grandma called, I asked my deputy to distribute this bulletin to every sheriff's office in the state. They'll all be looking for your father's truck and Derek's motorcycle. Trust me, Derek and his friends are not going to get away."

Ben mumbled a "Thank you" to the sheriff and they shook hands. When departing, the sheriff made a frightening pledge to Grandpa Thorne.

"Don't worry. We're going to catch the coward who hurt your grandson and will make him pay."

Chapter 16

The next day, Ben visited the sheriff's office for an uneasy photo session. The discomfort began with having to strip down to his briefs for the deputy who shot the photos. It intensified when answering the sheriff's questions about how Derek bruised his back and thigh. To support his previous claim, he invented details to create a complete story.

The interview and photo session drained Ben emotionally and made it difficult to focus when he returned to school. He thought about the problems caused by his lies. If Derek was arrested, he would call Ben a liar and ask the sheriff to check his story with Joe—and Ben knew his brother would tell the truth.

When classes ended for the day, Rachel picked up her sons at school and already had her daughters in the car. She came with good news—the kids could visit their father.

"Your dad woke up with a bad headache and a sore back, but the doctor thinks he should be able to leave the hospital in a couple of days."

Rachel warned her children that they needed to be very quiet during the visit. "Because of the accident, loud noises upset your dad. So we'll need to whisper when we're in his hospital room and when he comes home."

Ben didn't know why his mother wasted her time telling them to be quiet. They already obeyed that rule to avoid their father's wrath. Creating noise had always been one of the quickest ways to provoke him.

If their father would be crankier than normal, they faced an impossible task in trying to keep "mad Dad" from being unleashed.

Despite the "noise" warning, Ben still wanted to visit his father, especially with so much news to share. "Mom, have you told Dad what Derek did?" Ben asked, leaning forward so she could hear him from the back seat.

"No. And you shouldn't mention it either. Your dad woke up just a few hours ago and needs time for his brain to calm down before he hears upsetting news."

"OK, how about the wreck? Can I ask him what caused the car to flip over?"

"Hmm, that wouldn't be good either. Your dad might think you're criticizing his driving."

When Ben stepped into the hospital room, he lost interest in saying anything because of how old and feeble his father looked. It shocked him. He had never seen his father in bed during the day or with so little energy.

"What's going on with all the sad faces?" Al asked, slowly raising his head. "Why are you looking so grouchy?"

The questions came with a playful "fun Dad" tone, not the usual "mad Dad" slap-down. Receiving a sunny welcome warmed Ben's heart and he wanted to hug his father, but Ben didn't think he should touch him because of his injuries. Instead of hugs, the children quietly lined up next to their father's bed and stared at him.

"Are you boys taking care of the farm?" Al asked. "I hope you're not slacking off just because I'm not there to crack the whip on you."

"Grandpa takes us there," Joe said. "I've been feeding and milking the cow and Ben helps out with the other chores."

"That's good, Joe. I'm glad you learned how to milk. I knew that skill would come in handy."

"Both boys have been very helpful," Rachel said. "I don't know what we would have done without them."

"I'd like to have seen that," Al said with a smirk. "It usually takes a battle just to get their lazy butts out of bed."

"You'd be real proud of how hard they've been working," Rachel said, smiling at Joe and Ben.

"And how's Derek doing at the station?" Al asked.

Rachel hesitated and fussed with Becky's hair before answering. "Derek is doing fine. But that's nothing to think about right now. You need to focus on resting."

"That's utter nonsense. I'm raring to go. Find my clothes. I'm checking out of this dump right now."

Before Rachel could gather Al's clothes, a nurse arrived, briefly listened to his plan, and then firmly told him to stay in bed until a doctor came to see him. It took about a half hour, with Al becoming more determined to leave, but the doctor finally showed up and made it clear that Al wouldn't be discharged that day and probably not the next one either. The hospital staff had more tests to conduct before he would be cleared to leave.

Al groaned about his situation and mentioned what "big things" he needed to do at his service station and the farm, but the doctor never backed down and Al surrendered. Rachel politely excused the doctor before another argument could begin and then told her children to say goodbye to their father.

"Kids, we have animals to feed, a cow to milk, and dinner to cook," Rachel said, using one of her husband's favorite excuses for making a sudden departure from anywhere he didn't want to be.

Rachel and her children left the hospital room with quick goodbyes and no hugs. For two nights, they relaxed at home before their father's return. Joe and Ben were in school when it happened, so they missed his reaction to the news that Derek had robbed the station and taken the prize money. But they saw the aftershocks.

"Al, didn't you listen to anything the doctor told you?" Rachel asked while Al stormed about the house cursing Derek and vowing to get even. "You need to rest and stay calm. Getting upset will create more problems, not fix them."

After a few minutes of suffering through his father's tirade, Ben snuck out of the house to do his barnyard chores. While there, he prolonged his break from the shouting by cleaning the chicken coop. He stayed outside until Debbie came to get him for dinner.

"Dad already ate and went to bed because his head was spinning," Debbie said. "The rest of us are going to eat now, so Mom wants you to come in quickly."

With Al sleeping, the rest of the family ate silently at the kitchen table with no questions asked and no stories shared. "You're doing a wonderful job keeping the noise down," Rachel said, breaking the agonizing silence in the room. "After cleaning up the kitchen, let's all stay in here doing homework or reading books quietly—no TV, no games, no talking or running around the house. OK?"

None of the kids objected, but Ben wanted to talk. He had many questions: *How would his father fix customers cars with no tools? Would it be possible to stay in business if he could only sell gas? Would the family end up in the poor house?*

Ben hoped his mother would reassure him that things would work out. Instead, she glumly ate her meal, providing some assistance to Becky but avoiding any conversation with the other children. In the past, Joe took the lead when tension needed to be swept aside. On this day, he imitated his mother's silent sadness.

With no talking, dinner ended quickly, and the boys helped Rachel with the dishes—getting the task done quietly. Ben spent the rest of the evening looking at his homework but not really doing it. Fears about the future gripped his mind and allowed no room for his math assignment.

With the station closed, Joe and Ben resumed riding the bus to and from school. When they came home, their father paced in the kitchen, appearing tired and angry. Debbie sat at the table and Becky in her playpen.

"Where's Mom?" Ben asked.

"She went back to work. She already missed two days and we couldn't afford to have her stay out any longer. I can't go back to the station for two more days, so my job for now is babysitting."

Joe came up with a plan to deal with his father's irritability. "Do you want us to take care of all the evening chores?" he asked. "I'll milk the cow and Ben can handle the other stuff."

"You bet. I have a splitting headache and can't imagine having to use my head to push Daisy around tonight."

Daisy complained with loud, bothersome mooing when she wasn't milked at the same time twice a day, but she also rarely cooperated with the process. When milking, Al gave her a small bucket of grain to keep her occupied and then would place his head on her left flank and move her gently toward the right sidewall of the stall. He applied enough pressure to keep her from stomping around while being milked. If he didn't hold her in place, she would step in or kick over the milk bucket.

Joe and Ben quickly pulled on their work boots and headed to the barnyard. When finished with the milking and their routine tasks, Joe said, "Instead of going back in there, let's find a few other things that need to be done. I'd rather stay away until Mom comes home, so she can deal with him."

Ben agreed and helped Joe clean the cow's corral and stall. After leaving the corral with the last load of manure, Joe paused while Ben latched the gate. He took a deep breath as he surveyed the barnyard.

"We could run this place without him," Joe said. "Mom can depend on us."

Chapter 17

Usually Rachel stayed home on the weekends, but the Saturday after Al was released from the hospital she told Joe and Ben that they would be on their own. She asked them to do their chores and stay out of trouble. Rachel planned to drop off Debbie and Becky at their grandparents while she went on a job interview.

"We need extra money to pay the hospital bill," she said. "And without any tools, your father can't repair cars, which means we won't have that money coming in. If I don't make more money per hour and pick up overtime pay, we'll be in serious trouble."

"I'm sure you'll get the job and everything will be fine," Joe said with a confident smile.

"I hope you're right," Rachel said. "But if I get this job, I'm going to need both of you to help out around here even more. Can I count on it?"

"Of course," Joe said without hesitation, and Ben nodded to indicate his support.

By mid-afternoon, Rachel returned from her interview with a beaming smile. As Joe predicted, she got the job—front-desk manager at the Green Park Inn in Pleasant Grove. Her first day at the inn came in two weeks and she liked the work.

Despite her increased pay, the Baker children still heard their parents argue about money almost every night. Living in a small house made it difficult to ignore the fights, especially when their father lost control of his emotions. Rachel would plead with him to be quiet and warn him that "you'll wake the children." It didn't matter. They had already captured the attention of their children.

One of their most heated arguments took place during dinner. Rachel began with a reply to Al's complaints about the hospital bill. "Don't blame anyone else," she said. "You should have known that your insurance wouldn't cover injuries from racing cars."

"I don't know why we bothered to pay for insurance if it doesn't take care of things I do to grow my business," Al said.

Ben followed Joe's lead and continued to eat as if the conflict in the room didn't exist. He kept his eyes off the action and on his plate.

Making no effort to conceal her frustration, Rachel said, "Thanks to your business schemes, I don't see how we're going to be able to pay the hospital bill and still make the house payment."

"Ah, don't be such a worrywart," Al said with a dismissive snort. "I'll take care of it by working something out with the bank."

"No more loans! We're still paying off the loan for all the tools you bought and then lost because of your pal Derek Dean."

"We'll get the tools back and then everything else will work out fine. You'll see."

"Why didn't you keep your old job instead of gambling on the station and that ridiculous race car?" Rachel asked.

"Why don't you show a little faith in me?" Al asked, presenting his question with the harsh tone that warned he had reached his boiling point. Showing anger usually caused Rachel to back off. This time she kept going and did the unforgiveable—she wept.

"Al, I can't bear to face a stack of bills without enough money to pay even half of them. You need to start being more careful about how much you spend. Please help me."

"Drop that sad sack routine right now!" he shouted. "It's getting really old. What do you want me to do?"

"It's simple. Please close the station and get a new job."

"Fine! If that's what it takes to get you to stop nagging and criticizing me, I'll do it."

Rachel whispered, "Thank you."

"What choice do I have? Your whining and complaining is getting on my nerves."

To Ben's surprise, his mother's weepy plea worked. His father closed the station and made a deal with the bank for a new payment plan. He took a mechanic job at a car dealership in Provo and worked evenings and weekends for a construction company. He used Ben as his helper on many of those projects, traveling to the company's work sites and making repairs on forklifts, generators, and other construction equipment. For this work, Al used tools "borrowed" from the car dealership.

For Debbie and Becky, the new work schedules resulted in more time with their grandparents. For Joe and Ben, it meant more freedom. After finishing their daily chores, they could do whatever they wanted and go wherever their legs or bikes could take them.

Joe used his time to hang out with friends in Alma. For Ben, he either read library books in the barn while sitting on a hay bale or went hiking alone or with George Oaks. Ben liked George, but he didn't really know how to be a friend. It always felt like a struggle for Ben to do things with other kids.

By the time Al and Rachel returned from work, evening had arrived, and the entire family pitched in to help make dinner and wash the dishes. After a few months, that routine wasn't working for Rachel. She assigned cooking to her sons and wanted the meal to be ready when she walked in the door. If she had to work overtime, the kids could eat without her. Al usually worked until early evening and then had a long drive home, which resulted in him returning home after dinner.

Ben admired how hard his father worked, especially because it didn't seem to make him happy. Something happened, though, about six weeks after beginning his new job that cheered him up—the arrest of Derek Dean.

Chapter 18

Derek's teenage girlfriend kept him from getting away with the crimes committed at Al Baker's Service Station. After a month of constant companionship, Derek grew tired of Susan and dumped her on the side of the road in Vacaville, California, without any money or luggage.

Susan called home, crying about having made "a terrible mistake." Her parents immediately forgave their prodigal daughter and drove to California to pick her up. They blamed Susan's actions on the influence of an evil man who had seduced and deceived their young, naïve child. While they welcomed Susan back, the Meadows' forgiveness didn't extend to Derek. They went after him with a fierce desire for revenge.

Sheriff Kort visited the Bakers' farm to share the news and included Ben in the discussion because he would need to testify against Derek after his arrest.

"I expect that Derek will be in custody soon because Susan has given us the make, model, and tag number of his new car," the sheriff said, with Ben and his parents sitting across the kitchen table from him. "Susan told us that Derek purchased the car in Las Vegas with money made from selling his motorcycle and your truck and tools."

The sheriff mentioned that they drove the car around Nevada and California, staying in flea-bag motels and snatching things that people made easy to steal. "When they ran out of money, Susan suggested that

Derek find a job. She wanted to rent an apartment in a nice town and settle down. Derek ignored Susan the first two times she brought up the idea, but he stopped the car when she mentioned it again, told her to get out, and then drove off without her."

Susan thought Derek would calm down and come back to get her, but she soon admitted that the romance had fizzled and started walking. "Susan found a diner where she placed a collect call to her parents and begged them to come get her," the sheriff said.

"I'm sure they were excited to hear from her," Rachel said. "Some people in town thought that Susan might have been murdered since her parents hadn't heard from her since she left town."

"Yes, they were very pleased and persuaded Susan to serve as a witness against Derek, which will help us convict him," the sheriff said. "And Susan's cooperation will be favorably recognized by the court when punishment for her involvement in the theft is discussed."

Rachel began to share her support for not sending Susan to jail, but Al interrupted. "When Derek is arrested, I expect that we'll be getting whatever money he has left plus his new car."

"Don't start counting that money," the sheriff said. "You're not likely to get anything because Derek is quick to spend every penny he picks up."

"But he still has the car. That's worth something."

"We'll see. He might have sold it by now. And Derek will have others coming after him to cover his debts. You'll have to get in line."

Sheriff Kort's comments frustrated Ben because they sounded much more likely to happen than the more positive outcome his father imagined. "I need to do my homework," Ben said, hoping to escape this uncomfortable discussion. "May I be excused?"

After getting an approving nod from the sheriff, Al said, "If you're ready to do your part to send Derek to prison."

Ben mumbled that he would do it, but he worried that the sheriff might find out that he had lied to him. He also expected Derek to say that Ben had stolen money from the cash register many times. It would show that Ben wasn't trustworthy.

While thinking about these possibilities, Ben dropped his preference for Derek being arrested. Instead, he hoped that Derek would drive to Canada and disappear. For Ben, nothing good was likely to come out of Derek's arrest.

Instead of going north, Derek and Denny ended up in Southern California about a week after Susan's homecoming. Grandpa Thorne picked up the story from the rumor mill and shared it with the Bakers the next day.

"A police officer near Los Angeles found Derek and Denny driving around a warehouse after midnight," Grandpa Thorne said. "He pulled their car over for driving without lights and, being suspicious of the duo, he asked both men for their IDs. He radioed in a request to check warrants for them and found out that they were wanted for theft, kidnapping, and other charges. The men were arrested and are coming back here for their trial."

News of the arrests dominated every conversation in Alma for weeks. People began debating how severely the men should be punished and speculating about what they had done to Ben before his escape. Rumors about Susan being pregnant soared when she suddenly left town to live with relatives in Salt Lake City.

Ben became one of the primary checkpoints for gossip. Instead of being ignored or teased, kids asked him all kinds of questions. "How did you escape? What did it feel like to get hit by Derek? What did you see Derek doing to Susan? What are you going to say to Derek when you see him at the trial?"

Even adults at church and the grocery store noticed Ben and shared their thoughts. They encouraged him to be brave when testifying against the men. "We're counting on you to put those evil men in prison for years and years," said one man. "Don't let us down."

After a month had passed since Ben gave his statement to the county's lawyers, Rachel received a call that he needed to meet with them again at the courthouse in Provo. Ben would miss a day of school and Rachel would have to take time off from her job to drive there. Ben didn't mind making the trip until his mother added a new piece of information—the lawyers representing Derek and Denny would also be at the meeting.

"I'm supposed to warn you that these lawyers won't be nice to you at all. They will ask you a lot of tough questions and try to get you to change your story."

With a smile, she added, "But don't worry. All you need to do is tell the truth and everything will be fine."

Chapter 19

Telling lies came easy at first for Ben. The one about the bruises on his back and thigh rolled off his tongue without much thought. Sheriff Kort recorded the story and thanked him for providing so much valuable information.

When Ben needed to present his lies a second time, the county's lawyers made the effort more difficult because they asked him for details and he struggled to remember what he had already told the sheriff. He did his best to say it the same way and survived the second round. When it came to the third round, he faced a much tougher opponent.

"Your original statement to Sheriff Kort didn't include any mention of Derek Dean threatening to kill you when you claimed that he hit you on the back with a board," said the leader of the three lawyers defending Derek and Denny. "Now, you're saying that my client hit you and threatened to kill you at the same time. Is that what happened?"

"Uh, yes sir," Ben said, feeling uncertain if he should include a few more details to make his story more believable.

"Would you be surprised to know that Derek Dean, Denny Siegen, and Susan Meadows all have testified under oath that Derek never hit you with a board?" the lawyer asked with a piercing stare. "They don't even recall a board being available that Derek could have used for this alleged attack."

"They probably didn't remember with so much going on that day."

"Are you sure the memory issue isn't yours, not theirs?"

"Huh? I don't get what you're saying."

"Let me be clear. Have you forgotten that your father pushed you onto a ladder shortly before the alleged robbery? Please let me know if that fall caused the bruises on your back."

"I don't remember that."

"Derek Dean saw it happen because you had asked for his help to find the ladder. He said that a few minutes later, your father knocked you down because he was angry about you not being able to hold a light for him. And when you fell, you landed on the ladder. Do you remember that happening?"

"The light slipped out of my hand—that's all."

"After dropping the light, do you remember your father knocking you off the ladder?"

"I remember slipping off the ladder, but I didn't get hurt. Sometimes things like that happen when working on cars and trucks."

The defense team members whispered briefly before the questioning resumed. "When you claim that you didn't get hurt after slipping off the ladder, are you saying that the bruises on your back didn't come from the fall?"

"Well, no, I'm saying that it didn't hurt me. I bounced back up and then Joe took my place holding the light. He's a lot taller than me and could do it better."

"So, did the fall off the ladder leave bruises on your back?"

Ben hesitated as he thought about how to get out of this trap and then replied cautiously, "I'm not sure. I think that I might have had a few bruises the next day."

"Did you or didn't you have bruises on your back that resulted from falling off the ladder?"

"I don't know what you're saying," Ben said, recognizing that his lie had trapped him. He didn't know how to respond without revealing that his father's fit of anger caused the bruises.

"I'll simplify my question," the lawyer said. "Did you end up with bruises on your back from the fall off the ladder?"

Deciding that he could mix the truth with his lie and still be on safe ground, Ben said, "Yes, but Derek gave me more bruises by hitting me with a board."

"However, you didn't mention the bruises on your back until Sheriff Kort noticed them. Is that correct?"

"I guess."

"Ben, please answer with a 'Yes' or 'No' so that we all can be sure what your testimony is."

"All right."

"Did you mention the bruises on your back before Sheriff Kort noticed them?"

Ben paused, considering the impact of his answer, and then replied as the lawyer had instructed with a firm "No."

"Thank you. And did you mention the bruise on your thigh before the sheriff asked you about other injuries?"

"No. I didn't think it was important. Derek took our stuff—that's what matters!"

"Please focus on my questions," the lawyer said, giving Ben a forced smile. "It's my job to ask them."

Ben stared at the lawyer but said nothing. The lawyer continued. "You didn't hesitate to tell the sheriff about Derek allegedly slapping you in the face and hitting you in the chest. Is that true?"

"Yes."

"Why didn't you think the bruises on your back and thigh would be as important? From looking at the photos, they appeared to have caused you much more pain."

Ben replied by shrugging his shoulders.

"Ben, please answer my question with a clear verbal response."

"OK."

The lawyer took a deep breath and let it out slowly before asking the question again. "Why didn't you mention the bruises on your back and thigh to the sheriff when telling him about the slap in the face?"

Ben lost control of his emotions and yelled at the lawyer. "I wasn't thinking about the bruises because I have them all the time! I never think about them and nobody has ever cared about them until today. I wish you would stop asking me about bruises and talk about what really matters—Derek took our stuff and we want it back!"

Rachel put her hand on Ben's back and calmly said, "You need to settle down. These gentlemen are only doing their jobs and trying to make sure we all know exactly what happened."

Still angry, Ben leaned away from his mother's touch. "My dad pushed me off the ladder and then I fell on it. When I tried to run away from him, he kicked me. That's how I got the bruises."

"Then, Derek didn't hit you with a board. Is that what you're saying?"

"He slapped me and punched me. Isn't that enough?"

"Did he hit you with a board?" the lawyer asked, raising his voice.

"No!" Ben shouted with his face reddening from anger and embarrassment. He wanted to run out of the courthouse.

At that point, the lawyer asking questions nodded toward the corner of the room and all three defense lawyers met there for a lengthy conversation. They conducted it in whispers and pointed at Ben a few times. Rachel looked away from Ben and the lawyers during the discussion.

When the lawyers returned to the table, the questions focused on what happened when leaving the service station. The lead attorney for the defense asked, "Did Derek Dean force you to leave the station with him?"

"No, I rode with Denny in the truck because they said we were going to the racetrack so we could fix my dad's car," Ben said. "It sounded like a lie to me, but I went along with it until we started driving the wrong way and stopped on a dirt road south of Santaquin. Then I escaped because I knew for sure that Derek had lied."

"Did Derek or Denny chase you?"

"No."

"What did they do?"

"They drove off and left me there."

"Did Derek or Denny ever say that they were kidnapping you?"

"No. That's what the sheriff called it when I first talked to him."

"So, when you were with Derek and Denny, did you think they were kidnapping you?"

"No. I was trying to find a way to stop them from stealing my dad's tools."

"So, you went with them voluntarily. In other words, you made the choice to leave the station in the truck with Denny."

"Yep."

Ben's reply led the defense lawyers to hold another whispered discussion in the far corner of the room. When that meeting broke up, the lawyers returned and asked Ben a few more questions before announcing that they were done for the day.

"Thank you, Ben," said the lawyer who had asked the questions. "You've been a tremendous help today and we appreciate your cooperation and honesty."

For a few seconds, Ben took the remark as a compliment, but the discouraged looks of the county's lawyers and Sheriff Kort told him that he had helped Derek and Denny, not the citizens of Alma. While everyone else stayed in the room, Ben followed his mother down a short hallway and out the courthouse exit. The bright sun and fresh air felt good to Ben as he walked to the car.

Rachel didn't say anything until in the car. She quietly went through her usual drill of searching in her cluttered purse for car keys and then coaxing her old car to start. Breaking the silence, she said, "You did fine in there. It was hard for me to hear it, but you told the truth and that's what we'll have to live with."

Chapter 20

Derek and Denny ended up in prison despite Ben lying about some of the details of what happened at the service station. The interview in the county courthouse became the last time he had to testify against them because the opposing legal teams worked out a deal to drop the kidnapping and assault charges if Derek and Denny pled guilty to theft. As a repeat offender, Derek received a sentence of five to seven years in the state prison. For his first felony, the judge set Denny's prison time at two to three years.

Not being required to testify in a trial thrilled Ben. His interviews with the lawyers gave him a preview of what he would have faced in the courtroom—a stressful and humiliating experience. While enjoying that reprieve, the public disgrace of his actions still caught up with him. People viewed Ben as the boy who let two detestable criminals get off easy. The rumor mill generated stories about what led to a "mere rap across the knuckles" for the criminals. Many people assumed that Ben had refused to testify because he thought the men might escape from jail and kill him.

The lies Ben made up to protect his dad remained known to only a handful of people and none of them, including the sheriff and his mother, followed up with Ben about what truly caused his bruises. Ben knew that nobody told his father what he said. Otherwise, his father would have whacked him for embarrassing the family.

Over the next few months, chatter in the community about the crime story faded. At school, though, bullies kept it alive by calling him a "coward" for not helping the sheriff give Derek and Denny all they deserved. Ben did his best to ignore the teasing.

When Spring arrived, Ben began riding his bike to school instead of taking the bus because he preferred the solitude. On the bus, he became an easy target for boys who found it hilarious to sit behind him and make snorting sounds to imitate sucking snot into their mouths. Then they would pretend to spit a "loogie" into his hair. The boys usually didn't deliver anything, but he still had to listen and hope that he wouldn't go to school with saliva and snot in his hair. At times, they released a vile payload that he had to wipe away while listening to their giggles.

After enjoying a few days of not having to take the bus, three of his classmates noticed Ben unlocking his bike from a rack near the school's rear entrance. One of them, Scott Graham, said, "Hey, Benny, I want to take your bike for a ride. Give it to me."

Scott and his friends laughed when Ben turned to face them. Ben's glum expression let them know that they had humiliated him again. "So, are you going to give me your bike or do I have to beat you up first?" Scott asked.

Ben ignored the question and completed the combination to open the lock that secured a chain wrapped around the rack and the rear wheel of his bike. He kept his back to Scott, but he turned his head slightly to the side to keep an eye on him.

Scott handed his books to his friends and walked toward Ben. While approaching, Scott loudly repeated his demand, "Give me your bike!"

Ben answered by pulling the chain free from the bike rack and whipping it into the side of Scott's head. Being completely caught by surprise, Scott didn't have a chance to raise his hands to deflect the blow and it dropped him to the ground. He clamped both hands to his head and rolled to turn his back to Ben.

Scott's friends stood still, staring at Ben with stunned expressions. Ben thought they might come to save their buddy, so he started spinning the chain over his head like a lasso and took a step toward them. He liked the deadly noise the chain made when it whirled above him.

Both boys responded the same way, dropping their books and running to the school entrance while shouting for Mrs. Adamson. Ben turned his attention back to Scott and stopped spinning the chain. Scott hadn't moved since the attack and remained on the ground holding the side of his head. His knees were pulled to his chest and he cried. As Al Baker would say, "Like a girl."

Seeing Scott crying iced Ben's fury. When driven by anger, he had been ready to bash Scott again, but he suddenly felt sorry for him. The boy looked shattered and Ben knew what that felt like. He hated it and gave up any thoughts of a second strike. Instead, he quietly wrapped the chain around his bike seat and locked it.

After pushing his bike away from Scott, he jumped on and calmly pedaled for home. Within a few seconds, he heard Mrs. Adamson calling his name and turned to see her standing at the side entrance with Scott's friends. She waved Ben back to the school and then hurried to Scott's side, bending down to look at him closely.

Ben sat on his bike, debating whether he should keep riding or return and face serious trouble. Nobody stood between him and escape, but he decided to go back, simply because he liked and respected Mrs. Adamson. He rode to where Scott still cried and cowered on the ground.

Mrs. Adamson told Scott's friends to get Principal Smith. "He's at the bus lines. Tell him it's urgent and that he needs to come here immediately. Run, boys!"

After they left, she asked, "Ben, what made you do something so cruel? You're not that kind of boy."

Instead of trying to explain the intensity of the anger inside of him, Ben shrugged his shoulders and replied, "Don't know."

Ben didn't explain that Scott had threatened to take his bike, knowing that had little to do with it. He wanted to hurt someone because he had grown tired of being bullied every day—and Scott's threat added the extra scrap of motivation that compelled Ben to smack the boy in the head with a chain.

Mrs. Adamson found it shocking what Ben had done because she couldn't see the fury building up inside of him. She wasn't scolding a boy struggling with immaturity and throwing an occasional temper tantrum. Ben's mind had become a constant battlefield, with a wish to live peacefully on one side and a ruthless desire to seek vengeance on the other—and the brutal side threatened to control, shape, and devour him.

Chapter 21

After Principal Smith discussed the chain attack with Scott's parents and Ben's mother, he decided that expelling Ben from school wouldn't be an effective punishment, recognizing that he would be glad to stay home. Instead, he made significant changes to Ben's school routine with a four-week in-school suspension. He needed to make sure every student knew that what Ben had done wouldn't be tolerated.

Ben also received a stern lecture from the principal about proper behavior and the importance of kindness and self-control. While being scolded, Ben applied skills his father had taught him about dealing with a reprimand and showed neither a "smart mouth" nor a "sad face." He listened to the principal, agreed with all his points, and presented a "happy face."

"Thank you for not arguing with me," Principal Smith said. "And remember that we're friends. You can come to me for help whenever you need it."

Ben spent the next four weeks in a small windowless room that primarily served as a place for filing cabinets. The principal added a small desk and chair. In this detention cell, he received and completed assignments from Mrs. Adamson. Office staff members also came in to add documents to the filing cabinets.

While always being polite, Ben worked hard to keep up with everything handed to him. He didn't receive recess, physical education, or the "privilege" of going to the lunchroom with the other students. Even his bathroom breaks were timed for when the halls had emptied. Ben saw these punishments as wonderful gifts. The only drawback was the requirement to take the bus because he wasn't allowed to ride his bike to school.

Ben loved the solitude of his private classroom and would have gladly accepted his punishment being extended until the summer break, but the principal sent him back to the classroom for the remaining weeks of the school year. The kids on the bus had avoided him since the chain attack, so he returned to the classroom with optimism that he would also receive a cold-shoulder there.

As always, Julie gave Ben a warm, sincere welcome. "I hope you stay out of trouble and will be able to come to class every day. I don't like seeing your empty desk."

"I'm never the one looking for trouble. But it usually finds me, so I can't make any promises."

Even though his school time became more tolerable, Ben began each day by looking at the calendar on the classroom wall and counting down the days until summer break. He also became obsessed with checking the clock, wondering if it had stopped and nobody had noticed.

When Ben finished fourth grade, he gathered his things and went home, planning to hide from the world for a few months. He set a goal to take care of his chores quickly every morning and then head into the mountains to hike or read.

His plan worked except when his father had time off from his job at the dealership. On those days, Ben helped his father fix cars, trucks, and anything mechanical for a variety of businesses. Al often struggled to complete these projects as quickly as he wanted and became irritated when that happened. At those times, Ben served as the anger release valve, which kept him on his toes—ready to jump out of the way when his father's frustration led to a tool being thrown at him.

Ben made it through the summer without many bruises, but one of Al's flare-ups delivered a blow that soared to the top of the pain meter.

While working in the family's barnyard, Ben struggled to rake a mass of wet, heavy cow manure into a pile at the edge of the corral. He needed to move the manure to a place where he could load it into a wheelbarrow and take it to the dump zone. Being small, he lacked the strength to move the large amount of manure quickly. To offset his disadvantage, he dragged it one "pie" at a time.

Through this approach, Ben made progress in getting the job done, but it happened too slowly to satisfy his father. After seeing Ben's technique, Al walked briskly toward him, muttering profanities as he came. Ben anticipated a head slap or kick in the pants. Instead, Al reached around him and grabbed the rake out of his hands.

"Let me show you how to do it. Why do you always make the simplest things look so hard?"

Before Ben could move away, Al yanked the rake backward and drove the end of the handle into Ben's belly. The blow caught him by surprise and pushed deep into his relaxed stomach muscles. It felt like he had been impaled on the rake. Ben cried out in pain before remembering that he should never give that reaction.

"Quit crying, you sissy!" Al shouted and then roughly pushed Ben out of the way, so he could rake the manure at a furious pace.

"There, did you see how easy that was? If you put your back into your work and give it more than a halfhearted effort, you'll get a lot more done."

Without warning, Al finished his demonstration by throwing the rake at Ben. After dodging the flying tool, Ben scrambled to retrieve it while watching his father in case he had more "discipline" in mind. Instead, Al cooled off and merely ordered Ben to "get with it." That ended the lesson in how to rake cow manure.

Chapter 22

At school, Ben showed up every day expecting pain and humiliation. At home, he received the same and usually worse. To keep going, he tapped into the occasional moments when "fun Dad" showed up. On those days, Al tossed aside his view of Ben as the "stupidest and laziest boy in the world" and trusted him to help achieve the impossible. One of them happened that summer.

Al had offered to trim three branches from a tall oak tree next to his father-in-law's two-story home. Joe and Ben volunteered for the project and rode in their father's truck for the short drive there, chatting about how much fun it would be to work as lumberjacks. Ben begged his father to shout "Timber!" when the branches fell.

When the "lumberjacks" arrived at the house, Grandpa Thorne pointed out the branches to be cut. He needed them taken down because they touched the house's roof and rubbed on the shingles when the wind blew. Al studied the situation for a half minute and then announced confidently that his crew could handle the job.

"Boys, get the saw and axe. We have big things to do."

Al decided to start with the two smallest branches as a warm up. To reach them, he drove his truck under the tree as close to the trunk as possible. Next, he placed a long extension ladder in the bed of the truck, which allowed him to easily reach the first branch.

To cut the branch, he used a bucksaw with a three-foot blade. After getting the cut started, Al tied one end of a long rope to the middle of the branch and then tossed the other end to Joe.

"Now, boys, I want you to stand behind the truck and pull on the rope as hard as you can when I give you this signal," he said, waving his left hand above his head. "That's when you're going to play tug of war with the tree. You need to pull the branch away from me and into the back of the truck. Are you ready?"

Joe, the optimist, said, "Sure. We got it."

Al resumed sawing the branch while Joe and Ben gripped the rope.

"Dig your feet into the ground," Joe said. "Good footing is the key to winning at tug of war."

Ben followed his big brother's advice, twisting his sneakers on the patchy grass until he could feel the firm, flat ground underneath them.

In less than a minute, the branch cracked, and Al gave the signal to pull.

"Go!" Joe shouted, and the boys leaned back, tugging the branch with all their strength. Popping free, the branch fell into the truck while the boys' momentum carried them backward to the ground.

Al celebrated the achievement by waving the saw over his head. "Bravo, boys! We did it!"

Joe and Ben giggled, feeling giddy that they had pleased their father. Grandpa Thorne watched the victory from a safe distance behind the truck.

For the middle-size branch, the crew repeated the process. This branch fell faster than the first one and bumped Al on the way down, causing him to lose his balance. He dropped the saw and grabbed the tree to avoid tumbling into the truck bed with the branch. The ladder briefly danced under his feet before he stabilized it. The saw fell and bounced off the side of the truck, leaving a dent and scraping the paint.

Al pulled up his shirt and showed his sons a large, bloody gash on his ribs and stomach where the base of the branch had speared him. "Boys, this is what happens when you do a halfhearted, miserable job. I wanted you to pull it away from me, not into me."

It surprised Joe and Ben that their father didn't jump off the ladder to give them a kick in the behind. Al often made the boys pay when they had nothing to do with him getting hurt and, this time, they might have been able to prevent his injury.

Ben recognized that they had struggled with the second branch because it weighed much more than the first one. Based on that experience, the size of the next one deeply concerned him, but it didn't deter his father. Al fully expected his sons to defy the laws of physics and worker safety.

Grandpa Thorne shared Ben's concern and said, "Al, I'm getting a bit worried about what you're doing. Perhaps I should hire a professional."

"Nonsense," Al said. "The boys just need a little more grit. Besides that, we only have one more to go and I'm barely bleeding."

Al studied the third branch—the jumbo version—and decided that he needed to move the truck to a better position. Even then, the ladder wasn't tall enough to reach the third branch. When Al described his plan for getting higher, Grandpa Thorne grumbled that he couldn't watch "this insanity" another minute and went into the house.

Undaunted, Al pressed forward with his plan, setting up the ladder on the truck's cab to gain an extra four feet of height. Now, Al could reach the jumbo branch, but the cab's rounded, slick surface provided an unsure foundation. Ignoring the risk, he climbed to the top of the ladder—about twenty-five feet off the ground—with the bucksaw and rope in hand. There, he reached out as far as he could and tied one end of the rope around the branch. He tossed the other end to Joe.

"Wrap the rope around your waist and tie it in a knot that you're sure won't slip," Al said. "You'll need to put all of your weight into pulling this one. I don't want it to land on the cab and knock my ladder over. From this high up, a fall could be the end of me."

Joe tied the rope around his waist and then positioned his little brother to stand between Joe and the branch. Ben would provide some pulling power, but Joe would be the anchor—the one his father counted on to keep him from falling.

"That's looking good," Al said. "Now, give it all you've got."

Satisfied that they were ready, Al began sawing the branch. It took about five minutes before the branch cracked. Al paused briefly to see if the branch was ready to go, but it remained firmly in place and he resumed sawing.

A loud crack suddenly ripped through the yard, and the branch started to fall before Al could give the signal to pull. Startled, he shouted his favorite cuss word and grabbed the tree trunk when the falling branch swung within inches of the ladder. The severed end missed the cab and fell toward the house. The leafy end, which rested on top of the house, kept the branch from falling straight down. Like the fulcrum in a teeter totter, the edge of the house lifted the leafy end skyward and sent the heavier end plummeting toward the house.

When the branch fell, Joe echoed his father's profanity and ran away from the branch. Ben went with him. Their teamwork slightly changed the direction of the branch, but they quickly lost the battle to a bigger, swifter foe.

As the branch swung toward the house, its unrelenting momentum jerked the rope out of Ben's hands and knocked Joe off his feet, dragging him toward the house. Joe flew past Ben, sliding on his back. He had tied a first-rate knot because the rope remained tight around his waist.

While Joe didn't control the branch, his dead weight dragging on the ground caused it to slow down enough so that it didn't slam into the side of the house. The swinging motion ended less than a foot before the branch hit the house and the heavy end fell straight down. It momentarily looked like a small tree planted at that spot. The impression didn't last long because it began tipping over toward Ben.

From having dodged airborne tools, the slowly falling branch proved to be no match for Ben's quick feet. He dashed away from it, peeking over his shoulder to make sure it would miss him. Ben escaped, but when the branch slid along the side of the house, it snapped a black, plastic-encased wire that ran between the house and a nearby telephone pole.

A short section dangled from the house while the rest dropped to the ground next to Ben, looking like a long, black snake.

Al reacted with rapid-fire instructions. "Joe, untie the rope from you and the branch. Ben, get the electrical tape, needle-nose pliers, and dikes out of the toolbox—pronto!"

Ben glanced at Joe, pleased to see that he had escaped being hit by the branch. He jumped over the wire and ran to the truck where the toolbox was buried under the first two branches that had been cut. Al scrambled down the ladder, not showing any concern for how much it wobbled during his descent.

Based on Ben's experience in fetching tools, he knew that his father planned to strip, splice, and tape the severed wire at the break. Relieved to find all three items quickly, Ben ran with them to his father who was positioning the ladder against the side of the house. Al extended the ladder to the point where the wire had been snapped.

"Joe, hurry up with the rope! I need one end of it tied to the wire."

Joe worked on untying the rope from around the branch. He had already removed it from his waist and Al grabbed that end.

While Joe tried to complete his task, Ben handed his father the electrical tape and tools. Growing impatient, Al told Joe to "hustle up" and then dashed to the broken wire on the ground, dragging the rope behind him.

When he bent down to pick up the wire, Ben shouted, "Stop! You'll get electrocuted."

"Relax," Al said. "It's just a telephone line. I might get a bit of a tingle. That's all."

He proved his point by tying the rope around the wire without getting zapped. "And keep your big mouth shut. I don't want your fuddy-duddy grandpa coming out here and asking what's happening. We need to fix this problem quickly and quietly."

While Al climbed the ladder, he used the rope to pull the broken wire back to the point where it had previously been connected to the house. Then, he exposed the wires inside the phone line, twisted them together, and wrapped the splice in electrical tape. Finishing the job in minutes, Al quickly moved the ladder while Ben put away the electrical tape and tools. Grandpa Thorne walked outside moments later.

"I'm glad to see all three branches down and nobody is dead," he said. "Please come inside for a piece of pie to celebrate."

"That's tempting, but your daughter is waiting for us to come home for our family dinner," Al said. "We should get going as soon as we're done loading this last branch into the truck."

Seeing the disappointment on Ben's face, Grandpa Thorne promised to send a pie home with him. After finishing more of what Al called "waste-of-time chitchat," the crew went back to work. Al cut the large branch into three sections and Joe and Ben loaded them into the truck. Al tied the ladder to the top of the truck cab and wrapped more rope around the mass of branches in the truck's bed. The load looked ready to fall out if the truck went around a corner too fast.

Before leaving the house, Joe complained about the rope burns he received when being dragged across the yard. He lifted his shirt to show the red marks across his belly and back. Al looked at them briefly and then unveiled his wound again.

"Look at this. I got it worse, and you don't hear me complaining. So toughen up and stop whining! And let's keep all this a secret, especially the broken telephone line."

Joe and Ben nodded in agreement, understanding that being quiet would make things better for them. When their mother asked how it went, Joe and Ben replied "Fine." She smiled and didn't ask for details or notice Joe's rope burns or Al's bloody gash.

About two weeks later, Joe and Ben faced Grandpa Thorne's questions about how the telephone wire outside of his home ended up being cut and then wrapped in electrical tape. "We were having problems making phone calls after you boys were here with your dad for the tree-trimming project," Grandpa Thorne said. "When repairmen from the phone company came out to see what was wrong, they told me that it looked like someone had cut the line and then taped it together. Because of the poor job splicing the broken line, our phone stopped working. Do you boys have any idea about what might have caused that problem?"

Joe skillfully shrugged off Grandpa Thorne's questions with a simple "Don't know." Ben came up with a story that seemed plausible to him but not his grandfather.

"When we were working here, I saw three men from the telephone company cutting wires in your neighborhood. I asked them why and they said that they were checking the wires for rust. I bet that's what caused the problem."

Chapter 23

Growing up with a trained mechanic gave Joe and Ben firsthand experience in how to use tools to build and repair many things. Some of their best lessons came through working side-by-side with their father on innovative projects that taught them valuable lessons in creating a design to best fit the need and selecting the right materials to implement it. One of the most memorable learning experiences resulted from their participation in something else with a huge influence on their lives—scouting.

As with most Mormon families in the 1960s, the Bakers embraced Cub Scouts and Boy Scouts. Rachel helped her sons get off to a fast start by serving as their den mother when they were Cub Scouts. In her role, she helped plan a chariot race to create fun competition between the three dens in their cub pack.

Al's face lit up when Rachel mentioned plans for the race during dinner and he jumped into design mode. "I have exactly what you need—an electrical wire spool that would make perfect chariot wheels. I've been saving it for something special."

His designs usually involved junk salvaged from a construction site or vacant lot. When driving around Alma and neighboring communities, he would hit the brakes and back up his truck whenever he spotted something that might come in handy later. That's how he found the wheels for the chariot race.

After finishing dinner, the entire family walked to Al's dump site behind the barn where he pulled the spool from underneath other garbage. He smiled while presenting the spool as if it were a priceless heirloom. "Can you imagine the chariot we'll be able to build around these wheels?"

Rachel moved a little closer to the spool and examined it carefully. She knocked on the top piece, treating it like the door of an outhouse and grimacing at the thought of what she would find inside. "Well, it certainly would be solid," she said. "But I don't understand how you can turn this into a chariot."

"There's nothing a man can't accomplish with a little know-how and a generous scoop of elbow grease. Boys, am I right?"

Joe and Ben excitedly nodded in agreement, already imaging themselves as Ben-Hur winning the race with their magnificent chariot. Their father's plan sounded ideal and they wanted to get started that night.

"It seems a little too heavy for the boys to pull," Rachel said.

"There's your negative thinking again," Al said in a harsh tone, tossing an old board across the junk pile to express his frustration. "You never get it. Quit second-guessing me. You might be stupid, but I'm not."

Rachel looked away to hide her tears while Joe and Ben wrestled the spool out of the garbage pile. They pretended to not hear the insult or see their mother cry. At times like these, they had learned to shut their mouths and put smiles on their faces.

The next evening, Al and his sons started working on the chariot. Al's inspiration—the spool—resembled the small spools used to hold sewing thread, but it was giant-sized and had held heavy duty electrical wire. While driving home from the station one evening, Al along with his sons had found it on the side of the road where the power company had left it after replacing a line.

"Is it all right to take this without permission?" Ben asked.

"Of course, we're doing the power company a giant favor," Al replied. "They would have to pay someone to haul this junk away and we're doing it for free."

Despite Al's justification for taking the spool, he still painted over the highly visible warning on both sides about it being property of the power company. When doing it, he said, "We don't want anyone to get the wrong impression about where this came from."

Breaking off the ends of the spools created two wood discs about four feet in diameter and two inches wide. Al connected the wheels with an axle and created a cart that would sit above the axle for the rider. While doing this work, Joe and Ben struggled to hold the wheels in position for their father while he connected the other pieces of the chariot to them. It became obvious to the boys that the weight of the wheels would make it difficult to pull the chariot when completed. Not wanting to be accused of negative thinking, they buried their concerns.

On race day, Rachel's den showed up with the biggest, best-looking chariot. All the other cub scouts gathered around, making comments about the chariot's impressive size and design. The other two dens had used old bicycle parts to build chariots that looked more like wheelchairs—and were half the size of Al's creation.

With race-time soon approaching, Rachel's den members pulled the massive chariot toward the starting line and a few of them immediately began complaining about the weight. Their grumbling increased when leaving the parking lot and traveling over the race course—the softball field behind the church. The dens would race in the outfield, traveling about 250 feet over uneven, thick grass. The soft, bumpy surface made it much more difficult to pull the chariot than when it had been on the hard, flat parking lot.

Joe told everyone to "shut up" as soon as the grumbling began. "Just pull the chariot and save your breath. I don't want to hear any more griping."

He knew that his father would be upset if he heard complaints about his masterpiece. The grumblers toned it down, but they still whispered about the difficulty of pulling the chariot. They all desperately wanted to win the race and now it seemed impossible as they struggled to even make it to the starting line.

After a couple of minutes, they arrived at the line and paused there to listen to the pack leader go on and on about the glory days of Rome and the emperor's favorite sport of chariot racing. The long speech helped Rachel's den because it gave the cubs a chance to catch their breath. For Ben, the rest period didn't matter. As the smallest member of the den, the team had designated him to be the required rider. He would sit on the chariot while the rest of the team pulled it.

To start the race, the pack leader stood at the finish line, holding a red scarf while the chariot pullers leaned forward ready to run. When he dropped the scarf, the three teams took off. While the other two sprinted ahead, Rachel's den moved forward at a slow trot. From the beginning, a tight gap developed between first and second place and it stayed that way through the end. And while the winners celebrated, Rachel's den still had about half the course to cover.

When it became clear that his team would finish far behind the others, Ben jumped out of the chariot to push it. Joe, guardian of the rules, glared at him and shouted, "Get back in. We're going to finish this without cheating."

That was Joe. He worried about "cheating" while pulling a chariot with stolen wheels. Joe would whack him if he didn't obey, so Ben jumped back into the chariot and watched his team slowly trudge over the finish line. The last-place cubs dropped to the grass more out of discouragement than fatigue and refused to be consoled by their parents who applauded their "good try."

A few of the parents joked that the chariot would have been more suitable for building the pyramids of Egypt than racing. Ben didn't laugh. The race had been a serious matter to him and he hated to lose.

The winners jumped up and down when the pack leader announced their first-place finish in "world-record time." They received blue ribbons. The second-place team members won red ribbons for a heroic effort. Rachel's cubs left with white ribbons for having the most authentic design.

"You guys just weren't strong enough to pull this beauty," Al growled to the discouraged cubs as they hauled the huge chariot to his truck. "You should have trained for the race instead of sitting around like lazy bums while I did all the work."

The lecture didn't bother Ben. He had suffered tougher reprimands from his father. While he took it as merely another slap in the face, Al's harsh words and angry tone disturbed one of the younger cubs. He started to cry and darted away from the group, heading for his parents.

Joe jumped in to prevent a mass exodus. "Hey, guys, we'll do better next time. Let's get our chariot in the truck and be glad we won the award for best design."

Even though Joe often bossed Ben around and thumped him for being too loud or messy, Ben admired him and felt proud of his big brother. He also wanted to be proud of his father and didn't like it when other people viewed him negatively. The chariot race became one of those days when people whispered about him being a "total jerk." He found it easy to agree with them, but he wished it wasn't true. He wanted to love and respect his father.

Chapter 24

The chariot returned to the place where it came from—the junk pile behind the barn. Ben helped his father dump it there after the race and, about a month later, noticed that one of the wheels had been ripped off and used to reinforce the back wall of the pig pen. His father must have placed it there to keep the pigs from escaping. They had learned to lean on the pen's walls to dislodge the boards and create paths to freedom.

As he often did that summer, Ben rushed through his chores and then settled into a comfortable place on top of a broken hay bale, with his head on a pillow made of empty grain sacks. His bare feet hung over the end of a hay bale where the rising sun warmed them. In his hands, Ben held his latest book from the Alma Public Library—a biography about the explorer and frontiersman Kit Carson.

After reading the first two chapters, Ben heard Duke, his family's dog, barking. He set his book aside and stood up to see what the fuss was about. He spotted his friend George Oaks approaching.

"Duke, knock it off!" Ben shouted, which Duke interpreted as "Come, let's play!" Duke ran to Ben's resting spot in the barn with a broad smile and his tongue hanging out. The large dog, a German Shepherd and Siberian Husky mix, looked more like a wolf than a dog and often acted like a wild animal, running off into the mountains for days at a time. When he finally came home, Duke reeked of dead animals, skunks, and sagebrush. He usually came back starving, which Rachel joked was his sole motivation for returning. Duke wanted food from his family and that's it.

Shouting at Duke alerted George that Ben was in the barn and he walked toward it.

"Hey!" George shouted, waving at Ben who waved back and returned the "Hey."

"What are you doing?" George asked as he approached Ben's spot in the barn.

"Reading a book," Ben said while petting Duke.

"Why? School's out."

"You should know by now that I like to read."

"Yeah, but it's the summer. We should be doing something fun. Have you finished your morning chores?"

"Yep, I took care of them and now have the rest of the day off because my parents are at work. What gets you out of the house today?"

"My ma told me to leave. She had cleaning to do and griped that I was in the way," George said while Duke greeted the farm's visitor by licking his hands.

"Man, you're lucky. When my mom wants to clean the house, she makes a list of all the chores and then writes my name next to things for me to do and says that if I don't work, then I don't eat."

"That's awful. I'd starve if I lived here."

"No, my dad would knock some sense into you with a few shots to the head and a strong kick in the butt," Ben said, demonstrating how his father would deliver the blows. "Then, you'd be willing to work—or he'd kill you before you starved."

George frowned, looking around to see if anyone might be listening to their conversation, and then changed the subject. "So, what book are you reading?"

"It's a biography about Kit Carson," Ben said, showing George the book. "He explored the Rocky Mountains and fought in the Mexican-American War and Civil War."

"Why would you want to read that?"

"My mom told me that I should start reading biographies because they would show me the kind of person I need to be if I want to be successful. There's a whole section of these books in the library. I've already read biographies about Thomas Edison, Alexander Graham Bell, Marie Curie, and Wilbur and Orville Wright. And I liked them."

"That sounds boring to me. I'd rather read comic books, especially *Archie*."

"That's because you don't know what you're talking about. The only thing Archie does is hang out at the malt shop with Jughead, Betty, and Veronica. And Archie isn't even real. But Kit Carson—a real person—explored places that only Indians had ever seen and fought in great battles. How can you call that boring?"

"Uh, you're starting to sound like my teacher. Are we going to talk about books all day or do something fun?"

Ben thought about the question for a few seconds, wanting to continue reading, but he looked at George's spindly legs and the pleading look in his eyes and decided to take his friend on a tough hike. After placing the book in his bedroom and filling a couple of canteens with water, Ben led George away from his daily world of TV and comics to the raw beauty of the steep mountain behind them. And Duke followed, panting and looking from one side of the trail to the other as they started climbing the foothills.

While hiking, Ben told George about other explorers he had read about—Jim Bridger, Jedediah Smith, and Peter Skene Ogden—and how they would start at the mouth of a river and then go upstream to the headwaters. They filled in gaps on maps with the records of their journeys.

"I've never heard of any of those guys," George said.

"Well, I've also read about Daniel Boone and Davy Crockett. I'm sure you've heard of them."

"Yeah, Davy Crockett—king of the wild frontier! I've seen him on TV."

"When I grow up, that's what I want to be—a great explorer like Davy Crockett and the others I've read about."

"That's not possible. Everything has already been discovered. You'll probably end up being a mechanic like your pa."

"No! I told my mom that I want to be an explorer and she thinks it's a great idea. She showed me a magazine at the library called *National Geographic* and said that I could explore the world and then write magazine articles about what I found."

As he often did on these hikes, Duke suddenly shot off the trail and the boys caught glimpses of him charging through the scrub oak in pursuit of a mule deer that had been nearby.

"Look at Duke go!" George shouted.

"Yeah, but he'll never catch that deer unless it's wounded or sick. Duke won't quit trying, though. I bet he doesn't come home until morning when he's hungry for breakfast. I hope he stays away from the porcupines this time."

Duke had returned from one of his recent mountain trips with his mouth full of porcupine quills. Some of them shot through the roof of his mouth and protruded a couple of inches above his nose. The quills caused him to yelp in pain and made it impossible for him to eat. While Joe and Ben held Duke, Al attempted to pull the quills out, but the pain kept Duke from cooperating and a veterinarian had to finish the job.

"Where are we going?" George asked.

"I found a cliff that gives you a view of the town and everything all the way to Utah Lake. It's a tough climb, though."

"I'll be able to make it if we stop for a few breaks," George said, expressing his need early because he knew Ben would rather hike until exhaustion forced him to stop.

When the boys reached the cliff with the long-range view, they sat near the edge, sipping lukewarm water from their canteens and chatting about the distant scenery.

"I can see why you like hiking," George said, leaning back to watch a large, white cloud drift slowly above through the blue sky. “It’s pretty up here.”

“It is, but I want to see more,” Ben said with a sweeping gesture toward the western horizon. “I want to explore places most people can’t even find on a map—places in New Zealand, Norway, Argentina, and Kenya. Even if every inch of the world has already been explored, I haven’t seen it and I want to go there.”

Relaxing on the mountainside, Ben imagined himself following in the footsteps of famous explorers and reaching bright horizons—far from the shadowy world where he lived.

Chapter 25

For fifth grade, Ben returned to Alma Elementary School with muted optimism. He thought the bullies might leave him alone as they had at the end of the past school year. And it happened most of the time. His classmates usually obeyed the hands-off policy, but Ben remained on the fringe of social circles. Trying to fit in led to the year's most memorable event.

His teacher, Mrs. Wright, taught music daily, using a piano shared with two other classrooms. After the lesson, four boys from her class took the large upright piano to the third-grade classroom. The heavy piano could be easily moved because it had wheels like small tires that rolled smoothly on the school's tile floors.

Pushing it became an honor, and each year the teacher selected four strong, trustworthy boys for the task. As the smallest boy in the class, Ben didn't make the prestigious piano squad, getting assigned to taking out the trash instead. Each afternoon, he carried the classroom's metal wastepaper basket to a large dumpster outside the school.

Ben enjoyed trash duty and didn't ask to be reassigned, but his path took him down the same hall as the piano squad. Daily, he watched the squad members make their trek and thought it looked fun.

"Hey, can I push the piano with you?" he asked one day when the squad sped by.

"No," said Ted Goodwin, squad captain. "You're not strong enough."

"I'm stronger than I look. At home, I push a full wheelbarrow of cow manure uphill almost every day. Pushing a piano would be easier."

Ted didn't believe him. Determined to show the squad members that he could do it, Ben repeated his request the next day.

Ted surprised Ben by responding with a new idea. "Jump on the back and we'll give you a ride."

Ben decided to go for it. He jogged alongside the moving piano, set the wastebasket on top of it, and then stepped on the board at the bottom and back of the piano. He leaned over the top of the piano and held on to the front, becoming a passenger without the squad having to stop for the boarding process.

The squad showed off by picking up the pace to a slow jog while sailing down the hall to the third-grade classroom. Before reaching their destination, Ben pointed at the hallway that would take him to the school's rear entrance.

"That's where I need to get off," he said, expecting them to stop.

"Hold on," Ted said. "We'll take you there."

Ted and the boy next to him turned the piano so that it started heading toward the rear entrance, but the boys behind the piano kept pushing ahead at the same brisk pace. The squad's lack of experience in making a high-speed turn caused the piano to tip over.

Normally, a falling piano would have made a loud crash, but it fell on Ben and his body cushioned the fall. Because he used his hands to save the wastepaper basket from hitting the floor, Ben provided no resistance to the falling piano. His chest absorbed its full weight, expelling the air from his lungs.

After recovering from the shock of what happened, Ted and his squad frantically lifted the heavy wooden monster off Ben and back onto its wheels. Getting the weight off made it possible for Ben to start breathing again, but he couldn't do it. He remained flat on his back, still holding the wastepaper basket and feeling a surge of panic. A dozen tense seconds passed while he fruitlessly tried to take a breath. Ted rescued him. He grabbed the basket out of Ben's hands and helped him sit up.

"Try to take deep breaths, not short ones," Ted said calmly. "It's like in football when you get the air knocked out of you. You need to take deep breaths."

Even though Ben had never played football and didn't know what Ted meant, he trusted him, and the technique worked. He soon started breathing again and the fear of suffocating faded. Ben flexed his legs and, to his amazement, found that they hadn't been shattered.

"Are you ready to stand up?" Ted asked.

"Sure," Ben said and slowly rose to his feet with Ted providing some of the lift. The movement confirmed the good news that his legs were intact, but it also warned him of major problems elsewhere.

Ben's back and ribs screamed in pain, especially when he tried to continue taking deep breaths. The pain made any breathing difficult, so he returned to short, shallow breaths to ease the impact. Being mindful of his duty, he bent over to pick up the wastepaper basket and uttered a slight groaning sound when pain waves shot up his back.

"Are you OK?" Ted asked.

"I'm fine. Thanks for the ride, guys."

The piano squad watched Ben as he slowly walked to the school's rear entrance with the basket in his arms.

"Hey, let's keep this to ourselves," Ted said. "We don't want to get chewed out by Mrs. Wright. OK?"

Ben turned to the squad and gave them a thumbs-up sign.

They all nodded and flashed nervous smiles before resuming their trip to the third-grade classroom. When Ben raised his left hand to open the school's back door, the pain caused him to hold his breath and grimace. The same thing happened when lifting the basket to eye level and emptying it into the bin. After making that move, he noticed a blood spot on his shirt.

Ben pulled his shirt away from his body and saw a four-inch-wide red stripe across his chest where the piano had scraped his flesh. Blood oozed from the wound in several places. Ben made a detour to the boy's bathroom where he used toilet paper to cover the torn flesh. He wanted to keep his blood from exposing the secret he shared with the piano squad.

The toilet paper trick worked, and Ben made it through the rest of the day without Mrs. Wright saying anything about the piano being tipped over in the hallway. The fall apparently didn't damage the piano because Mrs. Dugmore, the third-grade teacher, made no complaints. And to keep the secret, Ben concentrated on not frowning or flinching despite frequent, agonizing spasms exploding in his back and across his ribcage.

For the next three weeks, Ben put on a show at school and home to hide his injury. It took great focus to ignore the persistent pain and to take a deep breath without wincing in agony. Slowly the pain lessened, but Ben's ability to endure pain went unrewarded.

The downfall came because one of the piano squad members couldn't resist sharing the story with a buddy. And the drama of "little Benny Baker being squished by the piano" soon spread. When the news reached Mrs. Wright, she took immediate action.

"Class, before today's geography lesson, we need to discuss another subject—honesty," she said with a stern tone.

Ben thought someone might have been caught cheating. He had no worries about that problem, but Mrs. Wright quickly wiped out his sense of security.

"We had a recent problem in the hallway where someone was seriously injured and five boys from our class knew it happened, but none of them told me about it. And that's unacceptable, dishonest behavior."

The guilty party of five sounded like Ben and the piano squad. In case her verbal clue didn't catch the culprits' attention, Mrs. Wright delivered her statement while looking at Ben and then shifting her focus to Ted.

"You need to understand that being honest goes beyond not lying, stealing, or cheating. It also requires sharing vital information instead of hiding it."

To illustrate her point, Mrs. Wright told a story about a mistake she made as a teenager. Shortly after learning how to drive, she put a long scratch in her father's new car by brushing against a fence post. She worried that if she told her father about the scratch that he would take away her driving privileges. To avoid getting into trouble, she kept quiet about what happened.

The next day, her father spotted the scratch and blamed it on his wife. She denied having done it and Mrs. Wright's parents ended up in a heated argument. Because she couldn't stand to hear them quarreling, Mrs. Wright confessed that she had scratched the car.

"By not telling my parents about the scratch as soon as it happened, I caused them to argue and still ended up being punished. I learned a valuable lesson from that experience."

After pausing to make eye contact with Ben and each member of the piano squad, she asked, "Would any of you like to tell me about something that should have been reported immediately?"

Ben avoided looking at Mrs. Wright and waited for one of his fellow conspirators to speak up. Even if Mrs. Wright asked Ben directly, he planned to honor his agreement with Ted and say nothing.

After Mrs. Wright repeated her question, Ted spoke up from where he sat on the back row. "Ma'am, I think you might be talking about the piano tipping over when we were pushing it down the hall."

"Ted, thank you for sharing that information with me. But did you leave out an important detail?"

"Uh, I suppose so. The piano landed on little Benny Baker and squished him like a bug."

Most of the kids laughed at Ted's account of the incident, but Mrs. Wright shut down the levity with a stern look. When she glanced at Ben, he imagined that she wanted to see if he had truly been "squished," so he gave his teacher a happy face to let her know that all's well.

Mrs. Wright asked, "Ted, didn't you think that I should have heard about what happened so Ben could get medical care?"

"I thought about it, but I helped Benny start breathing again and then he picked up the trash can and went right back to work. He's a lot tougher than he looks."

It thrilled Ben to hear a popular boy compliment him in front of the entire fifth grade.

"Ben, did you stop breathing?" Mrs. Wright asked, appearing surprised by the news.

"Yes, ma'am, but Ted got my breathing started again. I only had the wind knocked out of me and it was no big deal."

Ben should have stopped with "Yes, ma'am." Mrs. Wright jumped on Ben's comment that the piano accident "was no big deal" and stated that she needed to know if any of her students gets hurt at school. She finished the lecture by asking Ben and the piano squad to remain in the classroom at the end of the day.

With the teacher's request hanging over Ben's head, the day crawled by slower than normal. When the interrogation began, Principal Smith joined Mrs. Wright in asking for every detail of the piano mishap and why it landed on Ben. Until Ted started telling the story, Mrs. Wright and the principal didn't know that Ben had been riding on the back of the piano. Both interrogators also expressed surprise when they learned that the accident had happened three weeks earlier.

With the fact-gathering step completed, the punishment phase began. Mrs. Wright said she would reassign all members of the piano squad to chores to be done in the classroom. Ben lost his responsibility for emptying the wastepaper basket, being reassigned to dusting bookshelves.

"Boys, I know that some of you have missed your bus and the rest should have walked home from school by now," Principal Smith said. "Don't worry. We called your parents earlier today and they're here to take you home after we talk to them about this situation."

Ben couldn't believe that the principal included "Don't worry" in his announcement. He could make the long walk home from school—that wasn't a problem. Having his parents receive a call about Ben being in trouble at school again would result in him getting thumped by his father.

"Ben, your parents couldn't get off work to pick you up, so Mrs.

Wright will drive you home," the principal said, embarrassing Ben in front of his new friends.

"Oh, she doesn't need to do that. I can walk. It's only a couple of miles."

"No. Mrs. Wright will drive you home."

The principal told Ben to stay, but he sent the rest of the boys to wait for him in his office and promised to be there in a couple of minutes. The principal then asked Ben to show him his injuries. Ben pulled down the corner of his shirt collar and pointed at the red mark that still crossed the top of his chest. The principal asked Ben to remove his shirt.

"OK, but there isn't much to see now," Ben said, unbuttoning his shirt and slipping it off. "I'm nearly all healed and feeling much better."

While his teacher took notes, the principal examined Ben's chest and back. "Mrs. Wright, please record that there is a scrape across Ben's chest and several faded bruises on his back and chest."

When Principal Smith pressed his fingers gently into Ben's back, he said, "Tell me if you have any pain where I'm touching you."

Ben flinched and lied, "No."

The principal did the same thing with Ben's ribs and received the same response.

"We need your parents to take you to a doctor to be checked out. There might be a severe problem that X-rays could identify."

"But I'm fine," Ben said.

"You need to see a doctor because it's obvious that you aren't being truthful about having no pain. You cringe and hold your breath whenever I touch you."

Principal Smith turned to Mrs. Wright and asked her if she had seen Ben's reactions to being touched and received a solemn nod to indicate her agreement.

Ben desperately wanted to get out of going to the doctor. "We can't afford more doctor bills."

"If your parents need help paying for a doctor to examine you, I'll have the school cover the expense because the injuries happened here. There will be no debate about this—you're going to the doctor."

The principal handed Ben's shirt to him. "You can put your shirt back on. We're done here."

Mrs. Wright watched Ben button his shirt. "Having the piano fall on you must have been very frightening and painful."

"A little bit. But I'm used to it. Like Ted said, I'm much tougher than I look."

"What do you mean about being used to it?"

Once again, Ben realized that he should have limited his response to "Yes, ma'am." Joe often warned him to be polite and cheerful but don't provide more information than required. To answer Mrs. Wright's question, Ben made up examples.

"Sometimes I get hurt doing stuff that boys do," he said. "Like playing football, falling out of trees, and tripping over things. I'm someone who trips and bumps into stuff an awful lot."

Ben's examples omitted actual events such as his father throwing tools at him, breaking a broom over his head, or jabbing him in the abdomen with a rake.

"If anything like that happens at school, please come to me so we can talk about it."

"Yes, ma'am," Ben said, keeping his answer simple.

Ben followed Mrs. Wright and the principal to the school office, passing the corner where the piano had fallen. He resisted the urge to point out the spot. Instead, he joined the adults in silence for the entire walk.

In the office, Mrs. Wright briefly talked to the parents who had gathered there and then left them with the principal while she drove Ben home. They chatted along the way about Ben's schoolwork and she asked about Joe's progress in sixth grade. As expected, Mrs. Wright mentioned that Joe was one of her favorite students of all time. Ben told her that Joe still spent hours doing his homework every night.

"Joe has all the brains in the family. He's even the best at milking the cow."

"I'll tell you the truth about Joe," Mrs. Wright said. "He excels at school because he sets lofty goals and then works hard to achieve them. You could do the same."

"I don't know about that."

"You could be one of the top students this year and for years to come. I can see you going on to earn a college degree, but you need to focus on your teacher and take your eyes off the clock."

Ben laughed about the clock, knowing the criticism was true, but he also appreciated her words of encouragement.

When Mrs. Wright pulled into the Bakers' gravel driveway, Ben noticed his grandparents' car parked next to the house. "Ah, what are they doing here?" he asked with a loud groan.

"School policy doesn't let me take you home without an adult being present. I worked it out with your mother to have your grandmother meet us."

"You didn't need to do that. Joe is here and keeps me out of trouble."

"I'm sure Joe does a wonderful job. Today, your grandmother will be here too."

Having seen Mrs. Wright's car, Grandma Thorne came out of the house with Becky in her arms and waved from the front porch. Ben gathered his books and lunch box.

Before he could exit the car, Mrs. Wright said, "Ben, I hope you will trust me and let me know when you've been hurt. And I don't want you to think that you need to get used to being hurt. That's something nobody must go through. Do you understand me?"

Ben answered with a quick "Yes, ma'am," feeling uneasy about her touching the fringes of a well-protected area of his life.

As he exited the car, Mrs. Wright repeated the main point of her honesty lesson. "Remember, being honest is more than not telling lies. It's also speaking up about things that people need to know."

Ben nodded to her, closed the car door, and walked away briskly. He agreed with what she said, but he didn't know if her comments applied to family secrets. That's what he wanted to speak about for hours if anybody would listen—and if he had permission to mention those secrets.

When Ben reached the front porch, he waved goodbye to Mrs. Wright and waited for her drive off. He wondered what she would do if he told her about his "hurts" and who gave them to him. But knowing the problems it would create for his family, he pledged to suffer in silence—and keep his eyes on the clock.

Chapter 26

In the summer following Ben's sixth-grade year, his father received a phone call when the family was getting ready to eat dinner. After hanging up the phone, he took his seat at the table and made an announcement while loading his plate with mashed potatoes.

"That was Jeb Parker, my father's boss," Al said. "He called to let me know that my father passed away this morning. There's going to be a funeral for him on Saturday. I told Jeb we'd be there."

Al's family waited for him to explain why his father died, but he acted as if his father's death meant nothing more than an obligation to attend a funeral. Al ignored the stunned looks at the table and dove into his dinner with his usual speedy, silent approach.

Ben wasn't shocked by the behavior. He knew that his father came from a family that fell apart at the end of the Great Depression. Grandpa Baker abandoned his wife and four children on a small, rundown farm in Sandy, Utah, to look for work elsewhere. Because she had schizophrenia, Al's mother couldn't care for the children. When neighbors complained about the family's deplorable living conditions, social workers placed Al, his brother, and two sisters in foster homes. Al ended up in Alma where he met Rachel at school.

Ben had only participated in brief visits with his father's birth parents. The last visit with Grandpa Baker ended in less than two hours. He lived north of Salt Lake City in a small trailer on the farm where he worked. When the Bakers dropped in to see him, he gave them a tour of the farm, pointing out all the things he needed to get done that day. He made sure they knew what an enormous vital job he had and made it clear that they should leave because he didn't have time to chat. Al eventually took the hint and told his family, "Let's go." They drove away without hugs or promises to see each other again.

"Don't chase the chickens" were the only words Grandpa Baker spoke to Ben. Some of the chickens roamed about the barnyard searching for stray pieces of grain. As Ben often did on his farm, he reached down to grab one of the chickens by the feet, so he could carry it around like a pet. But the hen eluded Ben, squawking and flapping her wings. Grandpa Baker noticed the commotion and delivered his brief command with an angry tone and look that reminded Ben of his father.

"Al, I'm sorry about your father passing away and know that your heart must be very heavy," Rachel said, breaking the uncomfortable silence. "What happened? Was it a heart attack?"

"No, a train hit him while he was walking on the tracks west of the farm," Al said, looking up from his food. "What's wrong with you, idiots? Eat. It's getting cold."

The train story puzzled Ben. He didn't know how a train could sneak up on someone while walking through the quiet countryside. He imagined that the engineer would have blown the train's horn when he spotted a man on the tracks.

"What time is the funeral?" Rachel asked.

"Noon. We'll need to wake up early, get our chores done, and be on the road no later than eight. There will be no time for lollygagging around or stopping to pee every ten minutes. Got it?"

Joe and Ben nodded in agreement, but Rachel sat with tears in her eyes and looked at her plate. She asked, "Do we need to take food for the funeral service or help with the arrangements?"

"Nope, the Parkers will take care of everything. We don't have to come up with even a dime to pay for it. Jeb wants to cover the entire cost—and that's fine with me."

Al paused for a few bites of green beans before continuing. "But I promised that we would clean out my father's trailer."

The funeral took place in the LDS Church meetinghouse where Grandpa Baker had been an inactive member. It looked empty with only forty people in attendance. Ben recognized the Parkers, but nobody else. The other attendees had met Grandpa Baker a few times when the Parkers had talked him into going to church with them.

Because Grandpa Baker had been hit by a train, his casket remained closed for the memorial service, but it still sat in front of the chapel. Bishop Hyrum Hatch of Grandpa Baker's ward led the service and talked about what happens to a man after death, presenting the LDS viewpoint about three degrees of glory—the Celestial, Terrestrial, and Telestial Kingdoms and the many mansions there. He didn't predict which of these kingdoms Grandpa Baker would end up in or mention the other option—Outer Darkness where Satan and his angels would be sent along with Mormon leaders who turned against the church.

"Not many of us knew Brother Baker very well," Bishop Hatch said. "But the Parkers commend him for having been an exceptionally hard-working man. He always earned his paycheck by giving a full effort. Today, we celebrate his service to others."

Ben glanced to see if his father smiled when hearing that flattering remark, because the same thing could be said about him. Al paid attention to the bishop's message but showed no emotions.

After the memorial service, the attendees drove to a sprawling cemetery where men carried the casket to the gravesite. Bishop Hatch dedicated the grave and made a few more remarks. Ben didn't cry and never caught his father doing so either. He knew his father's opinion about crying—that's something only girls do.

Following the graveside service, the attendees returned to the church for a buffet lunch in the church's cultural hall. Enough tables and chairs were set up to accommodate one hundred people. Ben filled his plate until it overflowed and then found an empty table away from where his parents sat with the Parkers and Bishop Hatch.

Ben had gone through the buffet line ahead of Joe and his sisters, so he thought they might join him at his table. Instead, an older, large man with a gray beard sat next to him. He reminded Ben of Santa Claus, except he wore a conservative blue suit, not a flashy red one.

"I hope you don't mind me sharing this table with you," he said.

"No, but it looks like the adults are sitting over there," Ben said, nodding toward his parents' table.

"Hmm, not that table. Don't like being where everyone talks at the same time—drives me crazy."

"Same here."

"And, like me, you have a big appetite," he said, pointing his fork at Ben's plate.

"I do," Ben said, having followed his father's advice about buffets—"Load up, because you never know when you'll eat again."

Ben ate in silence while the man rapidly cleared his plate of everything. When finished, he pushed his empty plate aside and said, "I forgot to introduce myself. I'm Ray Spence, but most people call me Canada because I moved down here from Cardston, Alberta, Canada."

"I'm Ben Baker from Alma in Utah County. I don't have a nickname."

"We'll call you Lone Wolf since you like sitting by yourself."

"OK," Ben said, enjoying his new name. It certainly sounded much better than "Benny" or some of the far less flattering things he had been called.

Ben noticed Joe and his sisters exiting the buffet line. Ben waved at them, but Joe shook his head "No" and told the girls to sit with him at another empty table.

"Hey, let me tell you something about your granddad," Canada said. "He was a decent fellow. Hardworking like the bishop said. I've known him for eight years—that's when he wandered by and took a job at the Parkers' farm."

"Where did he live before here?"

"I have no idea. He kept his story private. I own the farm next to the Parkers and wanted to hire your granddad after seeing how hard he worked, but he was loyal to his boss and seemed happy to live in that tiny trailer."

"Did you know that he had a wife and four kids?"

"No, I knew about your family because you visited him a couple of times. He told me that your pa was his son and that's all I could get out of him. I suppose there were things in his past that he didn't want to discuss."

Ben had eaten all he wanted from his plate and pointed at the left-overs he didn't like. "Do you think it would be OK if I tossed this stuff in the trash and went back for more dessert?"

"Great idea!" Canada slapped his leg and stood up. Then, he paused and looked at Ben closely.

"Hey, before we go back, I need to say something else about your granddad. He might have made a few mistakes in his life, but he was still a good man. I don't know what caused him to end his life, but I hope it doesn't make you think any less of him."

Canada took a deep breath and then asked, "Can you forget about how he died and remember that you should be proud to call him Granddad?"

Ben mumbled "Sure," not knowing what else to say. The surprise attack by the train had always sounded farfetched to him. On the other hand, he didn't want to consider suicide as his grandfather's true cause of death.

Canada noticed that his comments had stunned Ben and muttered something about "saying too much." He suggested fetching a couple of pie slices before the good choices were gone.

Rachel caught Ben returning to the food table and waved him away, but his new friend shouted over the chatter in the room. "Sister Baker, your son is going back for seconds under protest," Canada said. "I begged him to join me in getting some pie, so I wouldn't be the only one coming back for more."

Rachel smiled in return but looked nervous. She always worried about her kids doing anything that people might find offensive.

For his second dessert, Canada selected a Dutch-crumb apple pie and took much more than a normal slice. He also cut a jumbo-sized piece for Ben and whispered, “Let’s get going before anyone judges us for eating like pigs.”

They quickly retreated to their private table. While devouring the pie, Canada told stories about how Ben’s grandfather would help him on his farm after working a full day for the Parkers. “Are you a hard worker like your granddad?”

“No. My dad says I’m lazy and I suppose that might be true because I’d rather go hiking or read a book than haul manure or pull weeds.”

“Who wouldn’t? Your pa is probably trying to encourage you to work hard like he does because that’s what his father taught him.”

Ben shrugged his shoulders, not wanting to tell Canada that his father rarely mentioned Grandpa Baker. When prodded to talk about his childhood, Al always told the same story about the two of them stumbling into a pit full of rattlesnakes when gathering firewood in a canyon near Salt Lake City. Both escaped without being bitten. That was the entire story—and his only story.

Within a few minutes, Al walked to Ben’s table and told him that it was time to go. “We need to get busy cleaning out your grandfather’s trailer,” he said before walking to Joe’s table.

Ben said goodbye to Canada, who called him “Lone Wolf” when they shook hands.

Al led his children to Bishop Hatch’s table where he announced his plan to stop at the Parkers’ farm before returning home. Several strangers hugged the Bakers and said they would be praying for them. Rachel reluctantly accepted donations of leftover food.

At the Parkers’ farm, Rachel took her daughters for a stroll around a well-maintained flower garden while Al inspected his deceased father’s trailer.

“Everything is filthy, and it smells like a cow barn in here,” Al said, shaking his head in disgust. “We’re not taking anything with us. It’s all getting burned.”

Al pointed to a barren area near the trailer. "Joe, I want you to build a fire there. Use your grandpa's old newspapers to get it started. If you can't find any matches in here, see if Brother Parker or his wife can spare a few."

When he opened the trailer's only closet, Al said, "Yuck! Something must have died in there."

He used his fingertips to move a few shirts and coats in the closet to get a better look at them before repeating his command, "Burn all of it. And clear out the drawers and any other place where you find junk stashed. I promised to leave this place shipshape."

Ben hauled clothes, boots, and garbage to the intended fire pit, but Joe hadn't found matches in the trailer, so he went to get some from the Parkers. His request led Jeb to return with him and inquire about Al's plans.

"What are you going to do?" Jeb asked. "Joe told me you might be burning everything."

"That's right. It's all worthless, disgusting trash," Al said. "I don't want it stinking up my car. But you can take all of it if you think it's of any value."

Jeb briefly sorted through the pile of old, worn-out clothes. "Not the clothes. They're past their prime, but I'd like to keep the dishes and other things in the kitchen. We loaned them to your pa and could use them for the next tenant."

"Fine," Al said, aggravated. "They're still in the trailer."

Al stormed to the trailer with Jeb and Ben following close behind. He yanked open a cupboard door and grabbed a few items, tossing them to Ben and telling him to carry them to Jeb's house.

"No, please wait a minute," Jeb said. "Let me get a box to store them in while you clean the trailer. When you're done, we can put them back in the cupboard."

Ben thought his father might blow up when hearing the request, but Al agreed to wait for the box. After Jeb left the trailer, Al pointed out a dozen other things he wanted Ben to haul to Joe's fire. They included dirty pillows and blankets, a tattered tablecloth, and old magazines.

After a couple of trips to the fire, Ben found a mechanical calendar and three paperback novels on a small, built-in nightstand next to his grandfather's bed. The calendar, which was made of bronze and stood about five inches high, featured a bear cub leaning against a sign that read "Welcome to Yellowstone National Park." The sign included two squares cut out of the metal that exposed the twelve months of the year on the left side and numbers one through thirty-one on the right. By turning little knobs on each side of the sign, the month and date could be set. Ben noticed the calendar remained set for the day his grandfather died. He must have changed it before leaving for his fatal walk on the train tracks.

The three books appeared to have been read many times and included "*How the West Was Won*" by Louis L'Amour, "*The Virginian*" by Owen Wister, and "*Riders of the Purple Sage*" by Zane Grey. Ben had read "*The Virginian*" and remembered how much he liked it. As Ben examined the calendar and books, Al returned to the trailer with a roll of paper towels and a bottle of Windex. He noticed Ben sitting on the bed.

"Hey, who said you could take a break?" he asked in an irritated tone. "We don't have time to dawdle. Get the rest of the junk out of here so I can wipe up this filthy mess."

Ben thought his father might find the four items interesting, so he held them out for his inspection. "I found these books and this cool calendar from Yellowstone Park. Would it be all right if I kept them?"

Al frowned at Ben's treasures. "Why do you want that junk?"

"They belonged to Grandpa Baker and must have been important to him."

Al glanced at them and then turned away and started squirting Windex on the counter next to the trailer's small sink. He muttered about what a "sickening pigsty" his father had created and wondered "how anyone could stand to live like this." Ben continued to hold out the four treasures.

"May I keep them?" he asked, cautiously repeating his request.

"Fine," Al said. "Go put them in the car and then hurry back and get busy. I want to be out of here in less than twenty minutes."

Before his father changed his mind, Ben dashed to the car and hid the items under the backseat. By the time he returned to the trailer, Jeb had arrived with a large box. Ben loaded it with old pots, pans, plates, cups, bowls and utensils. Most of it looked like stuff that even Ben's frugal mother would have tossed into the garbage, but Jeb said the trailer's next tenant would find all of it to be "perfectly acceptable."

"And as you've apparently learned, beggars can't be choosers," Al said with disdain, which caused Jeb to frown and walk away shaking his head.

After Ben had removed the kitchen items, Al looked inside the cupboard and grumbled about the mouse droppings he found there. He removed them with a paper towel, but it revived his rant about "the unbelievable filth." He continued cleaning the trailer as if every inch of it infuriated him.

The Bakers completed the cleanup effort in less than fifteen minutes and then restocked the kitchen. The trailer looked and smelled much better than when they arrived. Al inspected the work and seemed pleased with what had been accomplished in a brief time. He rated the result as "a work of art and a joy forever."

While Ben liked his father's good mood about the clean trailer, he found it sad that the evidence of his grandfather's existence had been burned in Joe's fire or washed away with Windex. Because the fire contained clothes and magazines, it would smolder for the rest of the day, but nearly all his grandfather's possessions had already been blackened or turned to ashes. Fortunately, he had saved four items from the fire and planned to display them on the nightstand next to his bed. They would be his connection to the grandfather he barely knew.

During the long drive home, Ben thought about what Canada had told him—the more believable version of his grandfather's cause of death. He wondered why his grandfather let the train to hit him. Al blamed the mistake on a hearing problem, but Ben had stood near passing trains and knew the ground shakes when they approach. Nobody needs to hear a train to know it is coming.

If Ben could have talked to his grandfather while he stood on the tracks, he would have asked a few questions. *What is so bad about your life that you're choosing death over life? Is suicide the only solution to your problems? Is there nothing in your life worth living for?*

Chapter 27

While Grandpa Baker's life remained a mystery to Ben because his father only had one story to share, the same was not true for Ben. He had plenty of stories to tell about his father. One of his favorites, featuring "fun Dad," took place a few months after the funeral.

"Ben, I need you to take a little trip with me this afternoon," Al said shortly after the family's weekly big lunch on Sunday. "We're going up Elk Canyon to pick up rocks for reinforcing the barn's foundation. If we don't get it done soon, the barn will tip over and roll down the hill."

"OK, is Joe going with us?" Ben asked, wondering why his brother hadn't been included in the plan.

"No, he's staying here to milk Daisy in case we run late. And the truck would be too crowded because we're taking Grandpa Thorne. He wants rocks for a flowerbed. So, get your working boots on, bring your gloves, and be in the truck in five minutes. Don't dawdle. I don't want to keep your grandpa waiting."

Ben hurried to get ready and arrived at the truck as his father tossed a pair of shovels and a pickaxe into the back. They made the short drive to add Grandpa Thorne to the team.

"Al, I'm looking for about two dozen rocks the size of cantaloupes," he said.

"That'll be easy," Al said. "We'll be able to pick up that many in a few minutes."

"Do we have to pay for the rocks or get a permit to remove them?" Grandpa Thorne asked.

"No, it's government land and nobody pays attention to what goes on up there."

"Oh, I'm not too sure about this idea. We might get into trouble."

"Don't worry. I pick up firewood there all the time. We'll drive a few miles up the canyon. Throw some rocks in the truck and be home before Sheriff Kort wakes up from his Sunday afternoon nap."

Despite Grandpa Thorne's concern, he still climbed into the truck. Within ten minutes, the rock-hunters entered Elk Canyon. The dirt road, with occasional patches of gravel and an abundance of holes, made the trip bouncy and noisy. The old truck squeaked with each bump in the road.

Al pointed at a narrow road that led to the dry creek running down the middle of the canyon. "There's a good place to start," he said, grinning as if he had discovered a goldmine.

He drove to a point where the road ended in a small clearing. Then he turned the truck around and backed up. "Let's see what we can find," he said with continued enthusiasm.

Ben followed his father and joined him in putting on work gloves and grabbing a shovel out of the truck bed. They found plenty of rocks, but most of them were smaller than the size Grandpa Thorne had said would be ideal for his project. When they returned to the truck with their first armful, Grandpa Thorne stepped out of the truck and examined the collection with obvious disappointment.

"Here's the deal," Al said with the strained tone he used when annoyed. If prodded, his smoldering mood could flare up and become a blazing fire. Ben couldn't bear to see his father aim one of his profane outbursts at Grandpa Thorne.

"We'll load the truck with rocks and then stop at your house first," Al said, continuing to make no effort to disguise his agitation. "You get the first pick and we'll use whatever is left over to shore up our barn. So, don't look at the rocks we're putting in the truck and act like they aren't good enough for you."

"That's fine," Grandpa Thorne said, forcing a smile. "I'm only peeking."

Al muttered "Good" and rushed back to the riverbank for another load. After seven trips, he announced plans to change locations. "This area is panned out. Let's drive up the canyon and look for bigger rocks."

He turned to make sure his father-in-law couldn't hear him and then said to Ben, "I don't want your uptight grandpa complaining to your mom that we didn't get him exactly what he wanted for his precious flowerbed."

After a short drive, Al pointed at a one-lane dirt road. It headed away from the river and made a short climb up a steep hill into a sparsely wooded area. He turned left onto the road, gunning the engine to ascend the hill. As the truck chugged forward, all the rocks slid to the back of the truck bed and piled up against the tailgate. Ben turned to inspect the damage and noticed a few smaller rocks bounce over the tailgate.

"Do we still have a load?" Al asked while keeping his eyes focused on the narrow steep road.

"Yep, we only lost two or three," Ben said, continuing to watch the tailgate and hoping that the load's weight wouldn't force it open. Scrub oak branches whipped and scratched the truck when it passed them.

When the road leveled out, Al shouted, "Hold on everybody, I'm going to move the rocks away from the tailgate."

He stomped on the brakes and the truck skidded to a loud stop with the rocks sliding forward. They smacked the back of the truck's cab.

"Now, that's what I call using your brains!" Al shouted. "You've witnessed one of the principles of physics—an object in motion remains in motion until it meets an unmovable object."

Grandpa Thorne muttered something that Ben couldn't hear while continuing to clutch the dashboard with both hands. He hadn't worked with his son-in-law enough to be prepared for big solutions to little problems.

Al waited for the dust to clear and then drove another one hundred yards. He stopped at a place where erosion had exposed a treasure chest of rocks, exactly the size and shape that Grandpa Thorne wanted. After Al and Ben loaded about two dozen into the truck, Al checked the tires to make sure they could handle the load's weight and then announced plans to drive a little farther to see what else might be available.

"Al, don't you think we already have enough?" Grandpa Thorne asked.

"Maybe for your little flowerbed, but I have a barn to save. What I'd really like to find are a few large slabs—two or three feet in length and about six inches thick."

Al waved everyone back into the truck. Because of road dust, Grandpa Throne rolled up his window and returned to clutching the dashboard with both hands. It annoyed Ben that he insisted on sitting next to the window and yet had closed it on a sweltering day. Fortunately, Al kept his window down so a slight breeze blew through the truck.

Al shouted, "Hold on!" as he turned a tight corner and accelerated to start climbing a series of switchbacks. The truck sped along the road, with the driver and passengers bouncing up and down in their seats. After completing two switchbacks, the truck had climbed so high on the hillside that Ben could see his hometown from one end to the other.

While Ben looked down the hill, his father focused on a washed-out area above them. "Do you see that gully? That's our next stop."

Al passed the target and then backed up, turning the truck so that the tailgate faced the rock pile. He shut off the truck and climbed out ready to gather more plunder.

When Grandpa Thorne stepped out of the truck, he examined the rocks already loaded. They nearly reached the top of the bed and caused the truck's tires to bulge under the weight.

"Al, let's not get greedy. I think it's time to call it quits."

Despite looking irritated, Al agreed to go, but then he spotted another "gold mine" after pulling away from the gully. "Oh! Look at that rock! It's exactly what I need."

Chapter 27

Al slowed the truck and turned toward the edge of the road—facing the side that dropped sharply to the series of switchbacks. With no guardrail on this makeshift road, Ben joined his grandfather in grabbing the dashboard when Al appeared to be driving over the cliff.

"Relax! You two are making me nervous."

Grandpa Thorne glared at Al while Ben slid back into his seat and tried to act "relaxed." Al had intentionally driven to the road's edge to give him enough room to back up. He completed the maneuver, left the truck running, and jumped out.

"Wait in the truck. I see a flat stone behind us that will make this trip a complete success. I'll throw it in and then we'll be on our way."

Through the mirror on the driver's side of the truck, Ben watched his father free the rock from the weeds and dirt holding it in place. Next, he dropped the truck's tailgate and lifted the rock into the bed. When he shoved the rock forward, the truck also moved, coming close to rolling over the cliff.

Ben turned to warn him that the truck had moved. Before Ben could suggest applying the emergency brake, Al slammed the tailgate with both hands. This action delivered another physics lesson—an object at rest remains at rest unless a man stealing rocks gives it a push. And if that object is pushed from flat ground to the side of a steep hill, gravity takes over. The object goes from being at rest to being in motion—fast motion.

Al's forceful tailgate closing moved the truck ahead so that the front wheel on the driver's side crossed the edge of the road and fell onto the steep hillside. When the wheel left the road, the truck tipped in that direction. Grandpa Thorne quickly braced himself against the dashboard as it appeared the truck might roll over, but the other front wheel also moved forward. When it dropped to the hillside, the truck straightened out with its entire front end hanging over the edge of the road.

For a moment, Ben thought the truck's momentum had stopped and they would be safe, but the truck started to slide forward and soon all four wheels were on the hillside. When that happened, the truck began a rapid descent. Ben turned to look for his father and saw him trying to catch up.

"Ben, grab the wheel!" Al shouted. "Keep her straight and hit the brakes!"

Ben heard the instructions, but he thought his grandfather, who had a driver's license, should take over. When Ben turned toward his grandfather who had his hands welded to the dashboard, it became clear that he had no plans to stop the runaway truck. Ben decided to go with his father's last clear message—*grab the wheel!*

He slid out of the middle seat and seized the steering wheel with both hands. At only four and a half feet in height, Ben found it nearly impossible to reach the brakes while steering the truck. To step on the brake pedal, he had to slide so low in the seat that he could barely see over the dashboard. And this off-road trip required him to keep his eyes on the mountainside.

He found that he could apply the brakes and still see where they were going by straightening his foot and using his toe to push the pedal. This approach worked, and the truck began to slow down. Grandpa Thorne offered no advice or assistance as he continued to stare straight ahead with a pale, terrified look. Ben remembered that his grandfather took heart medication and hoped it kept working for him.

Ben's first few seconds as a driver had succeeded in slowing the truck and keeping it heading straight. Things changed, though, when crossing the first of the switchbacks. The truck's front end gently kissed the road when crossing, but the backend slapped it hard. Grandpa Thorne and Ben bounced up in their seats and came down with a thump. Passing over the switchback also sent one of the rocks in the bed flying forward. It smashed the rear window of the cab.

While his grandfather pleaded with God for help, Ben pulled himself back into driving position and stretched for the brake pedal. The next switchback loomed two seconds away. He worried that crossing another one would cause him to lose control and roll the truck, so he made a quick decision. Ben slid lower in the seat and stomped on the brakes.

When the front tires contacted the switchback, the truck's nose slightly dug into the road. This helped act as another brake. Then, Ben made his first major turn as a driver and swung the truck to the left to get on the road instead of crossing it.

"Too close, too close, too close!" Grandpa Thorne shouted, pointing at the cliff on his side of the truck.

Ben thought he had plenty of room, but he wanted to please his grandfather, so he calmly steered away from danger. He finished braking and noticed that the truck was still running, so he turned off the ignition and applied the emergency brake. Ben decided that he didn't need his father's approval for using the brake. In his mind, he had become the captain of the truck and had full responsibility for its safe operation.

Despite having nearly lost his life in the truck, Grandpa Thorne didn't jump out as soon as it came to a stop. Instead, he rested his head on his right hand and leaned against the side window with closed eyes. Ben exited the truck and quietly shut the door. His grandfather needed to rest.

Al came bounding down the hillside grinning and laughing. Ben didn't know what kind of reaction to expect. They had never been through something like this. It pleased Ben to have "fun Dad" treat the runaway truck as an amusing event.

"Way to go, little buddy!" Al shouted as he ran up to the truck and peeked inside the bed. "You only lost a few rocks. I should let you drive more often."

"Sure," Ben replied, feeling confident that he could do it.

"How's your passenger?" Al asked in a whisper.

"He's taking a nap."

Al walked to the driver's side of the truck and looked inside. After a few seconds, he slowly opened the door and waved Ben toward the cab. Ben took his usual seat in the middle and his father slid in next to him without a word. Al restarted the truck and tried to drive forward, but the truck seemed reluctant to go.

"Somebody put on the emergency brake," Al said, releasing the brake and then driving away at a fast pace. "I suppose that was the sensible thing to do and I probably should have done it a few minutes ago, but think about how much fun you would've missed."

Ben smiled. He had finally bonded with his father—over a ten-second truck ride.

"Al, you're going a little too fast," Grandpa Thorne said sternly, lifting his head up from the window to glare at the driver. "God saved us once already today. Let's not test him to see if he will do it again."

"Yes, sir, I'll bring it down a bit," Al said, dropping his grin and focusing on the road instead of making eye contact with his weary father-in-law. Al looked upset and brooded briefly.

"Or I could let Ben slide over here and take the wheel," he said with a chuckle. "If Ben has God on his side, then we'd all be better off with him driving."

Grandpa Thorne didn't respond, and the trip home continued in silence until reaching the mouth of the canyon. Sheriff Kort in his patrol car approached them from the other direction. "Wave like a crazy boy," Al said.

Ben joined his father in waving at the sheriff and they received a subdued wave in return. Having been with his father on similar runs, Ben understood his philosophy—*if you don't act sneaky, you don't get caught.* It worked with Sheriff Kort. On the other hand, Grandpa Thorne reported all the details of the outing to Rachel. She agreed with him that taking the rocks wasn't honest and the near-death experience shouldn't have been treated as a joke. For Ben, it stood out as one of those days when "fun Dad" made his life worth living.

Chapter 28

"Get your working clothes on!" Al shouted the following Saturday as he stormed into the small bedroom shared by Joe and Ben. "We've got big things to do."

Joe and Ben had to fake enthusiasm for their father and never grumble about being thrown out of bed. Even though sunrise had yet to arrive, the boys jumped up as soon as they heard their father's voice. Al hated to see his boys "wasting the day in bed."

"Joe, I want you to milk Daisy. Ben, feed all the animals and make sure they have fresh water," Al said. "Then we'll grab breakfast and head over to the Armstrongs' farm to pick up a truckload of hay. I'm fixing their tractor in a trade for the hay. I don't know what's wrong yet, so this could be a long project or a quick fix. And when we're done there, I have another repair on a construction site in Spanish Fork. So, chop, chop, let's go."

Al often tried to fit twelve hours or more of work into his "day off." Satisfied that his boys were fully engaged in his plan, Al threw open the door to the girls' bedroom, shouting, "Rise and shine!"

Debbie responded by rolling over and pulling the covers tighter over her shoulders. She mumbled, "Be quiet. I'm tired and don't want to get up."

Al responded by imitating a bugle playing "Reveille" while kicking the headboard of Debbie's bed. When she still didn't jump to her feet, he grabbed the covers off her and tossed them across the room and then yanked the pillow from under Debbie's head and used it to repeatedly whack her behind. She resisted the command to get out of bed by curling into a ball and hiding her face.

By now, Becky had crawled out of her bed and stood silently by while she watched the noisy wake-up call. "What's wrong with you?" Al asked Debbie angrily. "Why are you so fat, dumb, and ugly?"

Ben cringed when he heard the "fat, dumb, and ugly" insult. His father often spewed the phrase when angry with Debbie. Ben knew that the words cut into her heart like a razor-sharp knife. He had experienced the same agony when his father called him "the stupidest and laziest boy in the world."

Debbie cried as she slid off the end of the bed to get as far away from her father as possible before staggering to her feet. She sobbed, "I don't know why you can't let me sleep until I'm ready to get up. Now, I'll be tired all day."

"I don't have time to waste with this nonsense!" Al shouted. "We're all working from sunrise to sunset today and that includes you. Your mother has already left for her job and you need to clean this dump before she comes home. And take a shower—you stink."

"No, I took one yesterday," Debbie whined.

"Don't give me that smart mouth!" Al shouted, stepping forward and slapping Debbie in the face. She reacted with hysterical crying and Becky joined her.

"What did I do to deserve such a bunch of bratty, bawling babies?" Al snarled before he turned away from his devastated daughters and stormed out of the house.

Despite the vile treatment of their sister, Joe and Ben, having grown numb to the abuse, shrugged it off and headed for the barnyard. When passing Debbie's room, Joe paused and said, "Way to go! He was already 'mad Dad' and now you've made it worse. When are you ever going to learn that he only wants to hear 'Yes' from us and to see nothing but happy faces?"

The morning for Joe and Ben went well as Al's mood improved. The Armstrongs' tractor only needed a carburetor adjustment and the work resulted in a favorable exchange—twenty-five bales of hay for less than an hour of work.

After unloading the hay and eating a quick lunch, one of Joe's friends showed up with a job offer. The friend had agreed to mow a woman's lawn and pick weeds out of her flower beds for eight dollars. The mowing would be easy, but he needed help with the weeding and would split the money with Joe if he could work that afternoon.

"Dad, would that be all right?" Joe asked his father. "I'd love to make that much money in a few hours."

"OK, it would be an excellent way for you to learn the value of work," Al said. "But be back here for your evening chores."

Ben stayed behind, feeling cheated. While Joe would be hanging out with a friend and making money, he would be going to Spanish Fork with his father and working the rest of the afternoon for no pay. Ben made the trip, helping his father fix an electrical problem with a small cement mixer

Despite needing to make two hardware store visits, Al succeeded in getting the mixer running and the entire afternoon passed without any signs of the smoldering anger that Ben had seen early in the day. After returning home, his father even helped Ben with his chores. Joe showed up at the same time and milked Daisy.

"Ben, it looks like your chores are done," Al said. "Run into the house and make sure Debbie has everything in order. I don't want your mother coming home to a mess and she'll be here soon."

As soon as Ben walked in the back door, he noticed that the lunch dishes hadn't been washed, which Debbie had promised to do. He found Debbie and Becky in their bedroom playing with dolls.

"What's going on?" Ben asked, shaking his head in sincere bewilderment. "Why haven't you done the dishes?"

"Becky wanted to play," Debbie said while helping set up a Barbie picnic on Becky's bed. "And I thought I was supposed to take care of her while you guys were gone. I didn't have time to do both."

"You must be as dumb as Dad says you are," Ben said, frowning because he knew the pleasant afternoon was about to turn into a rough evening.

"Yeah, and you're stupid and lazy!" Debbie snapped back.

Ben charged his sister and gave her a thump in the back of the head like his father had done to him many times. Debbie fought back and punched Ben in the arm. Even though she was four years younger, Debbie was as tall as Ben and heavier. She delivered a stinging punch that forced Ben to retreat from the room.

"OK, I'll do the dishes, but you need to start cleaning up this house before Dad comes in here. He's going to flip out."

"I don't care what he does," Debbie said. "I'm not afraid of him like you are."

Ben was more than afraid of his father. The man terrified him, so he rushed into the kitchen and focused on cleaning up the most visible messes. They included the remnants of an afternoon snack that Debbie and Becky had made. He scraped sticky clumps of Rice Krispies off the counter and floor, washed and dried dishes, and started putting them away. His father and Joe walked in the back door before he completed the last task.

"What are you doing?" Al asked Ben in anger.

"The lunch dishes."

"Why?"

"Debbie didn't have time to do them because she was taking care of Becky."

"That's not what I told her to do."

Al began shouting for Debbie while Joe carried the milk bucket to the kitchen sink where he would strain the milk to remove gnats and hay flakes before storing it in the refrigerator. Ben quickly finished putting away the dishes. After a long minute of listening to her father yelling, Debbie pushed open the kitchen door and stood in front of him.

"Why didn't you do the dishes?" he asked.

"I told Ben that I didn't have time because Becky wanted to play," Debbie said, pointing at Ben as if the fault belonged on his shoulders.

"I don't care what Becky wanted. Your job was to get the dishes done and then to clean up the house. From what I can see, Ben did the dishes and I bet the rest of the house is still a mess. Did you play all day?"

"No, I cleaned my room and made my bed—and so did Becky."

"What about the kitchen floor? Did you sweep it?"

"No, but I can sweep it now."

"It's too late. You wasted your time while the rest of us worked."

Al shook his head in disgust as he pointed at crumbs on the kitchen floor and then turned his attention back to Debbie. "When I was a kid, I learned to work hard and get the job done when promised. That's why my foster family let me live in their home for eight years. I kept their house spotless and never complained once about the work. When are you going to pitch in and do your fair share of the work?"

Instead of following Joe's example of keeping quiet in these tense moments, Debbie lost control of her emotions and asked in a loud, angry voice, "Just because that's what you did, does it mean that we have to do the same thing?"

Al's rapid-fire reply came as a backhand slap to the face and a demand. "Don't you ever talk to me like that. You know how much I hate smart-mouths."

He marched to the kitchen closet and pulled out the broom. "Now, take this broom, put a smile on your face, and sweep the floor and you'd better show me plenty of enthusiasm doing it."

"But you said it was too late," Debbie said as she took the broom from her father.

Al shouted a profanity and slapped Debbie again while the back door swung open. Rachel entered the battlefield. She ran to Debbie's side, took the broom out of her hands, and tossed it to the floor. She wrapped her arms around Debbie who had burst into a loud, terrified cry.

"Why did you hit her?" Rachel asked, shouting. "This is insane. Are you teaching your sons that it's acceptable to smack girls around? I can't believe you did that, and I will not allow you to do it again."

Shocked by Rachel's defense, Al stood speechless with the intensity of his bright red face disappearing like water down a drain. Rachel stared at Al for a few tense moments of silence and then slammed her purse down on the kitchen table.

"OK," she said, switching to a cheerful voice. "Let's all pitch in and get this house sparkling clean."

"Shipshape," Al added glumly.

"Right, I'm going to take Debbie to her room and check on Becky," Rachel said. "She's probably wondering what all the crying and yelling is about. Ben, please sweep the kitchen floor and then vacuum the living room. I'll come back and start working on dinner."

Eager to see the dispute end, Ben snatched the broom off the floor and demonstrated how a boy with enthusiasm sweeps the floor. The entire time he kept an eye on his father to make sure the lit fuse had been pulled out of the dynamite and the house would be safe. While sweeping, he wondered if his mother's new no-hit rule applied to both her daughters and sons.

A few days later, Rachel caught Joe and Ben teaming up against Debbie with name-calling and jabs to the ribs because she had done something to annoy them. Instead of telling them to stop, she calmly posed a question. "Are you being mean to Debbie because your dad treats you that way?"

Swallowed up in immediate and deep regret, Ben decided to start treating Debbie the same way he wanted to be treated—with kindness and respect.

Chapter 29

Ben's decision to show his sister kindness and respect didn't change how others treated him. He still had to endure frequent bullying at school and home. A speck of hope came through an experience created by his seventh-grade science teacher, Mr. Gaufin. It gave him the strength to keep going.

Mr. Gaufin offered all students in his classes the chance to do extra credit science projects. Most of them ignored the proposal while a few selected a project to boost their grades. Ben signed up for three projects because they looked fun.

The projects required learning more about biology or geology, conducting experiments, and preparing a report. Ben selected topics that blended science with his love for the mountains. They included tracking wildlife, analyzing water samples, and documenting tree species.

"I usually don't have a student eager to do so much extra credit," Mr. Gaufin said. "Perhaps you should start with one project and then see if you still want to do all three."

Having more ambition and confidence than normal, Ben promised his teacher that he would do all three—and planned to give each one of them his best effort. When he showed the project requirements to his mother, she praised his initiative and told him that she would be excited to see his research results.

The first project focused on tracking wildlife by searching for signs of animals traveling along streams and other places. Ben documented footprints found in muddy or sandy soil, recording when and where he discovered the footprints, and sketching them in his "scientific journal." Even though the journal was only an inexpensive, spiral-bound notebook, Ben pictured himself as a serious scientist.

After a couple of trips into the mountains, he decided to work on all three projects at the same time because they overlapped. He could document the trees he passed when collecting water samples and looking for wildlife footprints.

Eight weeks later, Ben went to his science class a few minutes early and submitted his reports to Mr. Gaufin who reviewed them with a smile.

"Impressive work, Ben," he said several times as he turned each page slowly and pointed out observations that he found "scholarly." Ben never expected his reports to receive such a careful and positive review.

"What amazes me is that you're already getting an A in class and don't need the extra credit," he said. "Why did you put so much effort into these projects?"

"I don't know."

"Sure, you do. Go ahead and tell me. I'd like to hear what motivated you."

"Well, it's what I love doing."

"OK. That's a good start. Why?"

"I like hiking in the mountains. That's how I spend my free time."

Mr. Gaufin smiled and asked Ben to elaborate.

"I might be weird, but learning more about the things around me is fun—like the names of the trees and animals out there. And the wildlife tracking project made me look for signs that I never noticed before."

"You've applied one of the keys to scientific research—observation!"

The teacher's dramatic statement became the end of the conversation and the beginning of the classroom discussion. "Let's talk more after class," he said while pointing at Ben's desk as a cue to sit down.

"I'm pleased to report that through extra-credit work, Ben Baker has shown the potential to be a scientist," Mr. Gaufin said, holding up the projects as he strolled across the front of the room. "He has combined his love of nature with science to produce outstanding work. I can see him someday working as a botanist or biologist for the National Park Service or a wildlife group dedicated to protecting our environment."

Ben wished his dad could hear this. He would be shocked that someone who had graduated from college with a science degree thought that Ben could become a scientist. He might be "stupid and lazy" in his dad's eyes, but a science expert could see him getting a respectable job.

After Mr. Gaufin delivered his encouraging remarks, the boy behind Ben blew a dark cloud his way. He leaned forward, punched Ben in the back, and whispered, "Quit wasting your time sucking up to the teacher. You'll never be anything but a chicken farmer."

Mr. Gaufin heard the whispering and turned to face the class, but Ben's antagonist quickly leaned away and held his tongue. The moment of glory for Ben had turned into another reminder that the wolves in the class still viewed him as the weakest lamb—and they wanted to make sure he remembered it.

A few other adults encouraged Ben to dream of a better life. They included the man who served as both his Sunday school teacher and scoutmaster, Gene Augustine—or, as the boys called him, "Brother Augustine," in line with their Mormon traditions. He led the Boy Scout troop on Wednesdays and for occasional weekend camping trips. On Sundays, he traded his scout uniform for a business suit and tried to teach a class of sullen teenage boys who deliberately made it an unrewarding task.

Behind his back, the boys criticized him for being a "nerd" and looking geeky, wimpy, and scrawny. Gene stood only five-feet, five-inches tall, weighed about 125 pounds, and wore thick glasses. He didn't look like an outdoorsman or someone who could do physical labor. He spoke softly, and his demeanor oozed with insecurity. He projected a sense of weakness that made him a "target."

Because Gene demonstrated a willingness to report unruly behavior to the boys' parents, they used sneak attacks to torment him. And when caught pulling a prank on him or making a rude comment, they would blow it off by saying, "We were just kidding."

The ridicule included his old tattered Sunday suit that was at least one size too large for him. The boys laughed when saying he must have bought it secondhand and that he looked like a beggar. They also joked about his suit being stained and smelling like vomit. With his four small children always clinging to him and spitting up, the observations about his suit were unkind but accurate.

Ben joined the jeering, not as a leader in spewing out the insults but as someone who laughed behind his back. Instead of taking a stand against disrespectful behavior, he chose the easier, less honorable route and played along with the cruel game.

When Gene tried to teach the boys in his Sunday school class, they leaned forward with their elbows on their thighs, staring at the floor and never volunteering to read or answer a question. They went overboard in making it clear that they had no interest in anything "Brother Augustine" had to say. Wanting to fit in, Ben followed the crowd with his actions, but he found it impossible to ignore his teacher.

Gene talked about treating others the way you want them to treat you, forgiving people who had offended you and honoring your father and mother even when it wasn't seen as the "cool" thing to do. He read verses from the Bible and Book of Mormon to support these ideas and used examples from his life that illustrated the advantages of taking the right path in life.

At the end of every class, Gene asked one of the boys to pray. He occasionally could convince someone like Ben's big brother to pray, but he usually ended up praying because all his students refused. When one of them agreed, the words shot out like a machine gun firing a blast of memorized expressions. When listening to Gene pray, Ben had the sense his teacher was talking to someone real, not an imaginary character. And his prayers touched on challenges in life that Ben understood.

The disinterest displayed in Gene's Sunday school class usually didn't rattle him and he only expressed frustration with his students on a few occasions. On one Sunday, they burned through his patience by going too far in demonstrating their apathy. He criticized the boys for ignoring him and said they had fulfilled prophecy—the same as people had done nearly 2,000 years ago.

He quoted Acts in the Bible, saying that their ears were dull of hearing and their eyes were closed. "If you would only listen, open your eyes and understand with your heart, God will heal you. How can you know what God wants to do for you if you continue to ignore what scripture says?"

Even though Ben continued to stare at the floor, he listened and thought about this message. He wanted to encourage Gene to say more. At the same time, he knew the other boys in the room would mock him for trying to be the teacher's pet.

Gene's passionate plea left Ben wondering about the promise—"God will heal you." He wanted to know what that meant because he had some sort of sickness. He couldn't easily describe the symptoms, but he knew that deep inside of him something wasn't quite right. And he desperately wanted to fix it.

Chapter 30

The "fix" didn't come through Boy Scouts, but Ben received comfort from the applause and compliments that accompanied his advancement through the ranks and collection of new merit badges every month. After two years of steady progress, the requirement to earn the lifesaving merit badge stood as Ben's only roadblock to becoming an Eagle Scout. He had already received the swimming merit badge, but the requirements for lifesaving went far beyond his skills. Excited about being so close to his goal, Ben enrolled in a lifesaving course at a pool in Provo shortly after his fourteenth birthday.

On the first day, Ben's instructor, Cliff Barrington, a student and swim team member at Brigham Young University, looked at him with concern and asked, "How much do you weigh?"

"Sixty-eight pounds," Ben said with assurance, having been weighed a week earlier. On each birthday, Ben's mother measured his height and weight, keeping track of the information in a scrapbook.

"Well, here's the problem. I don't know how you're going to be able to demonstrate a cross-chest carry on me. I weigh three times more than you."

"I can do it. Trust me. I'm much stronger than I look."

"We'll see. Keep coming to class and I'll test you in the final week."

Three weeks later, the door for Ben to become an Eagle Scout opened much wider. All his lifesaving badge requirements were completed except for the cross-chest carry. He faced his instructor poolside—ready for the final challenge.

When standing next to Cliff, Ben understood his instructor's concern about their size difference and recognized that this test presented a physical challenge beyond anything he had ever tried. But he had no choice. His mother believed that he could earn this merit badge and sat nearby to watch him.

"OK, lifeguard, save me," Cliff said as he jumped into the pool. "I'm a tired but cooperative swimmer and need you to get me to dry ground. To earn your merit badge, you must carry me to the far end of the pool and back without stopping."

"Got it," Ben said, joining him in the pool.

While Cliff imitated a tired swimmer, Ben played the lifeguard role and went through the procedure that he had learned. He began by making sure the person to be rescued was calm and ready to cooperate. Then, he swam behind Cliff and reached his arm across his muscular chest. Ben struggled to complete that step because his arm needed to be at least six inches longer to do the carry correctly.

"That's good enough," Cliff said. "Let's get going. I won't fight you unless you slow down or stop—and then you'll have a problem because I'll pretend to panic."

With one arm wrapped over the chest of the "tired swimmer," Ben used a side stroke with his free arm and a scissor kick to create momentum. The journey began slowly because of the weight issue. It took all of Ben's strength to move Cliff and the man's bulk pushed Ben down so that he had difficulty breathing without swallowing water at the same time.

When Ben choked and started coughing, Cliff asked, "Hey, lifeguard, are you all right?"

"Yep, don't worry about me. Lay back and relax. I'll get you to shore in no time."

Ben solved the breathing problem by taking a deep breath and then swimming slightly below the water's surface. This tactic made it much easier to tow Cliff.

When Ben neared the turnaround point, Cliff rolled over and lifted him out of the water. "Hey, are you drowning? You've been under the water a long time and are worrying me."

Ben took a few deep breaths and said, "I'm fine. Underwater swimming works better for me. Let's finish this. We're almost halfway there."

Cliff smiled and rolled back into his floating position. "OK, you're the boss."

Ben resumed his underwater technique and soon reached the wall. He popped up for a deep breath and spun Cliff around for the return trip. Toward the end of that lap, he started to feel a bit lightheaded and his body craved oxygen, but he swam the entire length of the pool without taking a breath. At the wall, Ben came up and pushed Cliff toward the pool ladder.

"There you go," he said while drawing in several deep breaths. "You're safe."

Cliff laughed as Ben clung to the side of the pool panting.

"Ben, there's no way I'm going to approve you to apply for a lifeguard job until you've grown about a foot taller and put on more muscle, but I'll definitely sign off on your merit badge. What you lack in size, you make up for in heart. Congratulations!"

They shook hands and climbed out of the pool. Ben's legs and arms trembled as he followed Cliff along the deck to where Rachel waited. Despite the fatigue, he felt great.

"Mrs. Baker, your son shows a lot of determination. I'll approve his lifesaving merit badge. Let me dry off and then I'll complete the paperwork."

Rachel congratulated Ben and handed him a towel. He dried himself and then slipped on a shirt and sandals for the trip back to Alma. "I'm very proud of you for setting a goal to become an Eagle Scout and doing what you needed to achieve it. This is something you'll value for the rest of your life."

Ben gushed with excitement when telling Joe that he had earned the lifesaving merit badge and now had all Eagle rank requirements completed except for his service project, which he planned to finish in a few weeks.

"That's not fair," Joe said. "I couldn't get time off work to take that course."

When Joe had joined Boy Scouts, he plodded along at a sluggish pace with the rest of the scouts in the troop for eighteen months. That's when his little brother entered the troop and launched a zealous pursuit of the Eagle Scout honor. Joe noticed the results and a race between the brothers began. Soon, Joe and Ben were advancing through the ranks as fast as the guidelines allowed.

Ben welcomed the competition, having finally found something that required his big brother to keep up with him. "The next course starts on Tuesday," Ben said. "You can sign up and still get it done this summer."

Motivated by Ben's proximity to winning the race to Eagle Scout, Joe took the next course and passed without any challenge, but the delay allowed Ben to qualify for his Eagle Scout award first. Even though Ben could have received his badge at an award ceremony before his brother, Rachel thought it would be special to have her sons receive their badges together. Ben reluctantly agreed to wait a month.

Joe and Ben received many compliments for their perseverance in earning the honor to be called Eagle Scouts. Ben especially enjoyed the moment of recognition because it provided proof that he wasn't stupid and lazy—he could accomplish an important goal. And he loved doing something that forced his big brother to scramble to keep up.

Chapter 31

Until Ben earned his Eagle Scout award, he needed to go on campouts to meet the requirements for certain merit badges such as camping and cooking, but he quickly lost interest after achieving his goal.

"Ben, I noticed that you haven't signed up for our campout next week," Scoutmaster Gene Augustine said at the end of a weekly troop meeting. "I hope that doesn't mean you're not planning to go. As an Eagle Scout, it would set an excellent example for the other boys. Can I count on you to be there?"

"Oh, I don't know," Ben said. "We're swamped getting the farm ready for winter."

"I understand, but it's only an overnighter and would be a perfect opportunity for you to teach the younger scouts their essential skills."

"I'd be glad to do that, but I don't think any of them would listen to me," Ben said, wondering why his scoutmaster thought he had the ability to teach other scouts when they viewed him as the prime target for pranks and teasing. When cooking over an open fire, Ben's mess kit would "accidentally" get tipped over or a handful of dirt would be added to his meal. At night, his tent collapsed when the stakes mysteriously disappeared.

Due to the scoutmaster's pleading, Ben signed up to go. Joe also agreed to attend even though he worked at a store in Payson on Saturdays and would miss the chance to work a full shift. The loss of wages would impact his goal of saving money to attend Utah State University as soon as he graduated from high school. While packing for the campout, Joe grumbled about it being a waste of time and vowed that it would be his final scouting activity.

Al also complained about the trip because he would have to take care of his sons' chores, and with snow in the forecast for the weekend, extra work would be necessary to protect the animals. He still gave the boys a ride to the church where the troop gathered for the trip. Joe and Ben jumped out of the truck and grabbed their gear from the back as soon as Al stopped.

"Be quick about it," Al said. "I don't have time to waste chatting with Brother Augustine and the other parents. I have the job of three men to do and need to get out of here fast."

While Al sped away, Joe and Ben carried their backpacks and sleeping bags to where the rest of the scouts waited. As they approached, one of the boys started to cackle like a chicken, tapping into a worn-out gag to announce that "the chicken patrol" had arrived. Because Joe and Ben raised chickens and had a reputation for not being fighters, the other scouts created a nickname for the Hawk patrol that stuck—the "chicken patrol."

Three parents had agreed to help the scoutmaster with transportation, but only one of them, Brother Sanderson, would be staying overnight. The other two would leave that evening and return the next day to bring the troop home in the late afternoon. Brother Sanderson worked for a road construction company and was driving a van he used during the week to haul work crews to job sites. He told Joe and Ben to put their stuff in the back of the scoutmaster's truck and then get in his van.

Before starting the drive, Gene announced that they needed to stop at Benanti's Groceries to buy more ice for the coolers and water jugs. The scouts all groaned about making the stop, especially when told that they wouldn't be allowed in the store.

"I'll go in with Brother Sanderson and Brother Franks," Gene said. "Everyone else needs to stay in their vehicle or next to it."

Every scout bailed out of the cars and van as soon as the vehicles stopped in front of Benanti's. The usual shoving, pushing, and poking started immediately. Ben moved away from the troop to avoid it.

While killing time, Joe and Ben walked toward the edge of the parking lot to get a closer look at the business across the street—Miss Franny's Fine Art and Collectibles or "Fat Fanny's Junk Store" as their father called it. Miss Franny's had taken over the space formerly known as Al Baker's Service Station.

Al's business had been converted into a gift shop and antiques store that attracted tourists looking for souvenirs and bargains while taking a scenic drive up one of the nearby canyons. The gas pumps had been removed along with the collection of old cars parked behind the building. The service bay doors had been decorated with stained glass, dreamcatchers, and posters.

"Do you remember the good times we had there?" Ben asked.

"I'm glad it's gone," Joe said lifelessly.

Before Ben could remind him of their driving adventures, the roar of motorcycles led him and all the scouts to turn around and watch three bikes coming toward them. The bikes rumbled down Main Street as the riders scanned the town's businesses. The lead rider pointed ahead to Miss Franny's shop.

When they passed the troop, the lead driver turned and looked at Ben. Even though the man wore sunglasses and a bandana around his head, Ben immediately recognized him—Derek Dean had come back.

Rumors had circulated for the past few weeks that Derek had been released from prison and lived in the area, but nobody in Alma had seen him. Now, Ben was getting a close-up view of Derek as he steered his bike toward him. Ben thought about running but Joe stood his ground, so Ben followed his big brother's example and didn't move. Derek stopped within inches of Ben's toes. The other two bikers parked slightly behind Derek with one on each side, looking like fighter jets flying in formation.

Even though the loud motorcycles had attracted their attention, the other scouts stayed away. The legend of Derek Dean kept most locals fearful of him. Derek reached down and shut off his engine, which led his friends to do the same. Ben glanced at the faces of the other two bikers to see if one of them was Derek's old friend Denny, but these men were new to him.

"So, if it isn't little Benny Baker," Derek said. "I bet you're surprised to see me again. Aren't you?"

Ben solemnly muttered "Yes" in response.

"Well, I'm not surprised to see you. I've been thinking about this moment since your lies sent me to prison. Guess what? The parole board let me out early for good behavior."

Ben didn't know what to say or do, standing still and shifting his eyes from Derek to his two friends. He again thought about making an escape, but he didn't want to give the entire troop the pleasure of watching him run off like a frightened chicken. So he acted calm and clenched his fists to fight his body's impulse to shake.

"I see that your dad's crummy gas station went out of business," Derek said. "I guess he couldn't keep it alive without me bringing in the customers."

"No, it closed because you stole his tools," Ben said.

"Oh yeah, that could be a problem. I guess I should say 'so sorry' but I'm not. Your dad is a jerk and deserved it."

"He's a great mechanic and working at a big auto dealership in Provo now. We're doing fine without you."

"Dream on, Benny."

Derek waved to all the scouts watching him. "So, what are all you girls doing today? Going shopping so you can have a little tea party?"

"No, we're going camping in Payson Canyon," Ben said before realizing that he should have kept the troop's plan a secret from Derek.

"Payson Canyon," Derek said, turning to look at his friends. "Didn't I tell you guys that we should ride over there next?"

They nodded and laughed.

Derek returned his focus to Ben. "I'll see you there, so we can catch up about old times. Expect me sometime around midnight."

With his thumb, Derek gestured over his left shoulder to one of his friends and said, "Of course, I'll be bringing Luke with me. He likes to start fires."

Luke grinned at Ben, showing his discolored chipped teeth, and added "Sure do" to support his friend's claim. Luke came close to Derek in height, but he lacked his powerful build and handsome features. His wiry frame gave the appearance that he had missed many meals and his thin, scraggly hair and darting eyes left him looking like a stray dog that might bite anyone who came to close.

Derek pointed over his right shoulder and added, "And my pal Wayne will be coming. He's handy with guns and can shoot the eye out of a magpie a half-mile away."

Wayne used his beefy right hand to simulate a pistol and made a popping sound when he aimed it at Ben. No hint of a smile touched his dark face when he took his imaginary shot. The man looked mean—the kind of person Derek had encouraged Ben to become.

Derek reached behind his seat and opened the saddlebag. He pulled out a large hunting knife, removed it from the sheath, and stuck the point into his left index finger.

"And I'll be bringing this friend with me," he said.

With his usual grin frozen in place, he punctured his finger and let blood trickle down the blade. "Look at that—he's sharp and thirsty for blood," Derek said before shaking the blood off the blade toward Ben and returning the knife to the sheath. He stashed the weapon in his saddlebag and told his friends, "Let's ride." The bikers restarted their motorcycles, made a U-turn on Main Street, and headed away from the scouts.

"Don't worry, boys," one of the scouts' adult leaders said, speaking loud enough to be heard by the entire troop. "They're just showing off and won't waste their time driving up the canyon to bother us. We won't see them again."

The scouts watched the bikers ride a few blocks and then turn toward Payson Canyon. Ben knew that Derek wouldn't consider the drive a waste of time after spending the previous five years in prison. And Derek had made it clear that he wanted revenge.

Chapter 32

Be prepared. That's what the Boy Scout motto challenged Ben to do in this situation. He took Derek's threat as much more than a mere taunt. During the drive to Payson Canyon, Ben set a plan for how to deal defend himself. He would wrap his Army-surplus web belt around his waist and attach his large hunting knife and sharp hatchet to it. He intended to make it clear to Derek that he was ready to fight even though he had no chance of winning the duel.

When the troop arrived at the campsite, the scramble began for the best spots to pitch tents. Joe selected an area for the Hawks and held it while the rest of the patrol members hauled their gear from the scoutmaster's truck. They set up their tents about thirty yards from the center of the camp. The Bears took the prime real estate—the closest to the parking area—while the Wolves staked out their turf behind the Bears. The scoutmaster selected a spot between the Bears and Wolves.

The Hawk patrol members stayed away from the jousting for domination. They didn't mind being considered in third place if the other scouts left them out of their contest. The Hawks' campsite was somewhat rocky but close to a wooded area, which came in handy in the middle of the night when needing an all-natural latrine. They pitched their tents quickly to allow time for a short hike before cooking the evening meal. With a snowstorm expected to hit the mountains before morning, this hike might be their only chance to explore the canyon during the campout.

Chapter 32

While the other patrols continued to argue about the layout of their campsites, the Hawks finished setting up theirs and Joe told the scoutmaster that they would return from their hike in less than an hour. The hike began on the road used to reach the campsite, with the Hawks heading up the canyon. About twenty minutes into the hike, they heard the unmistakable sound of motorcycle engines coming down the canyon road toward them.

"Uh, let's go back to the camp," Joe said as he came to an abrupt stop. "We probably should stay close to the rest of the troop."

"Why? Do you think it's that ex-con and his buddies?" asked Jerry Kearns, the youngest scout in the patrol.

"Might be," Joe said. "Better turn back now."

Nobody objected to Joe's plan and the scouts immediately reversed their course. Ben glanced at his belt and grimaced, noticing that he had forgotten to attach his hunting knife and hatchet. As the noise of the motorcycles grew louder, the scouts picked up their pace.

"Let's hide!" Jerry shouted when the sound seemed to be on top of them. He expressed exactly what the rest of the patrol had been thinking and triggered a dash off the road.

Ben crouched behind a large clump of twisted mesquite bushes and sagebrush that would prevent anyone seeing him from the road. The rest of the patrol spread out looking for places to hide. Within seconds, the noise from the bikes intensified, making it clear they were passing by. Ben peeked out from his hiding place and could see Derek and his friends slowing down and looking toward where the scouts had retreated.

His ability to see the bikers warned Ben that they could probably see him, so he dropped to the ground and stayed below the top of the mesquite bush in front of him. While on the ground, he turned sideways and looked for the other Hawks. He noticed that three of them had no idea how to play "hide and seek." They stood behind small, thin trees that only partially covered their bodies. One of them wore a red jacket, which Derek and his friends could easily notice.

Ben remained hidden until the sound of the bikes had passed them and then shouted and waved for the highly visible boys to get down. Instead of taking cover, they walked into the open. Knowing Derek well, Joe and Ben stayed in their hiding places.

"Hey, come on out! They didn't see us!" Fred shouted. "We're safe."

"Get down and be quiet," Ben said. "How do you know they didn't see you? They're probably turning around and coming back right now because you did such a crappy job hiding."

As Ben predicted, the sound of the motorcycles stopped going away from the scouts and came back up the canyon. "Let's run for the mountain!" Ben shouted, pointing at the steep hillside and taking steps in that direction.

Joe had a different plan. "No, find new hiding places and everybody shut up!"

All the Hawks obeyed their patrol leader and scurried to new, nearby locations. Ben found a place where erosion had created a small gully and dropped into it.

He could barely see the road from this position with the top of his head being the only part of him that might be visible to someone on the road. To correct that problem, he broke a small leafy branch from a scrub oak bush and placed it on his head. He had confidence that the branch served as camouflage. Because he hid farther from the road than the other Hawks, Ben could see most of their backs.

The bikers stopped on the road near the scouts and silenced their motorcycles. Ben spotted Derek and his friends about a minute later when they walked into the small clearing near the scouts. Derek's tall, thin friend, Luke, pointed at the ground as the men moved forward, using footprints in the sandy soil to track the boys.

Jerry noticed the men approaching him and took off running downhill toward the campsite. Derek laughed and asked, "Hey, pal, where are you going? Are you afraid of something?"

Jerry didn't respond and soon disappeared. Ben held his spot, feeling confident that he hadn't been seen and doubted that he would be found before the rest of the patrol had been flushed out.

Derek spoke loudly in his casual drawl, saying, "Boys, we stopped because we noticed someone hiding in the bushes and wanted to make sure nothing bad is going on."

Ben watched the bikers follow footprints to Fred's hiding place. Fred bolted when the men came close. He deserted the patrol, heading in the same direction as Jerry.

"What's going on here? Why do you boys keep running away?" Derek asked while scanning the woods for the next frightened rabbit to scurry away.

Evening had nearly arrived, but there was still too much daylight to move without being seen. Ben waited for a better chance to escape.

"We're only trying to make sure that everybody out here is safe," Derek said while Luke pointed out footprints that led the men to George, Ben's neighborhood friend.

Derek, Luke, and Wayne briefly whispered to each other and then spread out as they approached the spot where George knelt behind a small boulder. As Wayne went directly toward the boulder, Derek and Luke moved to opposite sides. They set up a trap. Unless George ran toward the mountain, one of the men would catch him.

Spooked by Wayne who approached him directly, George jumped up and started to run toward the campsite, but his jacket caught on a tree branch. The delay created by the snag allowed Luke to grab George by the shoulders.

"Son, slow down," Luke said. "You're going to tear your nice jacket."

After freeing him from the tree's grip, Luke retained his hold on George while Derek approached them.

"Man, relax," Derek said. "Like I told you, we're only trying to be helpful and make sure nobody is in danger."

"That's right, you can never be too careful in these mountains," Luke said. "Strange characters live out here, robbing hikers and making people disappear."

Without even taking a punch from Derek, George started to cry, failing to live up to the Scout Law and its requirement for bravery. Ben thought about surrendering to save George from more grief, but he liked the challenge of evading Derek and his friends and wanted to keep playing the game.

"Ah, come on, don't cry," Derek said. "What's your name?"

"George Oaks."

"George, we need to talk to all of your friends. Can you call them for me?"

"Well, I guess so."

George cleared his throat and then started shouting all the patrol members' names in a quivering voice. From two of Ben's favorite movies—"*The Great Escape*" and "*The Bridge on the River Kwai*," he had an image of how prisoners-of-war should behave. George failed the test, giving up his fellow soldiers without spending even a minute in the sweat box.

Despite having his name called, Ben didn't move, waiting to see what Derek would do. Joe took a different approach. He walked toward trouble and then stopped where Derek could clearly see but not touch him.

"What do you guys really want?" Joe asked. Ben admired his brother's sensible bravery. Instead of running away, he chose to face the bikers—yet at a safe distance.

"It's like this," Derek said, employing an expression that he often used when getting ready to lie. "We were driving by and noticed somebody hiding behind a tree and wondered why anybody would do that unless they were up to no good. So, we turned our bikes around and came back to check things out."

Derek paused and looked at his friends. "Isn't that right?"

"That's exactly what happened," Wayne said as if he believed it. "We're good citizens and doing our part to keep kids like you out of trouble."

"So, tell me," Derek said, looking at Joe and then scanning the terrain around him. "Why are you weirdos hiding here? I thought you went camping with the rest of the Girl Scouts."

"We're just hiking."

"Wait. Aren't Girl Scouts supposed to be honest? Why do you keep lying to us?"

"I'm not lying."

"And that's another lie. If you aren't hiding anything, then tell me where your brother is." At that point, Derek turned and looked directly at Ben who lowered his head as much as possible without losing sight of Derek. Ben assumed he had been spotted and prepared to run in case Derek charged his hiding place.

"I don't know. He took off. You know how he wanders away."

"Wow! Another lie! Or are you blind?"

Derek pointed at Ben's hiding place and said, "Joe, little Benny is right there. He's the idiot with the leaves on his head. Still acting like a stupid little goober."

Joe glanced where Derek pointed but didn't respond to him.

"Hey, Benny, come on out!" Derek shouted. "We don't have time to play games today. I want to tell you what it felt like to spend five years in prison because of your lies."

"Ben, run back to the camp!" Joe shouted.

Ben slowly crawled out of the small gully and walked toward the group. As he made his move, Jeff, the last member of the patrol to be seen, rolled out of a thick cluster of scrub oak and sprinted down the canyon road. Derek made no effort to chase Jeff or send one of his friends after him.

"Please let George go," Ben said. "Joe and I will stay here and listen to you."

"Now, you've finally turned into a brave scout instead of some frightened sissy hiding in the bushes," Derek said. He nodded to Luke who released George from his grip.

"George, go back to the camp," Joe said. "You'll find it if you stay on the road and head down the canyon."

George gladly obeyed. He soon disappeared, and Joe and Ben stood alone with Derek and his friends. Again, Ben wished that he had remembered his knife and hatchet.

"We didn't have enough time to talk in town," Derek said. "But now, we're all alone and I'm pleased to have your full attention. I want you to know that you ruined my life. You should feel like the lowest kind of trash for lying to the sheriff that I kidnapped you and gave you all those bruises. And the whole time, all I truly wanted to do was help your dad out of a tough situation."

Ben decided not to argue with Derek because he seemed to believe the twisted story trickling out of his mouth. So, Ben along with Joe listened as Derek rambled about how difficult his life had been in prison. "And since I got out, it's been impossible to get a decent job, so I'm stuck doing crap work," he said.

Ben kept his mouth shut, but he wanted to interrupt and tell Derek how hard life had been for his family after Derek took his father's tools, equipment, and truck. An interruption came through the sound of a vehicle coming up the canyon at a high speed.

"I hope that moron sees our bikes on the side of the road," Wayne said.

A truck came into view shortly before reaching the motorcycles and slid to a noisy stop on the sandy shoulder. Scoutmaster Gene Augustine had come to the rescue. He jumped out of the truck along with Brother Sanderson. They hurried toward the bikes and then noticed that they were being watched.

"Hey, fearless leaders, we found your lost boys!" Derek shouted. "They're up here. Come and get them."

"Joe and Ben, come with us," Gene said, ignoring Derek and gesturing for the boys to join him on the side of the road. "We're heading back to camp. Jerry told us that you might need a ride."

"Jerry? Is that one of the kids that took off like a frightened bunny when we stopped by to lend assistance?" Derek asked with a laugh.

"He thought you might be trying to harm our scouts," Gene said.

"Oh my, that boy is looney! Ben, please tell Mister Scoutmaster that we've only been catching up on old times."

Ben glanced at Derek before responding. "Yep, we've only been chatting about stuff. Nothing to worry about."

Derek smiled at Ben as if to say, *I own you*—and in some ways, he did. At first, he influenced Ben through his smooth style and rebellious attitude. After having been hit by Derek, he intimidated him because Ben knew Derek could beat him to death with his fists. And he had made it clear at the grocery store that he would enjoy killing Ben with his knife.

"Then, let's head back to camp," Gene said. "It's time to eat."

"Cool, don't let me hold you up, gentlemen," Derek said. "Go plug in your Easy Bake Ovens and cook up some hot brownies. My friends and I will be enjoying a few cans of beer we left cooling in the stream at our campsite. We're only a few miles up the road from you."

"Sir, I suggest that you and your friends stay away from our scouts," Gene said, again gesturing for Joe and Ben to join him. "We're here to learn scouting skills and don't need any distractions."

"Sounds good to us. We're only trying to be neighborly."

Following that fib, Joe and Ben hurried to join their rescuers and climbed into the truck with them. No words were exchanged until Gene had turned the truck back toward the campsite.

"That was tense," Gene said and then whistled and let out a deep breath. "I know that man is an ex-convict and expect his friends might also be men with criminal records. I'm glad you got away from them without any violence. Count your blessings! Like Daniel in the lions' den, God protected you."

Ben smiled because most men would have taken credit for intimidating his opponent through physical threats or superior intellect. In the scoutmaster's victory celebration, he voluntarily admitted that he needed help beyond his own strength to deal with someone as menacing as Derek. While Ben admired that humility, he preferred his hunting knife and hatchet. With them, he had confidence that he would be able to take care of himself—or die trying.

Chapter 33

The scoutmaster drove faster than he normally would and completed the return trip to the campsite in five minutes. The drive still gave him enough time to demand that Joe and Ben stay close to him for the rest of the campout. He also mentioned plans to discuss the Derek Dean encounter with Sheriff Kort as soon as the scouts returned to Alma.

"I'll be praying that God protects you boys," Gene said. "And Brother Sanderson and I will be super vigilant in doing whatever we can to keep those men away from you."

"Don't worry," Ben said. "If Derek and his buddies come after me when I'm in the mountains, they'll never catch me."

"Ben, you missed my point," Gene said. "I want you to stay near me at all times instead of running off into the mountains. And I suggest that you also seek God's protection and guidance through prayer."

"I'll let you do that. My mother taught me that God helps those who help themselves. That's my plan."

"Hmm, I don't think you're hearing me," Gene said. "Stay close to the troop—that's an order."

Ben wanted to argue with the scoutmaster, but he let it go as they had arrived at the campsite. After climbing out of the truck, Ben followed Joe to their tents where the other members of the Hawk patrol stood, waiting for them. Shaken by their encounter with Derek, they came back to the camp to discover that they had another problem.

"Somebody went into our tents while we were gone," Fred said. "They wiped their dirty boots on our sleeping bags and stole our candy bars and other things. Joe, tell the scoutmaster and have him get our stuff back."

"Let me look at my tent first," Joe said. "Then I'll go talk to him."

Ben ran to his tent and found dirt and leaves covering his sleeping bag. Instead of only missing a few things, his backpack and all the contents had been stolen. He didn't bring any candy bars on the campout, but he knew many of the boys envied his hunting knife and hatchet. Anger began to build inside of Ben and he stormed out of his tent ready to fight. He noticed Joe behind his tent, picking up clothes and other belongings from the ground and bushes.

"Remind me to never come on one of these stupid trips," Joe said. "I'm done with stuff like this."

"Have you seen my backpack?" Ben asked.

Joe pointed at a spot about twenty yards away. Ben dashed there and found his backpack—empty. Nearby, he spotted his clothes and food scattered behind a fallen poplar tree. He began gathering his belongings and returning them to his backpack, but he couldn't find the items he valued most—his knife, hatchet, and Boy Scout merit badge sash.

Ben brought the sash on the trip because the scoutmaster had mentioned plans to hold a special ceremony to honor Joe and Ben for becoming Eagle Scouts. Ben thought it might be an appropriate time to wear the sash even though he usually didn't take it on a campout. Everything ended up dirty from these trips and he wanted to protect his badges.

With assistance from the day's last glimmers of sunlight, Ben sighted his hatchet stuck into the trunk of a blue spruce tree. Its head was buried into the tree about seven feet off the ground—out of his reach. The sheath sat at the base of the tree. He found a stout, fallen branch and swatted at the hatchet to knock it free. Whoever stuck it into the tree hadn't driven it very deep, so the hatchet dropped to the ground after a few blows.

He sheathed the hatchet and attached it to his belt. In case the same thing had been done with his knife, Ben scanned the nearby trees and found it stuck in a Douglas fir tree about two feet off the ground. The knife had been used to pin his merit badge sash to the tree.

Ben walked to the tree and grasped the knife blade with one hand and the sash with the other. He quickly let go of both when finding them wet. He backed up slightly and noticed wet sand below the sash and wondered why the boys had dumped water on the sash and knife. Then he picked up the strong scent of urine and brought his hands closer to his face. One sniff confirmed his fear. After pinning Ben's sash to the tree, the scouts had urinated on it.

Words of frustration and hate swirled in Ben's brain. Having been in similar situations over the years, he could easily imagine the boys giggling while peeing on his sash and doing it to show him that it didn't matter how many merit badges he earned—they still could do whatever they wanted to drag him down.

Ben found the knife sheath nearby and attached it to his belt. Fortunately, it had escaped the urination ritual. Then he grabbed the wet knife handle and freed it from the tree. His sash fell to the damp soil below. He looped the knife blade through the sash and headed toward the huge fire blazing next to the Bears' campsite.

By this time, the sun had completely set. As Ben approached the campfire, he could see all the other scouts and the adult leaders gathered around it. He walked directly to the fire with the dripping wet sash dangling from his knife.

Gene Augustine spoke solemnly as he often did during his Sunday school classes and, as always, his audience stared at the ground. When Ben came close enough to understand his words, he heard Gene lecturing the scouts about the unacceptable behavior of some troop members that evening.

When the boys noticed Ben approaching, they moved out of his way because he held his large hunting knife in front of him. He walked to the edge of the fire, so close that the intensity of the heat shrouded him, and then dropped the urine-soaked sash into the middle of the roaring fire.

"Ben, what are you doing?" Gene asked in an anguished tone. "You worked so hard for those badges."

"They mean nothing to me," Ben said coldly, watching the flames engulf the sash and steam rise off it as the urine quickly evaporated.

"Hurry somebody, get a stick and pull it out of the fire!" Gene shouted, looking around frantically for either a helper or a stick to save the sash.

One of the Wolf patrol members stepped forward to meet his request, but the Bears had built a white-hot fire and the sash was blackened before he could drag it out. The sash landed next to the fire pit and continued to burn until one of the boys stomped on it and the flames died.

"Ben, why?" Gene asked sorrowfully.

"I found it hanging from a tree drenched in pee," Ben said, staring at the charred sash that included his hard-earned lifesaving merit badge.

A couple of the Bears laughed at Ben's statement and received harsh looks from their buddies. They needed to hide their amusement, so they could deceitfully express shock that anyone would do this to a fellow scout.

"Go ahead and laugh!" Ben shouted. "I get it. The joke is always on me because I'm little and you're so big. But you're forgetting one thing."

Ben paused to see if anyone would respond, but all of them, including the scoutmaster, looked at him in astonishment and offered no reaction to his speech.

Shaking with anger, he continued, "You've forgotten that I've spent a lot of time with Derek Dean and he taught me many valuable lessons. One of them is how to bring someone bigger than me to his knees. He showed me the power of a good weapon."

"Ben, calm down," Gene said gently as he moved toward Ben. "Let's talk privately about this."

"No, I'm done letting these jerks push me around," Ben said, waving his knife through the air to make it clear what he meant when saying "a good weapon."

The scouts backed away from Ben as he walked forward. Their retreat created an open path from the campfire to the Bears' tents. Ben marched in that direction, unsheathing his hatchet and letting his suppressed rage flow. With his knife, he slashed the first tent in his path and then used his hatchet to chop the ropes holding up the tent.

The darkening sky suddenly filled with threats from his fellow scouts, but nobody tried to stop him. They followed at a safe distance, staying away from the wild slashing motions he made with his knife. The Bear patrol members and Brother Sanderson yelled at Ben to stop when he slashed another tent and chopped a few more ropes, causing two more tents to collapse. Still enraged, Ben headed for more targets.

Undeterred by this erratic behavior, Gene ran to Ben's side and held out his hands. "Ben, give me your knife and hatchet. This must stop right now before someone gets hurt. Do you understand?"

Without a word, Ben handed Gene his weapons and retreated from the Bears' territory to the place where he had left his backpack. He grabbed it and crawled into his tent to hide. Having already calmed down, Ben recognized that he had let his anger lead him into a forbidden zone. He faced serious trouble and hid in his tent hoping that everyone would stay away.

Ben's reprieve lasted for about two minutes. Then Gene stood outside his tent and asked Ben to join him for a walk down the road. Ben followed, not wanting the other scouts to see the scoutmaster dragging him out of the tent.

"I understand that you're upset about your sash being spoiled, but we can get you another one. You need to handle such things in a calm, peaceful way instead of resorting to violence."

"That's a joke. Unless I make them pay for what they've done, they'll never leave me alone."

"There are other options. The Bible teaches us to not repay evil for evil and to wait patiently for the Lord to settle such matters."

"Where has God been for the last ten years?" Ben asked, feeling his anger return. "All I can remember since kindergarten is getting punched, kicked, pinched, poked and spit on. I'm tired of it—very tired!"

"I understand because I went through the same thing as a boy. Like you, I was smaller than the other kids and they liked to pick on me. It took a lot of prayer and perseverance to deal with it. Responding with violence isn't the solution."

"But it sure gets their attention. That's what Derek Dean taught me."

"Ben, do you really want to use an ex-convict as your role model? Look at what it's done for him. He's already been in prison twice and keeps doing things that are going to get him sent there again."

"Fine, then I'll disappear."

"Or you could do what I did and turn to God for your protection and strength."

Ben looked at Gene and chuckled, thinking about how all the scouts and members of his Sunday school class made jokes about him. He appreciated his scoutmaster's help in becoming an Eagle Scout, but he never considered him as an example to follow.

"I understand why you laughed," Gene said. "You look at me and think that I'm not the kind of man you want to become. But please try to see me as someone who has walked in your shoes and found a way to deal with the pain and frustration. I'll be praying that you turn to God as your counselor instead of listening to bad advice."

Gene waited for a reply, but Ben didn't know what to say, so he blurted out what stood at the forefront of his mind. "Fine, can I get my knife and hatchet back?"

"Not today, but I'll return them tomorrow night after we talk to your parents about what happened."

Ben would rather have the scoutmaster keep his valued possessions than get his parents involved. His mother would be embarrassed about her son going nuts with a knife, and his father would use it as another chance to point out his stupidity. He never wanted to come on this trip and now dreaded going home.

Gene and Ben returned to the campsite and parted ways, but Ben kept an eye on his scoutmaster and watched him stash the knife and hatchet under the seat of his truck. Ben planned to retrieve his property later before he stepped away from this horrible mess—and disappeared.

Chapter 34

Ben's chance to repossess his knife and hatchet came when he spotted Gene heading into the woods with a roll of toilet paper. Without hesitation, he grabbed his backpack and took an indirect route to the scoutmaster's truck, going around the fringe of the campsite. Because the other scouts avoided him, Ben easily made it to his target without being questioned.

After climbing inside, he turned off the cab light to conceal his actions and then reached under the seat. After sorting through the junk stashed there, Ben found his knife and slipped it into the sheath and then stored it in his backpack. Next, he looked for his hatchet and his fingers contacted a cold metal shaft that he thought was part of the hatchet. As he wrapped his hand around it, Ben's mind registered something else—the barrel of a revolver.

When the object reached the faint light of the truck floorboard, Ben confirmed his guess. He considered the consequences of stealing the handgun, but the lure of the gun overwhelmed his conscience and judgment. He slipped it into his backpack.

Ben resumed searching for his hatchet and located it. He also put it in his backpack. After exiting the truck, Ben quietly closed the door and crept away, attempting to stay unseen by the scouts gathered around the campfire. Instead of walking through the camp, he took the road past the campsite and then used the brush near the Hawks' campsite to hide his return.

When inside his tent, Ben closed the flap and pulled the gun out of his backpack. Using his flashlight, he inspected it more closely. He had stolen a .22 caliber revolver, a small gun primarily used for target practice or perhaps shooting squirrels. He decided to keep the gun even though it provided a poor option for self-defense.

After eating his evening meal, Ben walked toward the campfire to gather more food for his journey. He found a sandwich bag full of cookies and a package of hot dog buns and slipped them into his backpack. Because he stayed outside of the campfire's glow, he acquired these items without being seen.

If Ben rationed his food, he could hike for a few days without becoming too hungry. Depending on his ability to find trails, he expected to be able cross the mountains between his location and Nephi in two days. When reaching Nephi, he could beg for food and hitch a ride to Southern Utah. He planned to create a new home for himself in or near Zion National Park—one of his favorite places that his family had visited during vacations.

Ben rested in his tent while the rambunctious campfire party continued. All he needed to do was roll up his sleeping bag and tie it to his backpack. Then he would be ready to hike to freedom. He planned to leave shortly after the troop received orders to "bunk down."

Within the hour, Brother Sanderson told the scouts to go to bed. Ben stepped out of his tent when Joe and other members of the Hawk patrol returned to their area. When saying good night to them, he wondered if he would ever see them again. Ben kept his plan well hidden from Joe by not saying anything out of the ordinary. And Joe made it easy by ignoring him.

The scoutmaster stopped by for a quick chat with each of the Hawks, seeing if any of them had concerns about spending the night outdoors with a snowstorm coming. Ben exchanged greetings with him and lied that he was fine.

"Ben, I'll be praying for you tonight as I have many times in the past," Gene said. "I believe that God has plans for your life that are better than anything you might be expecting. Trust in him with all your heart and he will make your paths straight. You can begin that journey tonight."

Ben almost laughed when Gene mentioned beginning a "journey tonight" because that's exactly what he planned to do. Instead of replying, he merely nodded and waited to see if Gene would demand that Ben return the pistol, knife, and hatchet that he had taken from the truck. Instead, the scoutmaster said goodnight and walked away.

After a couple of stern reminders from Brother Sanderson, peace finally settled over the camp. Ben waited another twenty minutes and then rolled up his sleeping bag and got it ready to travel. He didn't want to delay his exit much longer because he might fall asleep. Peeking out of his tent, he surveyed the dark campsite and didn't see any movement. With only a half moon and cloudy sky, the scarcity of natural light would hide his escape.

Crawling from the tent with his pack and sleeping bag strapped to his back, Ben looked side-to-side to see if anyone noticed him. When his movement sparked no reaction, he stood up and walked bent-over to keep a low profile as he cut through the brush to reach the road. He left his tent in place because it would be too heavy to carry on a long hike and he wanted to give the impression that he remained with the troop. If all went as expected, his absence wouldn't be discovered until Joe decided that he had slept too long and came to his tent to shake him out of his sleeping bag.

Instead of hiking down the canyon to Payson, Ben went uphill, going away from civilization to avoid being spotted walking alone at night. He planned to stay on the road until morning because it currently had no traffic and would be faster than going cross-country. When daybreak came, he would look for off-road trails that went southwest and over the mountains to Nephi. He expected that anyone who tried to find him would never imagine a boy selecting the extremely challenging route he had in mind.

Confident of his plan, Ben pressed forward at a fast pace even under the weight of his backpack. His eyes adjusted to the faint light and he enjoyed the thought of freedom from the pain being left behind. Each mile completed brought him closer to Zion—the heavenly place of joy and peace.

Chapter 35

After ninety minutes of walking, Ben noticed the breeze coming down the canyon carried the strong scent of burning wood. Even though the canyon was popular for camping, especially with the fall colors on display, he supposed that the late-night campfire belonged to Derek Dean and his friends. Most campers would be sleeping by now, with their fire smoldering or extinguished.

After he began to see flickers of light through the trees ahead, a burst of loud laughter confirmed his guess about the smoke's source. Derek and his friends had set up camp and built a roaring fire in between Ben and his destination. He continued walking toward their campsite to see if he could pass it without being noticed.

The three men were about twenty-five yards off the road in a small clearing that opened to the canyon road on one end and a forested area on the other. Thick clusters of spruce and aspen trees as well as heavy underbrush marked the boundaries on the other two sides of their campsite. For Ben to continue up the canyon road, he had to walk near the huge campfire, making him visible to Derek and his friends. Taking a detour through the rough terrain around the camp would require using a flashlight, which would also lead to him being spotted.

Ben found a place in the trees where he could spy on the men and look for other ways to pass them. Because they appeared to be drinking beer, Ben hoped they would soon get drunk and fall asleep. While waiting, he frequently checked his watch, growing concerned about the loss of time. After a half hour, the party abruptly ended when Luke staggered to his motorcycle, pulled blankets out of the saddlebag, and carried them to a spot near the campfire.

When Luke stretched out on the blankets, Derek jumped to his feet and shouted, "Get up! We've still got a mission to accomplish."

"Hey, we've had a long day," Luke said. "Let's get some sleep and go scare the crap out of the boys tomorrow."

"No, we agreed to do it tonight while the little jerks are sleeping," Derek said.

"Yeah, but don't forget that I started working at six this morning," Luke said. "Give me a few hours to sleep and then I'll be ready to raid the scout camp."

Like Luke, Wayne pulled blankets out of his saddlebag and laid down near the campfire. For a few minutes Derek sat alone, watching the campfire and sipping beer. After tossing the empty bottle into a cluster of trees, Derek stood up and walked in Ben's direction. Ben thought he had been spotted, but Derek stopped a safe distance away to relieve himself and finish his current cigarette. Without bothering to extinguish it, Derek flicked the glowing butt toward the road and then zipped up his pants and headed to his motorcycle.

Derek had two blankets and used them to set up a bed on the far side of the campfire. Within a few minutes, Ben could no longer see Derek because the fire had started to burn out, casting a much smaller ring of light. Because Luke and Wayne were closer to him, Ben could see that they had already dozed off and he heard one of them snoring. He patiently remained hidden, waiting for the fire to grow even weaker.

When the clearing darkened, it gave Ben confidence that he could move undetected and triggered a new idea. The men had discussed plans to "raid" his troop, which Ben applauded when it came to the Bears and Wolves, but he wanted to protect the Hawks if possible. Damaging the men's motorcycles would put Derek on foot and keep the troop safe. And by preventing a predawn attack on the scouts, it would avoid drawing attention to Ben's absence earlier than what he was hoping for.

Ben left his backpack at his hiding place and crept toward the bikes, which were parked near the campfire. He silently inched toward his prey with his hatchet in one hand and knife in the other.

On the first bike, he cut all the hoses and wires he could find. Then he searched the saddlebag to see if it contained any snacks to boost his food supply. He had noticed the men eating chips when drinking their beer and hoped they might have some leftover. Instead of food, he found cigarettes and a liquor bottle. Feeling vindictive, he unscrewed the lid of the liquor bottle and drenched the cigarettes.

At the next bike, Ben repeated his process of cutting anything that might make the bike impossible to start. In the faint glow of the campfire, he noticed the cap on top of the gas tank and created another problem for his foes. He carefully opened the cap and let it slowly dangle to the side of the bike and then used his hatchet to create a small pile of sand. With his hands, he scooped up the sand and fed it into the open gas tank. The contaminated fuel would require draining the gas and then cleaning and refilling the tank before starting the engine. It served as an extra measure in case he hadn't already put the bike out of commission.

He left the cap undone so the men could see that sand had been added. The open cap would warn them to not even try starting the bike. He returned to the first bike to give it the same treatment, but the gas cap didn't cooperate even when he twisted it with all his strength. Wondering if it might be locked, he leaned against the bike to get a closer look.

Even though Ben only applied a small amount of weight to the side of the bike, it caused the kickstand to sink deeper into the sandy soil and the bike began tipping over. Ben desperately tried to keep it upright, but he stood on the wrong side of the bike to break its fall and it went down with Ben sprawled on top. The noise caused two heads to pop up next to the campfire.

Like a flash of lightning, Ben rolled off the bike, grabbed his knife and hatchet, and raced for his backpack. He ran fast, with no awareness of fatigue. After what he had done to the bikes, getting caught terrified him.

While running, Ben listened for signs of pursuit but the men, groggy after being awakened, didn't chase him. He only heard them talking.

"What's all the fuss?" Derek asked.

"Wayne's bike tipped over," Luke said. "And we think there was a big critter climbing on it, probably looking for food. We're not sure what is was because it's so dark and the thing took off running."

"It could have been a bear," Wayne said.

"That's stupid. There are no bears here," Derek said.

"Look!" Wayne shouted as Ben raced up the canyon road. "It is a bear! And there it goes."

"Where?" Luke asked. "I don't see anything."

"Open your eyes," Wayne said. "It's running up the canyon. Can't you see it?"

That's the last of the conversation Ben could hear, having left the clearing behind. He briefly stopped to put his weapons back into their sheaths on his belt and to slip his arms through the strap on his backpack. He glanced back and was pleased to see that nobody followed him yet. He resumed running up the canyon road, deciding to stay on it unless the undamaged motorcycle was used to chase him.

Ben ran for about five minutes before hearing the dreaded sound of a motorcycle engine. When a headlight flashed across the trees in the bend behind him, he abandoned the road and turned to his right. He aimed toward the mountains that overlooked Nephi.

At this point, the trees and underbrush stood far enough apart to drove a motorcycle through. To make it impossible for the bike to continue following him, Ben needed to blaze an off-road trail through a more densely forested area. For years, he had found the tall, rugged Wasatch Mountains to be his faithful friends. Now, on a midnight run from a vengeful man, he depended on them to become his trustworthy guardians.

Chapter 36

While Ben ran through the wooded area next to the road and then into a wide ravine, he frequently glanced over his shoulder to keep track of the bike. The darkness made its bright headlight easy to spot. When the light illuminated the canyon road at his exit point, he stopped and turned to see if the bike would fly by. He saw two men on the bike, with the passenger using a flashlight to scan both sides of the road. The light passed over the area where Ben stood and then quickly flipped back to freeze on him. He heard a shout and the bike slide to a stop.

Ben hadn't anticipated a backseat rider armed with a flashlight and reprimanded himself for standing in the open like a deer staring at the motorcycle's headlight. He spun around and charged ahead toward the steep, tree-covered hill on the ravine's far side.

As expected, the bike followed him, but the constant need to make sharp turns around trees made it a slow drive. Despite the obstacles, the motorcycle closed the gap and its headlight soon illuminated Ben's path. When he turned to see who was on the bike, he witnessed it flip because the front tire had hit a deep hole. The riders flew over the handlebars and landed on the rocky bottom of the ravine. The driver, Derek, slowly rose to his feet, massaging his left shoulder. The passenger, Luke, remained on the ground, holding his head in his hands.

Having confirmed that his pursuers survived the crash and could continue the chase, Ben turned away from them and went up the steep hillside as fast as he could go. A stout cluster of bushes stretched across the area and brought his ascent to a crawl.

"Hey, punk, come back here and apologize for messing up our bikes!" Derek shouted. "If you don't, we'll find you and make things twice as bad for you."

Ben didn't respond, saving his breath for the climb. While Derek and Luke recovered from the crash, he charged ahead, breaking through the brush blocking his way. He hoped it didn't include any poison oak or poison ivy. The darkness made it impossible to see these potential problems and other hazards. He stumbled frequently over rocks, roots, and branches. From his falls, he lost skin off both hands and drove pebbles and pine needles into his palms. One hard fall ripped a hole in his left pant leg and blood trickled from a cut below his knee.

While struggling up the mountainside, the abrupt roar of Derek's motorcycle engine startled him, and he lost his footing. While sprawled on the ground, he pivoted to survey the scene below. The motorcycle had left the ravine and was going back to the road. He could see that it only had one rider—Derek. Luke remained seated in the ravine. Ben knew that Derek wouldn't drop his plans for revenge so quickly, especially when provoked by the damaged bikes, and suspected that he only left the ravine to get Wayne.

Ben decided to keep moving and went straight up the steep hillside until he gasped for air and had to take a break to slow his breathing. Within a minute, the motorcycle's engine stopped. He scanned the area below him and the canyon road, but he couldn't see any movement and had lost sight of Luke. All he could hear were leaves rustling in the wind as the expected snowstorm approached.

In case Luke was following him on foot, Ben leaned into the hillside and resumed his climb. He had already started to wear out, so he focused on looking for the best possible path. He didn't want to waste any time or energy backtracking around obstacles. Ben continued for several minutes before pausing to take another break—the sound of the motorcycle coming back to the ravine gave him an excuse for stopping. All he could see was the headlight and no details to let him know what Derek was doing. It didn't matter. The bike's return compelled him to get going, and he plunged ahead with great determination to place more space between him and his hunters.

Despite only being a teenager, Ben had years of experience hiking these mountains and confidence that he would win the race. He rarely let a week pass without going for a lung-burning charge up the base of the mountain behind his home. For this challenge, Ben's strategy remained simple—keep going deeper into the mountains and smother Derek's desire to continue the chase by making it extremely painful.

In less than half an hour, Ben reached a ridge that gave him an unobstructed view of the back side of the mountains that loomed over Nephi and the other towns in Juab County. Even in the dark, he could see the peaks of Dry Mountain, Bald Mountain, North Peak and Mount Nebo. Determined to stay ahead of Derek, he started descending the other side of the ridge.

Instead of climbing the next hill in front of him, Ben selected an easier course that went almost straight south through a small valley. After going around the hill, he would search for a trail to take him west again toward the big peaks.

Even though relatively flat, the rugged terrain still required Ben to keep his eyes on the ground to prevent another fall. He only dared to glance up occasionally to make sure he didn't miss a trail going west. As he marched forward with tired legs, Ben found motivation in thinking about his new life. Some pain now promised better days to come.

Chapter 37

Snowstorms hit the Wasatch Mountains at any time between Labor Day and Memorial Day, requiring hikers and campers to be ready for cold, snowy weather. Ben came prepared for a snowstorm, but his plan included a campfire and his tent, not an overnight hike.

At first, the storm refreshed him. After three hours of strenuous hiking, the light snow melted on Ben's hands and face, washing away dust and sweat. When the snowflakes increased in size and frequency, his view of the storm quickly shifted from pleasant to unbearable. He dashed to a protected area under a pair of broad pine trees where he put on his hat, gloves, and heavier coat.

Ben looked back for signs of Derek and his friends following him, but he didn't spot a flashlight or any movement. With no pursuers in sight, Ben rested from his challenging hike, continuing to enjoy partial shelter from the snow.

Gusts of wind blew flakes on him, but the resulting chill and dampness was minor compared to what he would face if he left the protection of the trees. Storms in the mountains often came in waves, which gave him reason to wait for the current flurry to lighten up. Without intending to nap, Ben's eyes slowly closed, and he drifted into sleep. When he began to dream about being lost in the woods, he tipped over from his sitting position and woke up when his head hit the ground. To avoid falling asleep again, he decided to ignore the storm and keep moving.

Chapter 37

Ben clenched his fists and marched away from his shelter. The chilly wind welcomed his challenge with an icy slap to the face. As he hiked, the snowfall began to taper off and appeared to be ending, but then another heavy wave arrived and engulfed him. Walking became the only way to stay warm. Not knowing if Derek and his friends continued to follow him, he didn't dare stop to build a fire.

Snow kept falling for the next three hours. When hearing the crunch of the fresh snow under his boots, he looked behind him and noticed that he was leaving a clear trail of footprints. Speed served as Ben's only reliable strategy for eluding his enemy.

Snow stopped falling shortly before Ben finished climbing a small, barren hilltop west of the valley he had followed when heading south. From the hilltop, Ben studied the valley behind him and still picked up no signs of movement. So far, he appeared to be winning the race, and yet he felt compelled to keep going. He hurried across the hilltop to identify a landmark west of him.

He spotted a tight valley ending at the base of the mountains that would allow him to travel on relatively flat ground for at least a mile. A cluster of granite boulders at the valley's far end served as a highly visible target. He started hiking toward them, but pain throughout Ben's body reminded him that he had pushed the pace for nearly seven hours. It took thoughts of Derek catching him to resist the temptation to stop or slow down.

Things went well for about a half hour and then a staunch wind swept through the valley and provided a frigid warning of more snow coming. Ben trudged ahead and tried to ignore the plunging temperature and his fatigue. A promising change came when he emerged from a hearty growth of pine trees and discovered a small clearing with a trail crossing it. The wind had partially uncovered the trail or Ben might have missed it. He decided to follow the trail and see how far west it would take him.

While the trail boosted his speed, he suffered extreme pain where the straps of his backpack burrowed into his shoulders. The tenderness made him want to toss the backpack aside, but Ben kept his gear because it would be the difference between surviving the hike or freezing to death. Eventually, he would need to set up a camp where he could build a fire to cook a hot meal and dry his clothes that had become damp from melted snow. Stopping to build a fire would make it easy to be found, but he had nearly reached the point where it didn't matter. He wouldn't last much longer.

By the time Ben made it to the cluster of boulders, he had stumbled twice from dizziness and decided that a break was necessary. After a quick review of the rocky area around the boulders, he identified a ledge on the hillside south of the boulders where he could rest—and hide in case Derek remained in pursuit.

Before climbing to the ledge, Ben kept going straight ahead on the trail to create the impression that he had continued that way. He made sure his footprints stood out on the snowy trail until coming to a place where the trail had more rocks than snow. He used that point for his exit, carefully stepping on rocks while backtracking to the ledge.

When he reached the rock slide, it became easier to move without creating a trail of footprints. He soon reached the ledge and then looked for a place to set up camp. He found a small gap within a pile of small boulders and fallen pine trees that would keep him out of sight if he crouched or laid down.

Ben rolled out his sleeping bag inside his hiding place. Despite the bag being slightly damp from melted snow, he expected his body heat to warm it. Before getting into the sleeping bag, he unlaced his boots and pulled them off. He also removed his socks, finding blisters on all toes and both heels. Hiking in cheap boots for eight hours had left his feet in dreadful condition.

Next, he used his scout knife to open a can of peaches and devoured the contents, even drinking the juice that he normally would have tossed out. He ate a few of the hot dog buns and some of the cookies that he had taken from the campfire party. He considered heating up his can of soup, thinking how comforting it would be to have a hot breakfast, but he decided to save the soup—his only can—until he could safely build a fire.

Having relieved his hunger, Ben stretched out for a nap and hoped the shelter would keep him safe and dry. Despite being chilled, he began to drift off as soon as he rested his head on his backpack. The sound of the persistent wind rushing through the trees provided a soothing atmosphere for much needed rest. As exhaustion took control of his mind, Ben warned himself that he could only sleep for one hour. Then he should resume his trek to the base of the mountains that stood between him and Nephi, where he would begin the next leg in his journey to Zion.

Chapter 38

A familiar voice invaded Ben's dreams—Derek Dean. Hearing him wrenched Ben completely out of deep slumber. He crawled within his rock fortress to a position that allowed him to see the nearby area. He found the ledge empty, but he heard two men talking—Derek and the other had to be either Luke or Wayne.

In case he needed to start running, Ben put on his socks and boots, fighting through the pain of applying pressure to his blistered toes and heels. Until he had a firm plan for his next steps, he decided to leave the rest of his gear behind except for his canteen, hatchet, and hunting knife. He attached those essential items to his belt and slid anxiously out of the crevice to spy on Derek.

With sunrise now underway, Ben glanced at his watch and was surprised to find out that he had slept for more than two hours. Even though he might have collapsed on the trail, his long nap had allowed his pursuers to close the gap. And now he faced a likely end to his journey that promised to be painful and probably fatal. He imagined his body being buried in these rugged mountains—never to be found.

To his relief, the snow had stopped falling, and the rising sun fought to peek through the remaining clouds. Even the frigid wind had calmed down. Only a slight breeze swept the canyon. And the sunlight raised the temperature slightly.

Despite facing many challenges, Ben's hunters had followed him all night and now searched for him within speaking distance. When the chase started, Ben thought they lacked the willpower and stamina to pursue him for more than an hour. He also doubted that they had the skills to track him in the dark. On the other hand, he left a path through the fresh snow that even city boys could follow.

Looking over the lip of the ledge, Ben saw Derek and Luke studying the trail at the point where Ben had backtracked to his current location. "I'm sure he stopped here and then changed direction," Luke said, pointing at Ben's last visible footprint. "Even with this trail being rocky, we'd see something ahead of us, but there aren't any signs of him going past this point. And look at this. Can you see how his footprint is wider at the front and back than the others?"

"Yeah, so what?" Derek asked.

"It shows that the boy turned to his left and then jumped from this spot to those rocks," Luke said as he pointed out the path Ben had taken with frightening precision. "And then he probably climbed the hill to find a new trail or to hide in the rocks up there."

When Luke presented his conclusion, his pointing finger rose from the trail below Ben and came to rest at the spot where he watched the discussion. Ben quietly slid away from lip of the ledge and crept back to where he had left his gear. His only chance of evading Derek and Luke relied on his ability to stay ahead of them and force them to abandon the chase when he led them to a higher altitude.

As Ben quickly repacked, he tossed aside a few items to travel lighter and faster. He reluctantly kept one heavy item—the stolen gun. Before returning it to his backpack, he checked to make sure it was loaded and found bullets in all six chambers.

Ben left the rock pile, looped the backpack over his shoulders, and headed higher. During the climb, he could hear Derek and Luke talking. Not everything came through clearly, but he picked up enough to know that they continued to follow his trail and found his discarded items.

"Ben, I know you're close by and can hear me," Derek shouted. "You must be getting worn out by now. Why don't you come back with us to the scout campsite, so you can confess to messing up our bikes and make things right? We won't hurt you, but we think your father should fix our bikes for us at no charge. That's our only request. So, quit wasting time and let's go get a hot breakfast."

Ben didn't respond or slow down and soon reached the top of the hill. At that point, he took a narrow, overgrown hiking trail that headed west and downhill. Ben walked as quickly as he could over the uneven, slippery terrain. His body protested, having been challenged well beyond its normal range by the long, cold hike.

The two-hour nap in a damp sleeping bag didn't give him enough rest. His shoulders hurt from carrying the heavy backpack, his calf muscles cramped from climbing so many hills, and his head throbbed from only sleeping two hours. With every step, the blisters on his toes and heels reminded him of the damage already done and that he was compounding the problem.

Despite his weakened body, Ben set a good pace and soon connected with a trail at the bottom of the hill. When the trail entered a large clearing, he turned to see if Derek and Luke were following him. He immediately spotted them standing at the top of the hill. They waved and shouted his name. As an automatic reflex, he started to wave back and then quickly put his hand down, feeling silly for having treated this hike as a friendly outing.

"Come back!" Derek shouted.

Ben turned away from them and picked up his pace to make it clear that they would have to run to catch him. He had taken about twenty paces when a gunshot rang out across the valley. It caused Ben to sprint for the far side of the clearing. Even though nothing suggested that a bullet had landed near him, he treated the shot as more than a warning. For protection, he headed toward the trees along the edge of the clearing about thirty yards away.

Another shot came a few seconds later and he heard the bullet ricochet off a rock. It didn't seem to be close, but fear still gripped his stomach. Before the next shot rang out, he had left the clearing and ducked behind a fallen tree.

Ben raised his head to look for Derek and Luke. The fear that drove him to run and hide declined slightly when he noticed that Derek held a pistol, not a rifle. At this distance, even a skilled marksman wouldn't be accurate with a pistol.

Derek started shouting again about going back to the scout campsite. Ben thought about shutting him up by using the scoutmaster's pistol to fire a warning shot. He knew the small-caliber pistol wouldn't reach that far with any accuracy, but it might make Derek and Luke reluctant to continue chasing him, especially when every bend in the trail could be an ambush. He left the pistol in his backpack, deciding to save it as a surprise if he failed to outrun the men.

Seeing Derek and Luke still standing at the top of the rock formation gave Ben a morsel of encouragement. He decided to expand his lead by crawling away from the clearing and going higher into the mountains. When he had placed enough trees between him and Derek to block any lucky bullets, he returned to the trail and headed away from his pursuers. He felt energized and ready for a fast walk. Being shot at provided the fuel needed to stay ahead of Derek and Luke for at least a few more hours.

Chapter 39

The trail continued for about a mile and then split with a branch turning sharply to the right. Another branch veered slightly to the left. Ben checked his compass and took the path to the left because it headed toward Mount Nebo. Within a half mile, the trail became much steeper and changed direction again, heading toward North Peak.

The new path kept rising and taking him into deeper snow and thinner air. Already breathing heavily, the scarcity of oxygen at the higher elevation led to panting and a throbbing headache. Ben always loved hiking, but the stress of this painful journey stripped it of any pleasure. Instead of enjoying the scenery, he constantly surveyed the area for the best route and to check for how closely he was being followed.

When reaching a ridge that gave him a panoramic view of the mountain range, Ben looked behind him and could see Derek and Luke doggedly tracing his footsteps. The separation between them appeared to have only closed slightly. Encouraged, he continued upward.

After slipping on loose rocks and dropping to the snow on his hands and knees, Ben glanced to his left—eastward—and noticed a car on a winding road near the base of the mountain he was ascending. He didn't realize that he had come so close to a road and assumed it was the same road that ran through Payson Canyon. He knew that road looped around the back of Mount Nebo and ended in Nephi. He would have taken a direct route to that road if Derek and Luke weren't following him.

Staggering to his feet, Ben continued trudging up the bare ridge that left him highly visible to the hunters. When making one of his backward glances, he confirmed that his hunters continued after him and were at the base of the ridge. Based on the time that Ben had spent hiking on the ridge, he calculated his lead being less than fifteen minutes.

Ben tried to run to widen the gap, but his legs quickly grew heavy and his breathing raced out of control. He thought his lungs would burst and his head explode. He returned to walking, with regret for having wasted energy to gain a slight increase in speed.

When reaching a point where the ridge flattened out for about one hundred yards, he paused to consider his choices. The wind had moved enough of the light, dry snow off a side trail that he could see that it led from the ridge to a parking area next to the road below. This option tempted him again because it would be easy to go downhill and then he could beg for a ride to Nephi. But the drawback of making it easier for Derek to catch him remained.

The next option would be turning right and entering a long canyon on the mountain's west side that appeared to curve slightly to the south but continued all the way to the valley floor. He could see the small town of Mona, which would get him within ten miles of Nephi. And taking this canyon offered the advantage of going downhill. Ben almost selected this choice and started off, but he couldn't see any sign of a trail and worried about getting slowed down and providing Derek with a closer target for a pistol shot.

Ben went with the third option, hiking to the mountain peak. He knew it would be the most likely way to discourage Derek and Luke. At a fast but sustainable pace, Ben continued his upward climb, keeping his eyes focused on the wind-swept peak ahead. After leaving the relatively flat portion of the ridge, he found the grade even steeper than the section below and the footing became more treacherous as the snow-covered trail led to him stumbling frequently over hidden obstacles.

Ben's strategy to wear out his relentless hunters began to have that same effect on him. His exhaustion reached the point where his legs refused to cooperate with his repeated commands to go faster. With no trees to block the frigid wind, Ben started to shiver despite the heat generated by the hike. And his face, hands, and feet ached from the cold. He had learned about frostbite when earning his first aid merit badge and worried that he could be a victim if he didn't find shelter and build a fire soon.

Despite Ben's pain and anxiety, his resolve didn't weaken, and he gradually approached the peak. Even though snow had stopped falling on the peak, the persistent wind picked up the accumulated snow and sent it racing along the ground. While grimacing and cursing at the torment of snow blasting him in the face, he noticed that the wind was both hurting and helping him. The benefit came from his footprints being erased within seconds. When on the mountaintop, he might be able to hide and rely on the wind to give his hunters no path to follow.

When Ben reached the summit, he searched the eastern and western slopes for potential hiding places and selected a small tree grove on the west side as the best place to search. He hiked to the grove, but he decided not to enter it because the trees held the snow in place and his footprints would be visible. Next to the grove, he explored a rock slide that included dozens of large rocks and a few boulders.

While leaving no footprints behind, Ben climbed through the rock pile and found a tight gap below two boulders that wouldn't be big enough for most people, but he could squeeze into it. Water had washed dirt out from between the boulders, creating enough room for a small boy. To check the hole for snakes, Ben pushed a fallen branch into it a few times and scanned it with his flashlight. The place appeared safe and he wiggled into it, entering feet first and dragging his backpack with him. He wouldn't be found unless Derek or Luke squatted at the entry point and looked directly in the hole.

When hidden, Ben relied on his ears to know what happened around him. He wouldn't be able to see Derek and Luke unless they walked by. While waiting and listening, he focused on the small sliver of the horizon visible to him and watched dark storm clouds approach from the west. More snow would arrive within the hour.

After about twenty minutes of shivering in the hole, he heard voices in the distance. Because no reasonable hikers would climb the mountain in such weather, he assumed the voices belonged to Derek and Luke. When the talking suddenly came from the top of the rock pile, Ben's heart pounded.

"Do you see anything over there?" Derek asked.

"Nothing," Luke said. "No boy or any footprints."

As he finished his assessment, Luke's legs suddenly appeared in front of Ben's hiding place. Luke walked by without even slowing down.

"Keep looking!" Derek shouted from a new location. "He couldn't disappear."

"That's true, but the wind has blown away any trace of him," Luke said. "I'll give the kid credit for being clever. He picked the right trail to ditch us."

Ben enjoyed hearing the compliment, but he wished the men would give up in this location and search the east side of the mountain instead. His wish didn't come true.

Based on the sound of their voices, Derek and Luke had stopped near him. "We need a new plan," Luke said. "We're going to freeze to death if we spend much more time up here, especially with another storm coming. We should head to the road behind us and hitch a ride back to our bikes."

"Wait! Are you saying that you're giving up on me?" Derek asked.

"No, we're friends and sticking together. But it's time to admit this thing has gone on way too long. Let's get out of here before the sheriff comes looking for that stupid kid and wants to know why we've been chasing him. Do you want to end up back in prison?"

"Never again. I'll go down shooting first."

"Then, come on. Let's quit wasting time on an old grudge. By now, the little jerk has gotten the message loud and clear that you'd like to kill him. And who knows? He might keep running and die from trying to stay ahead of us while we're sitting in a restaurant enjoying a giant plate of pancakes, fried eggs, and bacon."

After a long pause, Derek said, "Fine. I don't like quitting, but I'm starving, worn out, and my feet feel frozen. Let's go."

Ben soon lost any ability to track the men as they moved away from him and wind gusts pounded his side of the mountain. Time crawled by slowly as he waited and listened for more conversation. After hearing nothing for ten minutes, Ben slid out of the hole to find out if they had left the peak. He didn't see Derek or Luke nearby, so he stood up to get a better view. When he still didn't catch sight of them, he began to feel optimistic that they had left the mountaintop—probably for a descent of the eastern side. But Ben doubted that they had given up the chase, so he returned to his hiding place in case the men came back.

While waiting, he reached into his backpack and pulled out the last of his ready-to-eat food—three hot dog buns and plastic sandwich bags with smashed potato chips and broken cookies. Even though the food didn't look appetizing, Ben devoured all of it and savored a few sips of water.

He thought about taking a nap in his hiding place but recognized it could be his last nap. With the temperature well below freezing, dozing off could be fatal. He fought to stay awake and to stop shivering. Suddenly, the new storm arrived, with a powerful wind driving more snowflakes into the mountainside.

Despite Luke's compliment about Ben's choice of trails, he wasn't feeling very clever as gusts of icy wind penetrated his shelter. Ben crawled out of the hole and started climbing up the rock pile, wondering what kind of mess he had gotten himself into. He had outlasted Derek and Luke, but his friends—the mountains—had betrayed him. A greater battle now followed—survival.

Chapter 40

Heavy, wind-driven snowflakes pelted Ben while he stood at the top of the rock pile and searched the mountain's western slope for a way to reach the valley. Within seconds, the storm forced him to turn around to protect his face and eyes from snowflakes coming at him like tiny darts shot from a massive blowgun. Going west into the storm at its current intensity would bring sheer misery.

To keep the wind at his back, Ben marched up the mountainside, continuing across the summit to seek protection on the eastern slope. He soon discovered a cliff about one hundred yards below the peak that jutted out from the mountainside. After climbing to the cliff's base, he crouched and relied on the rock formation above him to provide some shelter. Even with less wind and snow hitting him, Ben remained ice-cold, so he untied his sleeping bag from his backpack and crawled into it—with his boots, gloves, coat and hat still in place.

From under the cliff, Ben watched the snow whip across the peak and begin to accumulate in drifts against boulders or the few groves of trees near the peak. While trying to warm up, he thought about his desire to reach Nephi and eventually Zion National Park. It seemed like a perfect plan when he left the scout campsite. Now, he wondered if he should scrap it.

If he gave up and rejoined his troop, he faced profound consequences for taking out his anger against the Bears and for running away. If he kept going, he lacked the essential tools and supplies to live off the land. His possessions only included what he carried in his backpack and eight dollars in his wallet.

Ben remembered learning the word "despair" in school and thought it best represented the feeling of crushing darkness and desperation that descended on him as he evaluated his flawed plan to run away. No matter how Ben looked at his options, none appeared attractive. He couldn't go home. He couldn't live in the mountains. He couldn't think of any way to solve his problems. He felt trapped.

While Ben struggled with these thoughts, he remembered the many times, since Grandpa Baker's funeral, when he had wondered why his grandfather committed suicide. Ben imagined that he had reached a point where his life had become so dismal that any moments of joy failed to brighten the dark days. His problems, whether big or small, must have made death stand out as the best solution.

At times Ben considered making the same choice, but he always rejected suicide as dishonorable. The deepness of the despair Ben experienced while fighting to stay warm on the mountain helped him understand how his grandfather might have looked at his broken life and decided to end it. And Ben remembered the gun in his backpack. A single shot to the head seemed like a better way to go than freezing to death. While the result would be the same, taking charge of the matter promised to be much quicker and less painful than letting nature do the job.

After pulling the scoutmaster's pistol from his backpack, Ben changed his mind because he hated the idea that his ultimate action in life would be one that many people would consider cowardly—a legacy that he despised. Ben put the gun away and returned to thinking about which direction to head when the snowstorm ended.

Before long, the wind shifted and exposed his small sanctuary to the full force of the storm. Blasts of needlelike snowflakes battered him from the right side. He rolled up his sleeping bag and scrambled back to the top of the cliff in search of a new shelter. Instead of refuge, he discovered the wind to be swirling. No place this high on the mountain would spare him from being battered by the storm.

Ben wrapped his arms around his chest in a futile attempt to stay warm. He couldn't recall ever being so cold. As he shivered, thoughts of using the gun to end his misery returned. He still didn't want to shoot himself, but a new idea popped into his head. *Jump off the cliff and nobody will know that you killed yourself. People will think you slipped and fell to your death.*

He walked to the edge of the cliff and peered over it, looking for a place where a fall would certainly kill him. He found the ideal point and walked to it. The cliff dropped away to a cluster of large rocks about thirty feet below. If he dove into the rocks with his arms at his side, he envisioned his head splitting open. A quick death seemed certain. If not, he would be knocked unconscious and probably die from blood loss before waking up.

With the storm continuing to pound the mountaintop, "falling off the cliff" seemed like the perfect plan. All Ben needed to do was run toward the cliff, dive over it, and close his eyes. Committed to this plan, he dropped his backpack and examined the side of the cliff to make sure he could fall straight down and wouldn't bounce off rocks on the way. The setting appeared to be perfect for a death plunge. He took five steps back to create a running start and then charged ahead.

As soon as Ben ran toward the cliff, a force as tangible and strong as the relentless snowstorm stopped him and he staggered backward. Despite being unseen, it had the same effect on Ben as if someone had grabbed his shoulders and pulled him away from the cliff. At the same time, a clear thought entered his head. *No!*

Ben didn't hear a distinct voice or even a whisper, but his mind registered the command to stop. While staring at the edge of the cliff, he sensed a loud, rushing sound in his head that surpassed the noise of the wind whipping the mountaintop. At that moment, he received another clear message that dominated his thoughts. *Things will get better.*

Stunned by the physical sensations that accompanied the message,

Ben stood still and wondered what had happened. Nothing he had ever been through in his life matched this experience. The unseen hands and unspoken words seemed as real as if they came from someone standing next to him. And yet he remained alone.

Things will get better.

For unknown reasons, Ben believed what he heard and let it guide him. He walked away from the edge of the cliff and didn't look back.

Chapter 41

Ben retrieved his backpack and kept walking away from the cliff. He headed downhill, aiming for the distant road seen when climbing to the peak. Despite the deepening snow, the hike to the road passed quickly as he thought about the strange experience at the edge of the cliff. He struggled to comprehend what restrained him.

Even though he had attended church almost every week for as long as he could remember, Ben didn't really believe in God. To fit in with everyone else at church, he talked about God as if he were real. At the same time, he wondered if having faith in God was any different from believing in Santa Claus. The intent of adults when sharing stories about both seemed to be a trick to get children to behave.

Even though he doubted God's existence, Ben heartily agreed that people shouldn't lie, steal, or commit murder. Living a moral lifestyle appealed to him. At the same time, he listened with skepticism when people talked about God performing miracles in their lives or telling them what to do. Neither had happened to Ben.

Perhaps this day marked the first time God had spoken to him or the first time he had listened. As Ben thought about this possibility, he remembered his scoutmaster saying that he would pray for him. Ben didn't think much about the promise because he had heard this statement delivered by many people and it seemed to be nothing more than an expression like "Have a nice day." He pondered the idea that God might have been looking out for him because of the scoutmaster's prayer. It seemed farfetched, but the thought kept returning to his mind.

When Ben reached the road, he faced a decision. Turn right and head toward Nephi or turn left and go back to the scout campsite. He paused for a few seconds to see if the force encountered on top of the mountain would make the call, but nothing happened.

If Ben turned left and made it back to the campsite, he would be disciplined by his parents and the scoutmaster for his poor behavior. On the other hand, turning right stood out as a bleaker option. He might not survive if he didn't get a ride. So he turned left, toward whatever punishment might come.

After walking on the road for about fifteen minutes, Ben heard a vehicle coming toward him. Still swept up in anxiety about being caught, his first impulse was to hide, but he quickly rejected it. He had already dumped his fantasy to live off the land.

The vehicle soon appeared—the familiar patrol car of Sheriff Kort. It came to a slow halt next to Ben. Taking a deep breath, Ben turned to face the sheriff and was shocked to see Derek and Luke sitting in the backseat.

Sheriff Kort rolled down his window and casually leaned out, smiling and almost laughing. He asked, "Ben, how have you been?"

"Fine, thanks," Ben said, wondering when the sheriff's reprimand would begin and why he had Derek and Luke in his car.

"A lot of folks are mighty worked up about what you've been doing today. So they called me in a panic to help find you. I agreed to poke around to see if I could. And here you are taking a stroll in the snow."

"Yep. I thought it would be fun to go hiking instead of hanging out at the campsite."

"Oh, and I guess you didn't think about telling anybody that you were going off for a little sightseeing."

"Well, I started early and didn't want to wake anyone up."

"Things don't change with you, do they? You're still telling tall tales."

Not knowing what to say, Ben glanced at the sheriff's passengers and worried that Derek might have already complained about his friends' motorcycles being vandalized.

"I'd be glad to give you a ride home if you're done hiking for the day. Are you interested?"

Ben looked around as if trying to decide whether to accept the sheriff's offer or keep hiking.

"Uh, I was only joking," the sheriff said, chuckling at Ben's reaction to his question. "Get in the car and let's go. You're done."

"OK, a ride back to the campsite would be good."

"We'll stop there, but then I'm taking you home. Your parents have heard that you ran off and are worried about you."

Ben pointed at the backseat of the sheriff's car and asked, "Do you want me to ride back there with them?"

"No, no, no," Sheriff Kort said, chuckling again. "Sit up front with me."

After Ben hurried around the car and climbed in, the sheriff used his radio to alert his colleagues that "the missing scout has been found—alive and well." He made a U-turn and then used his thumb to point at the backseat.

"When hiking, did you happen to notice these two following you?"

Before responding, Ben glanced over his shoulder at Derek who held his right hand under his chin with the 666-tattoo visible. Ben understood the message—*keep your mouth shut or else.* He wondered if Derek had his gun or if the sheriff had taken it. Ben still had the scoutmaster's gun in his backpack.

After a long pause, Ben said, "No, I thought I had the trail to myself."

"That's interesting because we found a trail with your footprints and theirs going in the same direction."

Ben didn't reply and neither did Derek, but Luke jumped in, saying, "Like we've said before, we were only looking around for signs of deer, so we'd know if this is a good place to hunt. And, by coincidence, we happened to be going in the same direction as the boy."

Ben didn't look at Derek for confirmation, but he imagined him sending signals to his partner to keep his mouth shut. And Derek didn't volunteer any information.

"Son, is there anything you should tell me that would explain why the three of you went hiking on the same trail and in miserable weather?"

Having learned from his previous chats with the sheriff that he should limit his remarks to the truth, Ben decided to ignore the question. He didn't want to make up a story or admit that he had crippled two motorcycles.

Reacting to Ben's silence, the sheriff said, "While looking for you, I found Derek and his pal hitchhiking. I asked them if they had seen you and all I got in return was a dumb look."

Sheriff Kort paused to see if Ben would start blabbing, but he kept his mouth closed and so did the backseat passengers. The sheriff kept pressing for an answer and said, "I get the impression that all three of you are lying. Ben, do I need to remind you what happened the last time?"

"No, sir," Ben said, already feeling guilty about keeping secrets from the sheriff again.

"Your scoutmaster told me that you ran into Derek a couple of times yesterday and he thought a threat had been made. Did that happen?"

"Not really. Even if he did, I'm not worried about Derek. He could never keep up with me in the mountains and he can't shoot worth a darn."

With that insult, Ben glanced back at Derek to let him know that he didn't care about his 666-tattoo or any other intimidation trick he might use. Ben made a silent pledge to never fear Derek again. His confidence came from a simple belief—*things will get better.*

Chapter 42

Things didn't get better right away. In fact, Ben had a few rough months dealing with the consequences of his actions. Gene Augustine gave him an indefinite suspension from scouts for damaging the tents, stealing the pistol, and running away from the campout. Sheriff Kort kept prodding and pushing for an explanation of what happened with Derek and Luke, but Ben continued to reply "Nothing." And most of Ben's fellow high school students viewed him as even weirder than they already thought. He heard many whispers directed at him about being "the idiot who wandered off in the mountains and had to be rescued by the sheriff."

During math class, the teasing piled up to a level where Ben lost control of his emotions. After receiving a steady stream of insults from an especially obnoxious classmate, he yanked the boy from his chair and slammed his head into the wall.

"Are you picking on me because you didn't think I'd fight back?" Ben asked while punching the dazed victim. "Today, you guessed wrong."

"Ben, stop it! Did you hear me? Stop it, right now!" Ben's teacher shouted as he broke up the beating. "What are you doing? This isn't who you are."

While standing next to the teacher, Ben looked across the classroom and caught the eyes of Julie Winters whose disappointed look confirmed that, once again, he had gone too far in releasing his anger. He hated himself for showing no self-control.

The brief fight led to a conference with Ben's teacher, principal, and mother. The principal didn't suspend Ben. He merely warned him not to do it again and offered advice about how to handle similar situations in the future.

"Just relax. You need to learn not to take teasing so seriously," the principal said. "Remember, these knuckleheads are only trying to get a laugh."

Eventually, things for Ben improved. Derek left the area, with nobody knowing where he went, so the sheriff quit pestering Ben about him. The high school's "comedians" found new things to joke about and ignored Ben. Then came the miracle of Ben's junior year—he grew eight inches. And he added two more inches as a senior.

Instead of being shorter than all the boys and most of the girls in high school, he suddenly stood as tall as the average-sized boys and even taller than his big brother. Ben's growth spurt required him to buy longer pants about every three months, but it dramatically improved his life. The bullies moved on to smaller targets.

As planned, Joe left for Utah State University after graduating from high school and rarely came home during his freshman year. While Ben enjoyed having his own room, he realized what a challenging role Joe had played in trying to keep their home peaceful.

Even though Becky was only ten years old, she showed more courage or less common sense than her siblings and rebelled against her father's tyranny. And she paid a hefty price. Al unleashed his full fury on Becky through slaps, punches, and kicks. He held nothing back in trying to break her will. And yet, despite his extreme violence and vile name-calling, he never stifled Becky's desire to fight back.

In the past, Joe found ways to distract his father and calm him down. When that burden shifted to Ben, he felt helpless, not having Joe's skills or courage. During his senior year in high school, Ben stayed away from the house by going to the library and putting in as many hours as possible at his part-time job. He worked hard to avoid the challenge of trying to protect Becky and Debbie from their father.

At times, Ben still stumbled into Becky's battles. The most disturbing came when Ben arrived home to find his father chasing Becky's dog, Duchess, through the yard. To punish Duchess for killing two chickens, Al was trying to whip the dog with a tree branch. Terrified, Duchess ran at a frantic pace and sped down the road leading into Alma. Looking insane, Al continued to chase Duchess even though the neighbors could see his cruelty.

When Becky shouted at Al to leave her dog alone, he complied, sprinting back into the yard toward her. She fled into the house with Al close behind. Ben followed to see if he could get his out-of-control father to calm down. After Al cornered Becky in the kitchen, Ben stepped into the room's doorway, but he froze and didn't dare approach his father. The episode reminded him of his parents' fight in the kitchen years earlier.

While yelling at Becky for having a smart mouth, Al slapped her face several times. Instead of cowering and apologizing, feisty Becky answered back with profane insults. Al made it clear that he had heard enough by slugging Becky in the jaw with a vicious, anger-fueled punch.

She fell to the floor, crying hysterically and curling into a ball. Instead of recognizing that he had done something no father should ever do, Al began kicking Becky with his heavy work boots. His blows came quickly and with nothing held back. Ben couldn't believe that he would treat anyone this way, especially his own daughter.

Even though Ben didn't intervene, Al suddenly stopped and left the room, not looking at Ben or saying a word. Debbie had watched the assault and rushed to help Becky recover. She led her out of the room in case their father failed to cool down and came back to deliver more punishment.

Ben retreated to the barnyard to hide in the safety of "doing chores." He groaned deeply for letting fear of his father keep him from trying to stop the beating. Ben hoped that he would never see anything like that again in his life—and tried to flush that memory from his brain.

Chapter 43

After spending a decade at the bottom of the pecking order among his peers, Ben lacked the confidence to participate in typical high school stuff. He never attended the prom or dated. He rarely spoke in class and stayed far away from "guys being guys." Running on the school's cross-country and track teams became the exception. He loved to train and compete with his teammates.

His interest in running began when Joe joined the high school's cross-country team and soon became the team's fastest runner. Seeing how quickly his big brother excelled at the sport, Ben signed up for the team as a sophomore, but he came in dead last in his first five races. After beating three runners in the next race, he became a running fanatic.

Two years later, Ben stood at the starting line with a dozen teammates and fourteen members of the visiting team from Springville High School. For the last race of the season, Ben's coach changed the school's course to make it longer and more challenging. As a two-miler on the track team, the extra distance gave Ben an advantage over the cross-country runners who specialized in the mile and half-mile runs. He vowed to win the race, so that he would be the recordholder for the new course.

When the race began, Ben followed his usual practice of letting the inexperienced runners lead the way with a reckless sprint off the starting line. He knew their enthusiasm would soon cave in to fatigued legs and then he would glide by them as he gradually quickened his pace throughout the race. By applying this strategy, he ended up in ninth place with 500 yards to go.

His pace had been competitive and yet comfortable, so he approached the end of the race feeling fully equipped for a long sprint to the finish. He began by passing two Springville runners who had been only a few yards ahead of him. They glanced at Ben as he passed and made no attempt to match his faster pace.

Within seconds, he arrived on the heels of two of his teammates who were running side-by-side. At that moment, the boys held the top two spots for his team. To pass them, Ben accelerated to a speed he usually reserved for the final 200 yards of a race, wanting to create the impression that they shouldn't even try to keep up.

"Way to go, Ben!" one of them shouted. "We're right behind you."

Ben flashed a thumbs-up sign and kept going at the same fast pace. He knew the "right-behind-you" comment served as a warning that his teammates planned to respond to his early sprint when he began to falter.

The racecourse ended on the school's quarter-mile track that circled the football field. When Ben ran onto the track, he could see all the runners who remained ahead of him—four members of the visiting team.

Ben charged onto the track at his full-out sprint, pledging to tap into his energy reserves and use every ounce by the time he crossed the finish line. His momentum carried him onto the heels of the first of the four opponents he wanted to pass, and the runner peaked over his shoulder to see who threatened his position. That glance gave Ben all the encouragement he needed to keep sprinting. Ben made the pass and started catching up with the next two runners.

With the finish line about 200 yards away, Ben passed the pair. With his breathing now at a rapid, uncomfortable level, he could feel the burn in his lungs and knew that his legs would soon cramp. Hearing footsteps behind him, Ben kept sprinting. *Leave it all on the track! Finish the race—strong!*

The first-place runner still held a comfortable lead, but his coach urged him to sprint. "Get going, Tony," the coach said, running on the infield and waving his runner toward the finish line. "You've got a jet on your tail and two more right behind him."

A jet!

Ben embraced the compliment and lengthened his stride. He wanted to win this sprint and knew that nobody would catch him from behind if he did.

Seconds to go! Leave it all on the track!

Ben finished slightly behind the winner, but he outsprinted the two challengers for second place by more than a stride. After crossing the finish line, he slowed to a jog and moved away from the handful of spectators so he could discreetly throw up the contents of his overstressed stomach—three times.

While wiping his mouth, Ben turned to see how his teammates were doing. One had finished and stood in the infield, bent over at the waist with his hands on his knees and mouth wide open, gasping for air. Two more of Ben's teammates crossed the finish line only a second apart.

Ben staggered into the infield to watch other runners sprint for the finish line. The teammate who came in close behind him looked up when Ben approached and said, "Great run! Where did that sprint come from?"

"I don't know," Ben said, not wanting to admit that his competitive drive came from trying to prove that he wasn't "stupid and lazy."

Ben received a few other pats on the back for his run, but the thrill of his achievement soon blended into a tedious routine of completing school assignments, doing chores at home, and working four days a week at his paid job.

High school graduation couldn't come soon enough for Ben. Despite being a teenager, he continued to be treated by his father the same way he had since his early years of childhood.

A few months before leaving home, Al asked Ben to hold the base of a ladder for him while he climbed to the top and repaired loose shingles on the end of the house. A rainstorm had left the hard-packed soil on that side of the house slippery.

Chapter 43

"I need you to hold the base of the ladder so it doesn't slide out from underneath me," Al said as he started up the ladder.

Despite being taller than his father, Ben weighed much less than him because he had the lean body of a long-distance runner. "Dad, I'm not sure this is going to work because I'm not heavy enough. Maybe we should put a couple of rocks in front of each of the ladder's legs."

"No, this will be easy. Don't turn it into a big deal."

Ben nodded, recognizing that his father still didn't understand the laws of physics and wouldn't listen to reasonable solutions to problems. Al climbed the ladder with a hammer in one hand and roofing nails in his shirt pocket. Before he reached the top, the ladder started to slide away from the house even though Ben stood on the bottom rung.

"We're sliding! Do something—quick!"

Ben stepped off the ladder and placed his feet in front of the moving legs but failed to stop them. The top of the ladder and Al bounced down the side of the house while the bottom of it pushed Ben away. As the ladder picked up speed, it knocked Ben off his feet and he landed on the last few rungs when the ladder hit the ground. The fall dumped Al into a hedge next to the house.

Spewing profanities, Al pushed branches away and then charged Ben who had recovered from the fall and stood next to the ladder. When Ben saw his father coming, his training as a runner kicked in and he took off for the road in front of the house.

"You lazy, worthless bum! Why didn't you hold the ladder like I told you?"

Ben didn't reply, finding the question ridiculous and knowing there is never a correct answer for "mad Dad." He cut through the grassy area in front of the house while glancing over his shoulder to keep track of his father. When he noticed him picking up a three-foot pine branch from the ground, it reminded him of the weird scene he witnessed when his father chased Becky's dog down the road. Today, Ben had become the "bad dog."

Like Duchess, Ben easily outran his father. He only lost these races when very young. Now, the competition was lopsided, but Al kept coming.

Ben's escape was slightly hindered by a small, rail fence that ran along the front edge of the Bakers' property. Even though he didn't compete in the hurdles on the track team, Ben had experience jumping them and easily cleared the fence.

When Al came to the fence, he tried to imitate his son and nearly made it. His front foot cleared the rail, but his back foot caught the immoveable hurdle and Al sprawled headfirst on the road's gravel shoulder. Ben had turned to keep track of his father's progress and laughed watching the noisy landing.

Ben paused in the road long enough to see Debbie standing on the front porch and joining him in his laugh. Al staggered to his feet and the "mad Dad" switch appeared to have been turned off as he laughed and brushed dirt and weeds off his clothing. Even though the outburst seemed to be over, Ben turned away and kept running—effortlessly and loving the freedom his strong legs offered.

The two miles to Alma's Main Street passed quickly as he kept smiling about his father's botched hurdling attempt. Then he down-shifted to a walk and completed a circle through the town, not stopping to talk to anyone or visiting his grandparents to see if they could include him in their dinner plans. He merely killed time until sunset came and the cool mountain breezes compelled him to return home.

Ben slipped into the barn and made a bed in the hay bales where he rested while keeping an eye on the lights in the house. When they all went out, he crept in through the back door and quietly crawled into his bed. He lacked fear about what the next day might bring. By now, he knew the drill. His father would pretend that nothing happened and might even joke about the hurdling mishap.

Despite his lack of fear, Ben still hated being chased with a stick. He thought about his money saved in the bank that would help him escape his father's hateful house, not for an evening but forever. And his next escape wouldn't be on foot through the mountains: he planned to buy a car, pack his stuff in it, and drive away without looking in the rearview mirror.

Chapter 44

After graduating from high school, Ben left home for Southern Utah State College in Cedar City, to major in biology and run on the cross-country and track teams. The SUSC campus placed Ben within an hour drive of the main entrance of Zion National Park and even closer if he went to Kolob Canyon, an extraordinarily scenic part of Zion. While at SUSC, Ben spent his free time hiking in Zion and camping in the other national parks in Southern Utah. During the summer, he took jobs in the parks to help pay for school and to gain work experience with the National Park Service, his preferred employer after finishing college. Ben loved the parks, SUSC, and Cedar City, only making the four-hour drive back to Alma for Christmas and then not staying long.

While his move to Southern Utah provided the escape from home that he had planned for years, it became a lonely refuge during the school breaks, especially those connected to holidays. Most of the students left the campus to spend time with their families or friends. In his junior year, Ben faced the Thanksgiving school break with plenty to do, except on Thanksgiving Day when the hardware store where he worked part-time would be closed. On that day, Ben planned to go for a twelve-mile run and then stay in his dorm room in Manzanita Hall to catch up on reading assignments for his classes. He would cook his own Thanksgiving meal—a hamburger and tater tots. A lonely but peaceful day.

The campus emptied by mid-afternoon the day before the break officially began. It would be quiet for five days. After finishing his last class, Ben walked to the hardware store on Cedar City's Main Street to start his shift that would end when the store closed at eight. Ben worked the floor, helping customers with everything from finding tools to mixing paint. When not busy with customers, he stocked shelves.

At the front of the store, two cashiers handled the checkout process. One of them, Cindy Carson, approached Ben at closing time while he moved a few snowblowers from the curb in front of the store to inside to keep them safe overnight.

"Excuse me, Ben," Cindy said. "Do you have a second?"

"Sure," Ben said, sincerely interested in talking to his fellow SUSC student whose beauty and kindness he often admired when carrying things to the checkout line for customers.

"Are you staying in town during the Thanksgiving break?" Cindy asked.

"Yep, I need the extra pay and only go home for Christmas."

"Well, I'm serving Thanksgiving dinner at my church on Thursday and thought you might want to join us," Cindy said, handing Ben a sheet of paper with an illustration of a turkey and a list of what would be served. "I hope you'd be interested in coming as my guest."

Ben glanced at the ad for the event and noticed apple pie listed. The pie, all by itself, beat a hamburger and tater tots. Plus, he liked Cindy and thought this might be her way of starting a friendship. He still found the dating process to be well outside of his comfort zone, but he decided that accepting Cindy's offer would make it less terrifying to take at least one small step forward.

"Sure, thanks for the invitation. I'll be there."

"Great, the address for the church is on the flier and we start serving at one, but don't worry if you're a few minutes late. I look forward to having you join us."

"OK, see you then," Ben said, folding the flier and shoving it into his pocket.

"Oh, I'll see you tomorrow," Cindy said. "Like you, I'm working all day. Good night."

Ben mumbled "Good night" and walked to the rear entrance of the store to clock out and pick up his coat for the chilly walk home. He grimaced as he thought about how he ended the conversation with Cindy and wished that he had said more than "OK" when she mentioned that she looked forward to seeing him at the church dinner. He worried that Cindy interpreted his terse reply as either rudeness or a lack of interest.

While walking to his dorm room, Ben wondered what LDS ward Cindy belonged to and pulled out the flier. He stopped under a streetlight to read it and cringed when seeing "Cedar City Community Church." He had accepted an invitation to a non-LDS church. His mother would be horrified.

Suddenly, his interest in showing up for a free Thanksgiving dinner shifted. He had visited other LDS wards before and that had been a comfortable experience, but he had never attended a church of any other denomination. He felt obligated to decline Cindy's invitation out of loyalty to his pioneer ancestors who had been members of the LDS Church since its founding in the 1830s.

At work the next day, Ben avoided contact with Cindy as his way of dealing with his hasty decision to accept her dinner invitation. He didn't want to make up an excuse for not attending or to tell her the truth that going into a non-LDS church seemed like a betrayal of his heritage. The need to bring the snowblowers into the store at closing time forced him to face Cindy.

"Ben, I told our church's pastor that you're having Thanksgiving dinner with us tomorrow and he's very excited about meeting you," Cindy said, with a smile that instantly derailed Ben's plan to say "sorry, can't make it."

Ben nodded as he wrestled one of the snowblowers into its nighttime resting place by the cashiers' stand.

"I'll introduce you to him when you arrive," she continued. "Come in the main entrance and someone will direct you to the social center where we'll be eating."

Struggling to find the right way to say "No," Ben panicked and said, "OK. See you tomorrow."

Cindy smiled and returned to closing out her cash drawer for the day. Ben shrugged his shoulders as he returned to the curb outside to get another snowblower. "I guess I got to go now," he muttered to himself.

During his long run the next morning, he debated whether he should stick with his commitment or be a no-show and apologize later. He remembered Cindy's smile and her excitement about his attendance at the dinner and decided that he couldn't let her down. He would go, eat the free food, and leave out one detail if his mother asked what he did for Thanksgiving.

Not wanting to be late, Ben gave himself plenty of time to find the church and arrived fifteen minutes early. He warily approached the front door and glanced around to see if anyone noticed him. If a member of his LDS student ward saw him entering this church, he would certainly be questioned about it later. While clenching his fists to fight the anxiety shaking his body, he shot up the short staircase leading to the entrance and hurried inside.

Nobody stepped forward to direct him to the social center as Cindy promised. Despite seeing about a dozen cars in the parking lot, the church appeared empty. There was a light on in the entryway where he stood, but the chapel directly in front of him was dark, except for the natural light coming through three stained-glass windows. Being curious, Ben slipped into the chapel to get a closer look.

He noticed hymnals in racks on the back of the long benches, which looked like what he would sit on during sacrament meeting in an LDS meetinghouse. But next to the hymnal was a Bible. Mormons are expected to bring their own copy every Sunday—along with the Book of Mormon, Doctrine and Covenants, and Pearl of Great Price.

Like his church, this one also included a podium, choir seats, and piano. A difference was the giant cross in front of the stained-glass window directly behind the podium. Crosses aren't used in LDS churches or homes. Otherwise, Ben didn't see much difference between his church in Alma and this one. He picked up a hymnal to see if any of the songs were the same.

"Hello! May I help you?" asked a man behind Ben.

Startled, Ben quickly turned to face the man who stood at the entrance of the chapel. Concerned that he had broken church rules, Ben stowed the hymnal in the rack and then walked briskly toward the man.

"I'm sorry about wandering around," Ben said. "I came for the Thanksgiving dinner, but I'm a little early and didn't know where to go, so I waited in here."

"That's fine, this is the house of the Lord and open to all," the man said, initiating a firm handshake. "I'm Pastor Jonathan and glad you came. I apologize if we've already met and I've forgotten your name."

"We haven't," Ben said. "I'm Ben Baker, a student at SUSC and work with Cindy Carson at the hardware store on Main Street. She invited me here."

"Of course, Ben, I've been expecting you. Cindy told me that you're very hardworking, polite, and know everything about tools."

Ben laughed. "Not really. I learned a lot about tools from my dad, but I've found out that he gave me some bad information along the way. But thanks anyway for the compliment."

"And I bet your mother taught you to be polite."

"Yes, sir. She told me many times that it's an essential character trait of a successful person."

"She's a wise woman," the pastor said before turning toward the door when an older man and woman entered. He greeted them, pointed at the hall to the left of the chapel, and told the couple "follow the smell of turkey to the social center."

Returning his focus to Ben, the pastor smiled and said, "We should go that way ourselves." Ben walked next to the pastor as they headed down the hall.

"Did your parents teach you about the Bible as well?" the pastor asked, causing Ben to hesitate as he worried that a Mormon wouldn't be allowed to attend the dinner. He didn't know if Cindy understood that he attended the LDS Church because they had never discussed religion at work. He decided to avoid mentioning his LDS Church membership.

"They tried and so did my Sunday school teachers, but I didn't pay much attention, so I know more about tools than the Bible."

With a laugh the pastor said, "You're not alone, even though the Bible is the perfect tool chest to use when you need to fix life's problems."

Ben smiled and answered a few questions about school—his major, favorite class, and other interests—before they reached a room filled with folding tables, which included some covered with trays of food and others with empty plates and utensils.

"As you can see, we're almost ready to eat," the pastor said. "We're only waiting for a couple more servers to show up."

Preferring to work instead of mingling with strangers, Ben said, "I'd be glad to help serve. My mother taught me that if you don't work, you don't eat."

"All right, we usually don't put first-time visitors to work," the pastor said, "but I'll accept your generous offer. Perhaps you'd like to work next to my daughter."

Without waiting for a reply, Pastor Jonathan waved at a group of men and women chatting in front of an open door to an adjacent room. He asked, "Is my daughter still in the kitchen? I have a recruit who needs instructions for working in the chow line."

One of the women shouted through the doorway, "Chef Cindy, time to get out of the kitchen. The boss needs your help."

Not expecting the "chef" to be Cindy Carson, Ben was surprised when she came through the crowded doorway. As she approached him, Ben smiled and hoped he could work next to her instead of only admiring her from a distance.

"Ben, thanks for coming!" she said, before glancing at Pastor Jonathan. "I'm sorry that my dad put you to work already. He usually gives visitors a month before presenting opportunities to serve."

"Oh no, don't give me any credit for recruiting this hard worker," the pastor said. "Ben volunteered. Please show him what to do while I greet our other guests."

Shaking hands with Ben again, the pastor promised to chat with him later and then moved on to talk to a stream of new arrivals. Cindy gently touched Ben's arm and said, "Thanks again for showing up. I wasn't sure if you really planned to come, but I'm glad you did and are willing to help me."

"Thank you for the invitation," Ben said, delivering the line he had rehearsed for this moment, and then improvised. "I'm impressed that you're the chef for such a large dinner."

Pointing at the woman who had called her "chef," Cindy said, "Don't believe what Sheila says. She was only joking. My mother is the chef and I'm merely her assistant."

Cindy assigned Ben to adding scoops of green bean casserole and herbed corn to the guests' plates, depending on their preferences, as they passed through the line. When serving began, he stood next to Cindy who dished out mashed potatoes and gravy. At the head of the line, Cindy's mother, Amy, handled the key job—distribution of the turkey slices. Other servers helped with cranberry sauce, rolls, salads and desserts.

As the guests went through the line, Ben learned that most of them belonged to the church, with only a few visitors included. The church members welcomed Ben and added comments such as "Hope to see you on Sunday." One guest pointed at Cindy and Ben and voiced her observation, "You two make such a cute couple."

"I hope Pastor Jonathan agrees with me and lets you date his daughter," the woman said while gesturing for Ben to add green bean casserole to her plate. "He has run off other young men that weren't suitable, so you'd better be on your best behavior."

"Thank you, Clara, for embarrassing me in front of my new friend who hasn't even asked me out on a date yet," Cindy said with a laugh. "Please move along before you scare away our visitor."

After the woman had reached the end of the serving line, Ben whispered to Cindy, "You didn't warn me that you're a celebrity here and that your father is in charge."

"Yeah, I wanted to keep my identity secret, but now I'll have to admit that I'm a pastor's kid. I didn't tell you because people have strange ideas about us and I was hoping that you'd get to know the real me first."

"I've only met one pastor's kid and one pastor—and both seem very nice to me."

"Thanks! If you haven't met a pastor before, does that mean you've never attended church?"

Ben regretted his error in guiding the conversation into church participation and reluctantly answered Cindy's question. "I have in the past, but lately I've been using Sunday mornings to go for long runs or hikes. When I went to church, the leader was called 'bishop.' That's why your father is the first pastor I've met."

"Bishop? Does that mean you're Catholic or Mormon?"

"I'm a Mormon," Ben said, wondering if that admission would lead Cindy's father to run him off for not being "suitable." Hungry, Ben hoped that he would at least get to eat first.

Chapter 45

Instead of being sent away, Amy Carson, Cindy's mother, insisted that Ben go through the food line as the first server to be fed. He followed his father's advice to always load up his plate when the food is free and enjoyed a robust Thanksgiving dinner with Cindy seated next to him. The meal lasted for two hours, which normally would have been far too long for Ben, but he never looked at his watch or thought about leaving the noisy social center.

He learned that Cindy had lived most of her life near Dayton, Ohio, with her parents leading a small church there and raising three children—Cindy and two younger brothers, Daniel and Matthew. Two years earlier, her father moved the family to Cedar City to take his current role. The move came shortly after Cindy's high school graduation, so she enrolled at SUSC to begin her work toward a bachelor's degree in secondary education. To Ben's disappointment, Cindy didn't know the explorer Kit Carson and whether they were related.

From Ben, Cindy received a firsthand description of scenic places to visit in Southern Utah. By probing, she picked up details about his academic plans, hometown, and family. He explained that he rarely traveled home due to a tight budget, saying, "I'm on my own when it comes to school. My parents can't help." He didn't get near any of the family problems that truly kept him away from Alma.

After most of the guests had left, Ben looked around and wondered if he should go before he wore out his welcome as a "first-time visitor," but he wanted to spend more time with Cindy. He noticed a young couple starting to gather plates and utensils from the tables and asked Cindy, "Should we help them clean up?"

"I *should*, but you've already done too much," Cindy said. "You should go and enjoy the rest of your day off."

"I'd enjoy helping you and there's plenty of work to go around."

Cindy said "Thanks" and they took the lead in washing and drying the dishes. Within an hour, they had cleaned and put away all the dishes. Cindy sent Ben out of the kitchen with a new assignment. "Mom and I will finish in here. Please see if my dad is ready to put the tables away."

While wiping crumbs and punch off one of the tables, the pastor noticed Ben approaching him and said, "It looks like the ladies finally let you out of the kitchen. Are you getting ready to take off?"

"No, Cindy asked me to help you put away the tables."

Despite the pastor's objections, Ben stayed to help fold and store the tables in a large closet. They completed the project within ten minutes. Seeing no other work yet to be done, Ben decided to go before being politely pushed out the door. He said, "Unless there's anything else I can help with, I'll be heading back to campus now."

"Thanks for your help and for spending your holiday with us," the pastor said. "You exceeded the lofty expectations that Cindy set for you."

"You're welcome and thanks for dinner. It was delicious. I'll have to run an extra five miles before work tomorrow morning to burn off the calories."

"Will we see you on Sunday? Our service begins at ten-thirty, plus we have Sunday school at nine. I teach one of the classes—it's for newcomers and might be something you'd find interesting."

"I'll think about it. I'm usually about ten miles into my long run at that time."

"Give yourself a break and only run eight miles. Then you'll be able to join us. We're casual, so you can even show up in your running clothes."

Ben repeated his promise to think about it and then headed for the exit after a quick goodbye. The pastor walked with him and said, "Before you go, let me tell Cindy that you're leaving. I'm sure she'll want to say thanks for coming and helping."

"No, she's busy," Ben said as he kept walking, not wanting to give the impression that he was dating the man's daughter or even considering it. "I'll see her at work tomorrow. Please tell her goodbye for me."

The pastor nodded and watched Ben leave. Despite having enjoyed the dinner, Ben still liked getting outside. Walking briskly in the chilly fall air was refreshing. With Main Street deserted and the campus empty, he found it easy to go deep into his thoughts. He reviewed the long afternoon in the church and the pastor's invitation to return. He wanted to go on Sunday to be near Cindy. At the same time, he worried that she might only be recruiting him to be a new member of her father's church and had no interest in them becoming a "cute couple."

Chapter 46

Fearful of rejection, Ben avoided Cindy the next morning, but she caught him in the paint department while taking her lunch break. "Hey, Ben, you left the church yesterday without giving me a chance to say goodbye and thanks for all you did for us," Cindy said. "My parents appreciated your help and enjoyed meeting you."

While transferring paint cans from boxes to the store shelf, Ben smiled and said, "I liked your parents. You're lucky to have such a good family."

"We're not good all the time, but I know that I'm blessed to have a wonderful mom and dad and brothers that aren't too annoying."

"I appreciated the invitation. That was my best Thanksgiving ever."

"Oh, that can't be possible. But I'll accept the compliment on behalf of the church and invite you to come back this Sunday. My dad would like you to attend his Sunday school class at nine. Will you be able to make it?"

Ben took one look at Cindy's beautiful brown eyes and warm smile and made a snap decision. "OK, I'll cut my morning run short and be there. Where do I go for the class?"

"Meet my dad inside the main entrance and he'll show you where it's at. I help teach a class for young kids, so I might not see you until we break for the worship service. That's at ten-thirty. If you'd like, we could sit together."

Ben agreed, hoping he didn't appear to be too eager. On Sunday, he again showed up fifteen minutes early. Only a few cars were in the parking lot, but he went inside the church and found the lights and heat on. As he waited for the pastor, church members began to arrive and greeted Ben when coming through the entrance. Most of them stopped to ask him if he was new and needed help. He declined, letting them know that the pastor planned to meet him there.

The pastor soon arrived, giving Ben a firm handshake and pat on the shoulder. "Ben, I'm pleased to see you," he said.

"Good morning, Pastor Carson, it's good to see you too."

"Please call me Pastor Jonathan. Nobody here uses my last name."

Ben nodded his understanding and followed the pastor down the hallway to a small classroom with eight chairs set up in a circle. "You're such an early bird that you beat me to the door," the pastor said. "I hope you didn't wait long."

"Only a few minutes. I'd rather be early than late."

"Me too, but I'm usually running behind schedule because someone has grabbed me for a quick chat, so I have to be flexible."

When they entered a classroom, the pastor added, "And as you can see, we have plenty of room for other class members, but it might just be the two of us today due to holiday travels. Instead of waiting, let's get started."

Pastor Jonathan prayed for wisdom and guidance for their discussion and then asked, "Do you believe in God?"

Ben stammered in trying to deliver an honest answer that wouldn't insult this man who had devoted his life to God. "I grew up going to church and talking about God as if he is real, but I don't know if I believe in him. I like the ideas that God represents and do my best to live a good life. On the other hand, I've never seen God and can't say for sure that he exists."

"That's a great answer," the pastor said. "It's honest and shows that you have a questioning mind, which is essential for you as a scientist. I haven't seen God either, but I've experienced him in my daily life, especially in times when I turned to him for help that I couldn't get elsewhere. Have you ever had one of those moments?"

Ben paused before responding because the question triggered a sudden, vivid memory that he had never shared with anyone. He studied Pastor Jonathan who patiently waited for a response. Ben wondered if he could trust this man he barely knew. Something had connected with Ben when getting ready to jump off the cliff in the Wasatch Mountains six years earlier, but he didn't know if God had touched him or if he had made up something in his head to explain his abrupt change of mind. The pastor didn't let him evade the question by asking a new one or launching into a sermon. He quietly waited, and Ben finally gave in to his patience.

"Something strange happened to me when I ran away from a Boy Scout camp in the mountains," Ben said. "I don't know where the thoughts came from that entered my mind that day, but the message was clear and kept me from making a terrible mistake."

Ben divulged the story of leaving the camp, disabling the motorcycles, and leading Derek and Luke to a frigid, snowy mountaintop. He talked about the harsh weather and the deep despair that led him to the edge of the cliff. Finally, he described the force that drove him back from death and gave him hope that things in his life would get better.

After Ben finished his story, Pastor Jonathan shook his head and said, "Ben, if that experience doesn't make you want to find out if God is real, then what would it take to get your attention? I believe God spoke to you that day through the power of the Holy Spirit. It's the same power that led me to invite you to this class today. I've strongly received the impression that God still wants to reach you."

"I don't know if that's true," Ben said. "What happened to me on the mountain might have been nothing more than a hallucination caused by nearly freezing to death."

"I understand that your science background has given you a desire for proof," the pastor said. "But have you ever researched the existence of God or are you relying on other people's views about God?"

"I grew up going to church every week and sat through hundreds of Sunday school lessons," Ben said. "I'd call that research and it didn't do much for me."

"Did you do more than merely hear the words of your teachers? Did you analyze their comments and study the message further to see if it was true?"

Ben felt compelled to be honest. "No, I had other things on my mind."

"Let's conduct an experiment to see what would happen if you truly studied this issue. Would you be willing to do that with me?"

"I don't know. I'm pretty busy."

"How much time do you expect to spend studying for your toughest biology class this quarter?"

"That's hard to say," Ben said and paused to calculate the time spent on reading the textbook and studying for quizzes and exams. "Probably more than a hundred hours, plus I'm writing a paper due at the end of the quarter."

"Then, here's the experiment," the pastor said, picking up a notebook from the chair next to him. He began writing on a page.

"Research a simple question about God, spending one hundred hours on it, and then give me your answer when you're ready. Be prepared to defend your conclusions. If you present a compelling argument, I'll buy you dinner at your favorite restaurant in Cedar City."

Ben chuckled about the pastor's plea to spend one hundred hours competing for a prize worth less than ten dollars. He didn't want to offend the pastor by telling him no, so he agreed to go along with the idea. Ben's mind raced ahead to a quick solution—find a book in the university library that shows God is the product of outdated thinking, not modern scholarship.

After Ben accepted the challenge, Pastor Jonathan smiled and said, "I'll be praying for you every day." Then he handed the page to Ben who accepted it with a nervous grin and read the research question.

If God is real and I ignore him, am I making a huge mistake?

Chapter 47

"How did you like my dad's Sunday school class?" Cindy asked when she joined him for the worship service. Ben had taken a pew near the front of the chapel at the pastor's suggestion because he would have "more elbow room." The spot suited Ben who continued to prefer sitting up front as he had done all through elementary school.

"Good, but I was the only student, so your dad spent the entire hour talking to me. And he gave me a homework assignment," Ben said, handing the research question to Cindy.

She read it silently and then said, "That's a great question. So, where are you in your walk with God? It sounds like you might not be a believer."

"I've never known what to think about God, but I don't see myself as an atheist or any other kind of nonbeliever. I'm only someone getting through life by working hard and being a good person."

"That's a fine plan, but you could have so much more out of life if you turned to God for help. He's a loving Heavenly Father who wants you to do more than just survive. If you trust in him, he will fill you with hope, joy and peace."

Ben laughed nervously. "I'm sorry about laughing, but you surprised me when you started talking like a preacher."

"Guilty, but that's my version of being a pastor's kid. I take my faith in God earnestly and believe in a powerful, unseen counselor who can guide and protect us."

"Why do you believe?" Ben asked. "Can you give me something that I can see and touch?"

Cindy handed Ben her Bible. "Read this with an open heart and see what it tells you."

Music interrupted their conversation as the service began. Ben continued to hold the Bible and thought about Cindy's faith. He admired her strong beliefs, but he wouldn't merely go along with her stance to make himself date-worthy. He hated being a phony and anticipated that she would spot his deception.

Returning to his hectic schedule on Monday made it easy to procrastinate the start of the research he agreed to conduct for Pastor Jonathan. When Cindy asked him to attend church the next Sunday, Ben accepted the invitation because he looked forward to sitting next to her for an hour. At the same time, he knew it meant facing questions from the pastor about the research project. Not wanting to be embarrassed, he made a trip to the campus library and skimmed a dozen theology books. The complexity of the information overwhelmed him. No quick, easy answer was found.

Ben showed up for the Sunday school class early and had a one-on-one conversation with the pastor before four other students arrived. The pastor sighed after listening to Ben's summary of his library visit. He expressed no surprise that Ben found differences of opinion among theologians on the existence of a higher power and what religion should offer people.

"With your approach, it sounds like you could spend more than one hundred hours studying my question and still not have a compelling answer," the pastor said. "May I offer you a different approach?"

"Sure," Ben said.

"Which sources do you consider the best when researching a subject? Primary or secondary?"

"Primary."

"Of course. And I believe the Bible is a primary source when it comes to discussing God. Do you think that's a fair conclusion?"

Ben agreed, and the pastor continued. "Why don't you begin your research by reading the Bible?"

"That's what Cindy suggested, but she also said that I should read it with an open heart."

"She's right. Did you do it?"

"No, I've read the Bible before and liked the stories and lessons about having good morals, but it didn't convince me that God is real."

"Consider applying Cindy's idea of reading with an open heart or, to be more precise, an open mind. Could you look at the Bible in a fresh way? Instead of thinking of it as a collection of stories with good morals, view it to be a biography about Jesus Christ—someone who most historians believe existed. Have you ever read a biography?"

"Sure—many. That's something my mother encouraged me to do."

"Good. Who have you read about from ancient times?"

"Julius Caesar."

"Great example. Was he a real person or fictional character?"

"Definitely real."

"How do you know that?"

"Through books written about him and things he left behind—buildings, sculptures, and other artifacts found by archeologists."

"And did he have an influence on world history?"

"Sure. He gets credit for the rise of the Roman Empire."

"And what influence does he have on our lives today?"

"Well, I don't know. I guess the month of July and perhaps Caesar salad," Ben said, laughing.

"Good enough. Was Jesus a real person or fictional character?"

"I don't know. To me, it seems like there's a lack of evidence."

"Are you sure that's true? Aren't there books written about him and sculptures, paintings or other artifacts that would suggest he was real?"

"That's true, but most of those things, including the Bible, were created long after he supposedly lived. They might have been things people came up with when telling stories about a popular legend. And over time, some people took the stories as facts."

"Would you be surprised to know that the oldest existing copy of the Bible is hundreds of years older than the oldest copy of a history of Julius Caesar even though Caesar lived before Jesus?"

"Yes, that would surprise me."

"It's true. If you're interested, I'd be glad to show you facts that you could use in your research project. And while those facts are compelling, the best piece of evidence is the impact Jesus has had on the world compared to Julius Caesar. Think about how much world history is connected to Christianity—whether good or bad—and the art, music, literature and other cultural influences like Christmas and Easter celebrations that can be traced back to Jesus. Do you know of any other legend or actual person to leave that kind of mark on the world?"

"Not off the top of my head, but let me think about it."

"If you can find one, be sure to include it in your research, but I recommend that you start somewhere else."

Pastor Jonathan picked up his Bible and said, "Cindy is right. You should begin here. Read the Bible as if you've never read it before and keep an open heart and mind when you're reading it. See if you can discover whether it's fact or fiction."

Ben exhaled slowly and said, "Wow. I don't know if I have time with classes and everything else I'm doing."

"Don't forget that you already promised to dedicate one hundred hours to researching my question. Being a college student, I'm sure you could read the New Testament in twelve hours. That would be an excellent start to getting your answer and you'd still have time to attend our Sunday services."

The other class members arrived, giving Ben a timely break in the discussion. He didn't have to commit to reading the Bible or continuing to attend church. After the class, the pastor shook hands with Ben, looked him in the eye, and promised, "I'll be praying for you and asking God to help you find the time to read his word."

The pastor gave Ben a new copy of the Bible, so he wouldn't have to check one out of the library and then hurried to the chapel to deliver his sermon.

While Ben waited in the pew for Cindy to join him, he turned pages in his new Bible while thinking about the pastor's pledge to pray for him. He recalled the last person who said it—his scoutmaster, Gene Augustine. He made the promise shortly before Ben left the campsite for his snowy hike up a mountain where his life nearly ended.

Ben worried about Pastor Jonathan's plan to pray for him. It seemed superstitious to be concerned, but strange things happened when the scoutmaster prayed for him and Ben didn't want anything to change. He liked the way things were going, especially when Cindy arrived in the chapel with a kind greeting and sat next to him.

Chapter 48

Thinking about his conversation with Pastor Jonathan kept Ben's mind too active for sleep that night, so he decided to follow the approach that the pastor and Cindy had suggested. Because his roommate was sleeping, Ben grabbed his Bible and quietly left the room for the dorm's shared area.

Ben found it empty and stretched out on a couch to read for an hour. He began in the New Testament with Matthew. With the first sixteen verses presenting the genealogy of Jesus, he thought this reading assignment would surely put him to sleep. But he stayed awake as Matthew transitioned to the familiar story of Jesus' birth in Bethlehem, the wise men from the east, King Herod, and the round trip to Egypt. Ben continued through the story of John the Baptist and his preaching in the wilderness.

The next chapter passed quickly for Ben as he remembered it well—Jesus being tempted by the devil and Jesus recruiting his disciples to become "fishers of men." When he reached the fifth chapter and started reading the Sermon on the Mount, his pace slowed significantly. Despite having heard these words often as a child, Ben paused to think about what they meant—as if reading them for the first time. And the message penetrated a well-protected area of his life—the anger he held toward his father and many former classmates.

The emphasis on forgiveness and an obligation to "love your

enemies, bless them that curse you" reminded him of the approach to life his scoutmaster had recommended. While Ben had already rejected Derek Dean's philosophy of attacking anyone who messes with you, he remained a long way from what Jesus taught.

Ben finished Matthew before he realized that an hour had passed. It surprised him that reading the Bible hadn't turned out to be painfully dull. While thinking about what he had read, Ben closed his eyes to rest them and dozed off.

The sound of loud talking and footsteps jarred Ben from deep slumber and he sat up to see two fellow students staring at him as they walked by.

"Hey, what's up?" one of them asked. "Did you pull an all-nighter?"

"No, I came out here to read for a few minutes and fell asleep."

The two students stopped and one of them pointed at the book in his hands as he slowly sat up. "Is that a Bible you're reading? No wonder you fell asleep."

"Yep, it works every time when I have insomnia."

Laughing, the students exited the dorm and Ben shuffled to his room.

Despite having a test to cram for, Ben read Mark that evening and Luke over the next two. After working a full shift at the hardware store on Saturday, he read John while eating dinner in the cafeteria. He placed a couple textbooks next to the Bible to disguise his reading material in case anyone he knew walked by.

With the four gospels completed, Ben had something to give Pastor Jonathan for his progress report on Sunday. Besides enjoying the pastor's pat on the back, he liked the class and soaked up the information. The small size of the group and interactive format allowed him to express his skepticism about religion. He also received counsel on ways to discern the truth about God without relying on blind faith or the belief of others.

In between the weekly Sunday school classes, Ben continued to read the New Testament, but he took it at a much slower pace than the twelve-hour timetable that the pastor had presented. Ben found his skepticism shrinking and becoming less of a roadblock to seeing that the Bible's promises might be feasible. He had previously tuned out all messages about hope, joy, and peace because he had little of that in his life.

Pastor Jonathan followed up on his progress every Sunday, so Ben created a chart to show him how many hours of research he had conducted. During one of the pastor's classes, Ben disclosed his struggle with deeply held anger due to abuse by his father and bullies. The pastor listened carefully, expressed regret, and prayed for Ben. He also suggested that Ben use the university's free counseling service for students. Thinking it could be an interesting discussion, Ben made an appointment to see a counselor.

The counselor began with a typical approach and asked Ben about his childhood. Ben told the counselor things that he had kept secret for years. The counselor found the abuse to be shocking and applauded Ben's ability to carry on a relatively normal life. Still, he suggested more sessions, including group therapy, and Ben went along with the idea.

From his individual and group sessions, Ben recognized the need to completely embrace the reality that being abused wasn't his fault. Like many survivors of abusive situations, Ben believed that he was "the problem." He had picked up that perception from his father and let it influence his thoughts and behavior for years.

Counseling also helped Ben understand that he should quit wondering what he could have done to win his father's affection and avoid his harsh disapproval. As with many abused children, he had adopted a faulty approach to life that made him dependent on someone else's emotions for his sense of worth and happiness. He couldn't control the abuser, so he tried to avoid him or any circumstances that would trigger his rage. When facing challenges in other relationships, Ben took the same path, running away from conflict, criticism, and rejection.

The Bible study and counseling provided comfort by helping Ben deal with his childhood pain. Both encouraged Ben to let go of the harmful things behind him and to reach for the better things to come. Even if he continued to view the existence of God with skepticism, he had found value in what the Bible taught, viewing it as a worthwhile guide for his life.

Within two months of starting the pastor's experiment, Ben read Revelation, the last book in the Bible, while sitting in his dorm's shared area—the same place where he read the first book in the New Testament. He remembered Revelation from a decade earlier when Derek Dean suggested reading it to learn more about "the beast."

Despite finding the book difficult to understand, Ben could see a connection between what the writer recorded and what he had experienced in his life—a continual, ferocious battle between good and evil. When he read in Chapter 11 about two powerful witnesses for God, it struck him that this wasn't creative fiction or a metaphor for a common struggle. In his heart, he believed that the book spoke honestly about things yet to happen.

While Ben read this chapter, he recalled what he had read earlier that "death is swallowed up in victory." The many promises in the Bible about the gift of eternal life through a savior suddenly seemed real to Ben, not wishful thinking as he had often viewed them. Something moved inside of Ben to give him hope that the people on God's team—those who believe in Jesus Christ—will have a life beyond their current mortal existence.

For the first time, Ben wanted to pray and to do it with sincerity, believing that God would hear him. He left the dorm for a walk, thinking about his new, intense desire to pray. Ben's path led him to the university's track where he had spent hours training and competing. Sunset had passed, so the track was empty and dark. He walked to the starting line for the distance runs and knelt there, clutching the Bible to his chest.

"God, I don't know if I'm asking this in the right way, but I want you to pick me to be on your team. I promise to give you my best effort to finish every race. I'm sorry that I have ignored you for so long and ask you to forgive me for everything I've done to let you down. Please let me know what you want me to do with my life, give me wisdom to understand spiritual things and help me always believe that you're there and have adopted me as a son. I pray for this in the name of Jesus."

As Ben said these words, something unseen touched him like it had at the edge of the cliff years earlier, creating a powerful sense of peace. It left Ben feeling overwhelmed with gratitude because God had heard him and accepted his request. Ben's belief that he had connected with a loving Heavenly Father, the almighty creator of heaven and earth, left him in tears. He remained on the track and allowed the tears to flow. He knew this eternal father wouldn't judge him for crying "like a girl."

Ben looked forward to presenting his report to Pastor Jonathan because he knew that he could defend his conclusions. And instead of a free meal, he would receive a lasting inheritance as a reward.

CHAPTER 49

When Ben delivered his report the next Sunday, Pastor Jonathan said, "Praise the Lord. That's an answer to prayer and there's rejoicing in heaven."

Over the next three weeks, the pastor held one-on-one sessions with Ben to discuss baptism and church membership. While Ben enjoyed attending the church, he hesitated about taking those steps because they meant turning his back on the LDS Church with its strong connections to his family's heritage.

"Ben, I understand that this decision is difficult for you, but I think it will be easy for you to make when you consider the source of your new faith in God. Where did it come from?"

"Studying the Bible with an open heart and praying to God for salvation," Ben said.

"Is your faith connected to the Book of Mormon, the LDS prophets, or your pioneer ancestors?"

"No, but I've always been taught that those things are important and to walk away from them feels like I'm losing my family and leaving a church that does so many good things."

"Frankly, it is likely to create friction with your parents and awkwardness with other family members and friends who are Mormons," the pastor said. "Jesus said that his message would create division in relationships because some would accept it and others would not. I'm challenging you to let go of the traditions that keep you from following the commandment to love God with all your heart, soul and mind—and to put God first in your life."

The pastor waited for Ben to acknowledge his challenge and then continued, "What I've also learned about the LDS faith is that you can't outchurch a Mormon—through the church's programs, the members receive a lot of support from each other and they live good lifestyles. I admire those results, but I believe you need to focus on the ultimate purpose of the gospel and that's to bring people to salvation through faith in Jesus, not by good works or religious ordinances. If you embrace that focus on faith and not on honorable actions that could be performed by Christians or nonbelievers alike, you'll discover that the clear message of the Bible is all you need to find the way into the kingdom of heaven."

For several more weeks, Ben continued to talk to the pastor about the saving grace he had experienced through Bible study and prayer compared to the complicated LDS Church plan of salvation. At the end of those discussions, Ben decided to be baptized by Pastor Jonathan and join the Cedar City Community Church. After his baptism, he received hugs and words of encouragement from many church members, including Cindy who he had started dating shortly before Christmas.

A year later, Ben asked the pastor to go with him to the Utah State Prison in Draper to visit a prisoner. When asked about his motive, Ben replied, "Didn't Jesus say that we should visit people in prison?"

"That's true," the pastor said and agreed to go.

Ben held back on providing details about the visit because he thought the pastor might discourage him from going when he learned more about the prisoner's history and the potential for a hostile confrontation. Despite that possibility, Ben felt compelled to go and wanted the pastor to accompany him in case he needed help talking to the prisoner about God.

Ben and Pastor Jonathan arrived at the beginning of visiting hours and followed a small crowd through the sign-in process. The first step was having a guard inspect the Bible that Ben planned to leave behind.

"Who are you here to see?" asked the guard checking them in.

"Derek Dean," Ben said. "He's a friend of mine."

"Did you go through the proper procedure to schedule this visit?"

"Yes, sir."

The guard found Derek's name on the roster of prisoners to receive visitors that day. "It looks like your visit is approved."

"That's good," Ben said. "I hope Derek still has time to meet with us."

The guard laughed. "Oh, he has plenty of time. We'll let him know you're here."

Ben and Mike sat in an area where prisoners mingled with visitors. Because Derek was in the minimum-security section of the prison, the setting was much more informal than what Ben had expected. Based on what he had seen in prison movies, he thought they would talk with Derek through a small hole in a thick window and bars would keep them apart.

"Are you nervous?" Pastor Jonathan asked.

"No doubt," Ben said. "I didn't think that we'd actually get this close to Derek and he frightens me."

"Oh, really, you told the guard that he's a friend."

"That's sort of true. We were friends until I sent Derek to prison for five years. And after he got out, we had another minor problem. I haven't seen him since then."

Derek soon strode through the door with the same swagger he had when working at Al Baker's Service Station, but he looked older and not as menacing. Ben took a deep breath and walked toward Derek to greet him with a handshake.

"Little Benny Baker is all grown up now," Derek said, grinning while crushing Ben's hand.

"Yes, and I'm here with a friend, Pastor Jonathan Carson," Ben said, gesturing toward the pastor. "He leads a church in Cedar City where I'm attending Southern Utah State College."

"A college kid and a churchman coming to see a vicious criminal.

Why? Are you making me part of an experiment for a psychology class or here to redeem my lost soul?"

"No, I've come to apologize for lying to the police about you and for vandalizing your friends' motorcycles. I'm sorry that I did both of those things. Please accept my apology."

Derek dropped his usual grin and stared at Ben, appearing to be perplexed by his comments. "Honestly, that's why you're here?" he asked, breaking the awkward silence that had fallen on the conversation.

Ben paused before replying to think of something more profound to say, but nothing came to mind, so he repeated his apology. Then, he suggested that they sit at one of the empty tables in the visiting area. Derek and the pastor followed his lead and took seats where they had a small amount of privacy.

"I should have apologized years ago, but my pride got in the way and, to be frank, you scared me."

Derek laughed and slapped both of his hands on the table, which drew a stern look from one of the guards.

"And I brought you a Bible to read," Ben said. "When we first met, you told me to go home and read the last book in the Bible—Revelation—because it talked about the beast. I thought you might want to read it again."

Ben turned to Pastor Jonathan and said, "The beast is Derek's nickname and that's why he has six, six, six tattooed on his hands."

Derek grinned, clenched his fists, and held them up for the pastor to see. "When Benny took one of these babies to the chest, it dropped him to the ground," Derek said. "I could have killed him that day if I really wanted to, but I didn't. I liked the little guy, especially after he took out those two punks with a steel pipe exactly the way I taught him."

Pastor Jonathan looked at Ben for confirmation and Ben nodded to admit his guilt. They now had new things to talk about on the drive back to Cedar City.

Ben handed the Bible to Derek and, to Ben's surprise, he accepted it with a mumbled "Thanks." Then, Derek asked, "Did you bring me any cigarettes?"

"No, I'm sorry. I don't smoke and didn't think about bringing you any."

"That's OK. I won't be here much longer. Like always, I'll be getting out early because of my good behavior. How did you know I was here?"

"Derek, you're a celebrity in Alma," Ben said with a chuckle. "Everyone in town has been talking about your latest prison stay. It didn't take long for the news to reach me even though I live in Cedar City. When I heard about you being sentenced to prison, God promoted me to apologize to you. So, here I am."

"Well, I'll have to say that this is a first," Derek said with a loud laugh. "I've never had someone visit me in prison to apologize. But, oh man, I've had other visitors. Do you remember my girlfriend Susan?"

"Sure, did she visit you in prison?"

"Not Susan! But her parents did and gave me a lecture about how I ruined their daughter's life. So this visit is much nicer, unless you're going to demand that I apologize to you in return."

"No, I came to let you know that I'm sorry and to give you a new Bible, so you can read the story about the beast. As you might recall, the beast ends up on the losing team. So, after reading about his defeat, I hope you'll want to read the rest of the Bible to see how you can join the winning team. That's what I did, and it changed my life."

"I guess that means you're Mister Righteous now and won't be stealing any more money from your old man or putting sand in people's gas tanks," Derek said, drawing another surprised look from the pastor.

Derek picked up the Bible and waved it in the air while imitating an old-time preacher, saying, "Brother Baker, the Bible declares that you shall not do such wicked and detestable things."

Ben smiled and said, "That's right. And I brought Pastor Jonathan with me to tell you what else the Bible teaches. Would you like to hear what he has to say?"

The pastor appeared surprised by the question, which Derek noticed and laughed in response. Derek opened his Bible and said, "Sure, I have nothing else to do today. Fire away!"

Pastor Jonathan accepted the challenge and asked Derek to turn to Romans, which led to a spirited debate about who should decide what's right and wrong. Derek attempted to rattle the pastor, but he also seemed to enjoy the discussion and never indicated that he wanted it to end.

When the guards announced that visiting hours would soon be over, the pastor asked, "Derek, would it be all right if we prayed for you now?"

"OK. Give it a try, but I doubt God is interested in having anything to do with me."

Pastor Jonathan prayed until one of the guards shouted that it was time to leave. When Ben raised his head from praying, he noticed that Derek had also bowed his head. Derek didn't say anything, but Ben thought that Pastor Jonathan had connected with him in some way.

"Derek, thanks for your time," Ben said, offering to shake hands despite the previous crushing. This time Derek gave Ben a firm but not hostile handshake and smiled.

"Ben, I always thought you were a good kid and now you've become a good man," Derek said. "Your parents should be proud of you. I'm glad you didn't turn out like me."

Ben let Derek know that he appreciated the compliment and would continue to pray for him. "I've had people pray for me and amazing things happened in my life as a result. I hope the same happens for you."

After starting toward the exit, Ben turned to wave goodbye to Derek. His old friend and foe nodded in return and then joined the other prisoners leaving the visiting area. Derek's usual swagger seemed to have been set aside for the moment.

"Wow, that was incredible," the pastor said. "You're full of surprises today. What's next?"

"This one was easy," Ben said. "Now, we need to go see my father."

CPSIA information can be obtained
at www.ICGtesting.com
Printed in the USA
LVHW082123041218
598715LV00015B/31/P